Praise for the Suspense Novels of Daryl Wood Gerber

"The frantic plot will keep readers on edge."

—*Kirkus Reviews*

"The novel's plot is thick and the prose is more than rich enough to sustain it. Its shifting perspectives will give readers an even greater sense of excitement as the many pieces of the puzzle fall into place. Readers will be shocked by this exciting, fast-paced thriller's twists and turns."

—*Kirkus Reviews*

"Daryl Wood Gerber has proven again to be a gifted storyteller and one to watch in this genre. An absolute must-read!"

—*Escape with Dollycas*

"This is an edge-of-your-seat, can't-put-it-down thriller. If you like Dan Brown's thrillers you will want to read this!"

—Goodreads

"*Day of Secrets* is an action-packed, suspense-filled, riveting book. I was glued to this story, could not put it down, and didn't want it to end."

—Goodreads

Books by Daryl Wood Gerber

The Cookbook Nook Mysteries

Final Sentence
Inherit the Word
Stirring the Plot
Fudging the Books
Grilling the Subject
Pressing the Issue
Wreath Between the Lines
Sifting Through Clues

The French Bistro Mysteries

A Deadly Éclair
A Soufflé of Suspicion

Writing as Avery Aames

The Long Quiche Goodbye
Lost and Fondue
Clobbered by Camembert
To Brie or Not to Brie
Days of Wine and Roquefort
As Gouda as Dead
For Cheddar or Worse

Suspense

Girl on the Run
Day of Secrets
Desolate Shores

DESOLATE SHORES

DARYL WOOD GERBER

Desolate Shores
Daryl Wood Gerber

Cover design and illustration by Dar Albert, Wicked Smart Designs

Beyond the Page Books
are published by
Beyond the Page Publishing
www.beyondthepagepub.com

ISBN: 978-1-950461-20-2

To my husband, Chuck.
There from the first book I wrote. Here, forever.

Acknowledgments

"Success is not final; failure is not fatal;
it is the courage to continue that counts." —Winston Churchill

This is a story that has haunted me for years. It was one of the first books I wrote, prior to my cozy mystery series. I had many early readers who enjoyed the story, but a few agents said they couldn't sell it. Deflated, I set it aside. Often I'd wanted to rewrite it and resubmit, but I couldn't find the time. Some author friends recommended that I let it go. But the story, as I said, haunted me. And I found the time to rewrite. Boy, did it need it. My style had changed drastically. I hope you enjoy the journey of Aspen Adams, a character who is close to my heart.

To my family and friends, thank you for all your support.

Thank you to those who have helped make this first in a new suspense series a success: my publishers, Beyond the Page, including Bill Harris and Jessica Faust; my cover artist, Dar Albert; my agent, John Talbot; and my sweet sis Kimberley Greene for your undying support.

Thank you to my talented author friends Krista Davis and Hannah Dennison for your words of wisdom and encouragement. Thank you to all of my author pals on Mystery Lovers Kitchen, Plothatchers, and to my fans on Delicious Mysteries. Thank you to my first readers from the Cake and Dagger Club who inspired me to move forward with other projects. Your enthusiasm for my suspense novels has been very important.

Thank you to all my readers, including librarians and booksellers, for taking the journey with Aspen Adams as she opens her heart to the new life she craved by moving to Lake Tahoe. Thank you for sharing your love of the story with a friend. An author's story cannot come alive without all of you.

Chapter 1

A wave cracked against the shore. A seagull cawed and shrieked. I snapped my head to look. The bird circled overhead and glided to a log on the shore. I stopped running along the pavement, peered harder.

Logs don't wear shoes.

I leaped over the fence and bounded down the slope, slipping on the snow. Even through the icy powder that dusted her face, I would've recognized her.

"Vikki, are you okay?" I yelled.

She didn't answer.

I skidded to a stop and gasped.

Silver-blue crystals clung to her face. Her lips were ghostly gray, her translucent skin pasty. Her chestnut hair flared around her head like fiery rays radiating from the sun. Her burgundy sweater clung to her torso. Her chest wasn't rising and falling. Dark goo pooled beneath her neck and hair. Blood.

I checked her pulse. Nothing. I straddled her and pressed on her chest. Counted to ten. Pinched her nose. Managed three short breaths. Pressed my ear to her mouth. Still nothing.

If only I could lift her, I could carry her to the road. But I wasn't that strong. She was much taller than I was.

"Somebody, help!" My voice echoed off the icy beach.

No reply. Even the most avid skiers in Lake Tahoe weren't driving to the slopes before seven.

Frustration clamped down around my guts. Tears stung my cheeks. My breath seemed stuck in my chest. I wasn't sure I could survive if someone else I loved died.

Sweat streamed down my neck as I pressed on her chest again. "C'mon, Vikki, breathe. One, two, three. Say, 'Hello, Aspen, tricked you.' C'mon."

Only last month she and I had celebrated her twenty-eighth birthday with chocolate cake and champagne. Vikki took ten tries to blow the candles out before I admitted they were stay-lit candles. I had laughed so hard.

"Breathe." Wind sliced my face. The usually invigorating aroma of pine made me gag. I slid back on my heels and stared.

What had led her to the beach in the middle of the night? An urgent desire to gaze at the stars? A tryst with a secret lover?

I keened at the top of my lungs. I wasn't sure I could stop.

It was predawn when I'd started my run. Now the sun was creeping over Cave Rock. A thin, shimmering path of sunlight streaked across the deep azure waters, promising a glorious day. Buoys danced as waves crested and receded. The beauty was why I had moved to Lake Tahoe. To start a new life. To heal.

I felt cold nausea clawing at my throat. I was going to puke.

Don't you dare. Hold it together.

Right palm over left hand, I pressed again on Vikki's sternum.

"Hey, you, down there," a man yelled from the road beyond the fence. I couldn't make out his face. "You need help?"

"Yes." I stood, but my feet slipped on the ice. I landed on my rear by Vikki's side.

"Stop," a woman shouted. "Don't move."

A little too late for that.

With the speed of a soccer player, the woman in the blue parka and jeans dashed through the gate and sprinted across the expanse. As she drew near, relief swept over me. Karen Brandon was a seasoned detective for the Placer County Sheriff's Office. A member of my book club. A friend.

"Aspen, step back."

I scrambled to my feet and obeyed.

"How long have you been here?"

"A couple of minutes," I said, sounding unsure, brittle.

Karen crouched and grabbed Vikki's wrist, checking for a pulse like I had. She placed two fingers on my friend's neck. After a moment, she looked up at me, sadness in her dusky eyes. For over two decades, Karen had worked Vice in Sacramento. Three years ago, in her early forties, she'd transferred to Lake Tahoe to get away from the stress. I would bet she was regretting that decision now.

"You want me to call the police?" the man on the road yelled.

"No, I'm with the sheriff's department." Karen flicked snow off the top of her boots. "Stay right where you are." She rose to her full height—a good six inches taller than me—and leveled me with a searing glare. "Do you know her, Aspen?" The odor of whiskey that leached from her mouth made me recoil. "Talk."

"Yes. It's Vikki Carmichael." Dear, sweet, funny Vikki who liked wine and cheese and bawdy jokes, and who just hours ago had chided me about my current profession. *You're a garbological explorer,* she had teased. I'd countered by saying I was a process server and up-and-coming private eye who sometimes had to dive into Dumpsters.

"Have I ever met her?" Cold breath billowed from Karen's mouth. She tucked her gold charm necklace beneath the collar of her turtleneck and zipped her parka to her neck.

"On the slopes, maybe."

A year ago December, Vikki and I had met at Alpine Meadows, a family-friendly ski resort located a couple of miles from Tahoe City. In the winter, she was a chairlift operator known for drawing smiley faces on people's ski tickets. In summer, she gave water-ski lessons. At the end of a bitter December day, I was standing in line when the chairlift broke down. While waiting for it to be repaired, Vikki and I chatted at length. We ended up going to dinner, where we discovered we had so much in common. Besides our love for photography, crossword puzzles, sports, and men with a good sense of humor—not necessarily in that order—we learned we both loved to bake.

"Aspen." Karen braced my shoulders. "Are you okay?"

"No. I don't know. I mean, it's—" My intestines wrenched with pain. The taste of dirty pennies filled my mouth.

"She's young," Karen said, as perfunctory as ever. Through book club, she and I had become the kind of friends who talked about life in general, but we had never shared the outdoors or dinners or movies. Not like Vikki and I had.

I shivered. "She looks so cold."

"Death will do that to a person. Did you move her at all?"

"No, I knew—"

"Let's get you away from the crime scene." She reached for my elbow.

"Crime scene?" I shoved my knuckles against my mouth and almost bit through the skin. "You think somebody killed her?"

"I don't see anything she might have struck her head on, do you? And there are no skid marks by her feet. Let's go." Karen was a bit of a control freak. I tried not to take her tone personally. "Come on, you've already messed up a lot of the area."

"Ma'am, I'm cold," the man on the road called. "I'm going to get a coat."

"Wait, sir." Karen clenched my arm and tugged me up the hill, taking care to follow in our previous footprints. At the top, she nudged me through the gate. "Find someplace to sit. You look—"

"Was the gate open when you ran down?" I spun around and looked back at the shore.

"Yes, why?"

"It's supposed to be locked."

Had the murderer had a key? Vikki had one. She'd been house-sitting the A-frame house across the street. Had the murderer followed her?

Karen ran her fingers through bleached-blond hair that never looked combed and faced the man who was none other than Vikki's food-mooching neighbor, Garrett, dressed in a pair of pajamas and boots. The sight of him made my skin crawl. More than once, he had shown up at Vikki's with the lame excuse of needing a cup of sugar. He would stand there ogling Vikki. Granted, she had been as attractive as a runway model with a lithe figure like Karen's, but the way he'd gaped at her had been beyond disturbing.

"Who are you?" Karen asked.

"Garrett Thompson." He stamped his feet on the ground and blew into his hands to keep warm.

"Stand over there. I've got some questions to ask you." Karen pulled a cell phone out of her parka and punched in a number. "It's me. We've got a homicide. The body is lying in the snow, near the edge of the lake. North of Tahoma. South of Tahoe City." She shook her head. "Yeah, yeah, I'm not going anywhere. Look, anyone can see the corpse from the danged road. Call the fire department, then get the others down here."

Garrett sidled up to me. He smelled of stale beer. "What's going on?"

"Vikki's been murdered," I whispered.

The guy turned ash gray and without so much as a goodbye darted in the direction of his home.

Karen, who was engaged in a shouting match with the woman on the other end of the phone, didn't notice his departure. "Well, wake him up if you have to. I don't care if he barks, we've got a dead body." She ended the call, shoved the phone into her pocket, blew a trail of steam from her mouth, and turned toward me. "What the blazes were you doing down there?"

"I was running. I saw her from the road and recognized her. Vikki is . . . *was* . . . my best friend. We skied together and . . ." Tears welled in my eyes. One slipped down my cheek. I batted it away. "She wanted to become a professional photographer."

"You said your friend worked at—" Karen glanced around. "Hey, where'd that guy Thompson go?"

"Home."

"Which one?"

"The blue one across the street. Next to the A-frame where Vikki was house-sitting." I glanced at the house and back at Vikki, and our final conversation came to me in a rush. She'd been teasing me and I'd responded with: *I hate you.* In jest. But still . . . "I left a parka there last night."

"You were with her?"

"We ate an early dinner, then I went to serve a subpoena." My heart ached as if it had been plunged into ice water.

"Is this the first dead person you've seen?"

"No." My teeth began to chatter. "My mom and dad—"

"Of course. Sorry. That was insensitive of me." Karen withdrew a pack of cigarettes from her pocket, popped one out, and rolled it between her fingers. One night after book club, she confided that she'd quit smoking a year ago. The rolling routine had started after she had annihilated her nails with anxious chewing. "They died twelve years ago, right?"

Died. I nodded. My father caught a robber rummaging through the silver in the dining room hutch. The guy shot him in the heart. When my mother came to my father's rescue, the robber shot her in the back.

"The police never caught the creep who killed them, did they?"

"No." At the time I was a student and extremely naive. I didn't know I could have pressed the police to do more.

"Don't beat yourself up," Karen said, as if reading my mind. "Not for that. I try not to." She was referring to her inability to prevent her father's fatal heart attack a couple of months ago.

A siren blasted in the distance, growing louder until a fire truck zoomed up and pulled to a stop near us.

"About time." Karen shoved a piece of gum into her mouth and dashed toward the driver, my presence all but forgotten as the machinery of solving a murder groaned to life.

Chapter 2

True to her word, Karen returned and questioned me at length about what I'd seen and done, until her sheriff's department colleagues arrived, at which point she stomped away, leaving me to flounder.

Suddenly alone, a realization hit me. I'd never see Vikki again. We'd never go skiing or talk about avalanches or argue over which guys were the cutest racers on the Olympic team. Our hot tub gossip sessions were finished; our revelations about new cookie or muffin recipes over; our visits to the Homewood Tavern for a glass of wine a thing of the past.

How I'd wanted to tell her about last night's process serving success. Lazar, an alcoholic who'd wanted custody of his kids, had faced me with a knife, ready to dice me like vegetables. I'd smiled disarmingly and asked him about his children—a boy and a girl. What did they like to do? He didn't answer. I mentioned their futures and their education. After the one-sided chat, he lowered his arm and handed over the knife, accusing me of using my pretty face to captivate him. Yeah, right. Vikki would've punched me in the arm and said, *Let's hear it for good DNA.*

"Dude, pull that tape tight," an officer in a blue parka yelled.

"Sure." A beefy man yanked on the yellow ribbon he was setting up to establish the perimeter of the crime scene. The cordoned-off area extended from the pier, along the highway, and down to the water. "Bro, keep those lookie-loos back."

The officer in the blue parka gave a thumbs-up.

Locals were crowding the yellow tape wanting to know what the hubbub on the snow-covered beach was all about.

"What's going on?" a stick-thin man asked a woman to his right.

"I don't know. Ask the brunette in the red-and-black running outfit." She pointed at me.

I tugged at the raggedy strands of hair that peeked from beneath my ski hat. When the man approached, I told him I knew nothing, and he trudged away in a huff.

Though I'd been working for my aunt's detective agency for

eighteen months, I hadn't had the opportunity to become familiar with the various law enforcement staff in Lake Tahoe. The snoop-and-serve stuff I'd been doing didn't bring me into contact with the big guns at the Placer County Sheriff's Office.

The PCSO, located in Auburn, maintained authority over Tahoe City as well as the other towns on the California side of the lake. The North Lake Tahoe Station staff had plenty of people to manage a peaceful resort area, but not enough for a homicide.

Now a dozen officers governed the scene. Some had volunteered from the Truckee Police Department. The emergency response team had declared the body dead, though Karen informed me that the coroner would make the official determination. Since the coroner had to come from Auburn, the formal pronouncement could be a while.

I took up residence on a huge boulder outside the chain-link fence, which put me no more than fifteen feet from where the officials were working. I wanted to observe everything that went on. After the mess the police made of my parents' murder case, no way was I going to let the sheriff's department screw up this investigation. A month of scream therapy, six shredded pillows, and two shattered mirrors wouldn't allow me to.

Sweet Vikki. Brutally honest Vikki. A little sister. Better than a sister.

Last night, while poking fun at me, she'd said, "Face it, Aspen, you abandoned your patients back in the Bay Area, and you despise yourself for it."

I argued, but she was right. What else could I have done? Sink or swim, fight or flight. Those had been my options. I'd chosen flight. I'd accepted my aunt's offer of a job, which was a satisfying alternative to being a therapist. Secretly, I relished the darker aspects and chaotic schedule of a detective. I'd never been content with the sedentary career of psychology, even though I'd convinced myself that healing emotional wounds was how I should devote myself to mankind. My ability to communicate with people was a gift, right?

Wrong.

The temperature had only risen a few degrees since I'd found Vikki, even though the clouds had moved on and the sun was shining. The chill from the rock I was sitting on was seeping through my jogging suit. I drew up my knees and focused on a pair of male officers who hovered near her body. I could hear them easily because their voices bounced off the ice. It also helped that they were yelling to be heard above the waves hitting the beach.

A third officer took pictures with a digital camera. A fourth wrapped Vikki's hands in paper bags. Near me, an older woman sketched on a pad, glancing from the road and back to the murder site, probably trying to make sure the drawings were to scale.

A baldheaded African-American deputy along with an athletic Asian female deputy scoured the perimeter while sharing a funny story.

Gallows humor was one thing, but a total disregard for Vikki ticked me off. I was about to jump up and confront them when I spotted Detective Sergeant Nick Shaper, a man I'd seen introduced at a city council meeting, pacing the highway. My first impression of the man had been positive. He'd reminded me of one of my favorite college professors. Young and hip yet informed and well spoken. Shaper seemed to be taking in the site. He stopped and scanned the crowd. For what, the killer?

Vikki's neighbor, Garrett Thompson, popped into my mind, but he was nowhere in sight.

Shaper rubbed both hands along his dark hair and then strode with the command of a general down the steps toward the murder site. "Deputy Kim," he said to the Asian woman, "what are we looking at?"

"Doesn't look like much of a struggle." Kim, who looked late thirties, about the same age as Shaper, joined him, eyes alert. "The body may have been arranged after death. Note the hair."

"Weapon?"

"We found a rock that looks suspect." She mimed something about the size of a basketball. "My guess, a basal skull fracture. Not a lot of blood."

"Have we collected trace evidence?" Shaper removed his black parka and slung it over his arm.

"Some short strands of blond hair. A few darker ones. Some bloody pine needles. All bagged. We can't contain the entire scope of this place." Kim pointed to a lean officer near the gate. "He's got a record of everything, if you're interested."

"Later. Have we got any witnesses?"

She gestured to me then Karen, who was conversing with another officer.

Shaper approached Karen. "What the heck happened? How could you let this area get wrecked? There are footprints and skid tracks everywhere."

Karen's cheeks flushed, but she covered by squaring her shoulders and setting her jaw. "We have photos of the virgin scene, don't panic."

"Tell me what happened."

"I was on my way to the grocery store. I had the window open. You know how my defroster doesn't work."

Shaper waved for her to pick up her pace.

"Anyway, I heard screaming. I parked and bolted down the stairs to help."

Shaper looked toward me and returned his gaze to his subordinate. "Go on."

"I checked for a pulse, realized the vic was dead, and removed Miss Adams from the scene."

I'd reverted to my maiden name after my marriage fell apart.

"I called it in," Karen continued, "and after the others arrived, we searched the area and found footprints leading to those bushes."

"There's a new layer of snow from last night. How'd you see them?"

"Faint depressions. We used a duster to brush the new stuff away, took pictures, and proceeded." She indicated a cluster of manzanita bushes. "We found the weapon lying beneath that bush there."

Karen was tempering her tone around her boss. Was it out of respect, or did he intimidate her?

"She's our sole witness?" Shaper glanced in my direction again.

"One other. A neighbor." She nodded toward me. "I know her. She's okay."

"I say who's okay."

"But—"

"Did you get her statement?"

"Yes." Karen glared at him. "But she was in shock."

"Where's the neighbor?"

"Sitting tight at his house."

Shaper spun around and, with his chin lowered, made his way toward me. I pictured the homicide detective who had handled my parents' murders. In no uncertain terms, the guy had told me that everyone, including me, was a suspect. Fury had shattered all sense of reason after that.

As Shaper slid under the yellow tape, I remained rooted to my boulder, refusing to be cowed. He stood before me, his black sweater clinging to his sturdy chest, muscular legs pressing at the seams of his jeans. Though I was in good shape and trained in self-defense, he could have felled me with one punch.

"Miss Adams?" His gentle tone surprised me. He'd been so brusque with his cohorts.

"Aspen, if you prefer." I rose to my full height, but he was still a head taller than I, with some gray in his hair. "And you are?" Okay, I knew who he was, but I felt a formal introduction was necessary. Call me crazy.

"Detective Sergeant Shaper. I'm sorry you've had to go through this. How did you happen to find the victim?" He didn't pull out a pen or a pad. His jaw was set, his moss green eyes attentive.

"I was on the highway running."

"You do that every morning?"

"Yes. I glanced toward the water and saw her."

"You saw a body from back there?" He looked skeptical.

"I assumed it was a log at first. I hopped the fence—"

"Why didn't you use the gate?"

"Because it's usually locked." I knew my terse responses were a result of my previous encounters with policemen. I tried to ease off. "I assumed it was, but Karen—um, Detective Brandon—came in through it."

"You live nearby?"

"Not far."

"How old are you?"

"Thirty. What does that—?"

"What do you do, Miss Adams?" Shaper ticked off another of his laundry list questions. Routine but necessary.

"I'm a process server."

"For whom?"

"My aunt. She owns the Maxine Adams Detective Agency in Incline." When I'd grown weary of being a family therapist, Max offered me a chance to start over. She said I'd be helping people in another way, in a brand-new location. I'd jumped at the chance.

Shaper and I stared at each other a moment, not sure whether we were allies or foes. From all I'd heard, law enforcement didn't think private eyes were worth their salt.

"Nick," the African-American deputy yelled.

"Yeah."

"Got something."

Chapter 3

The deputy approached holding up a baggie with a black waterproof pen inside.

Despite the freezing temperature, Shaper removed his gloves. "Where'd you find it?"

"Near the victim's right hand beneath the fresh snow."

Shaper focused on the pen. "Any paper? A note?"

"No. The top was in place."

"That's Vikki's," I said. "It was her favorite. She used it to write her smiley faces."

"Her what?" Shaper asked. "My apologies. Deputy Walker, Aspen Adams."

Walker tipped an imaginary hat.

Shaper said, "Go on about the pen."

I shivered. Though my toes had thawed, icy fingers still clutched my heart. "Vikki drew smiley faces on ski lift tickets. You know, all in fun, to brighten a day." I pointed to a piece of electrical tape wrapped around the lid of the pen. "See that? Vikki put that on a few days ago because the pen was leaking."

Shaper said to Walker, "What else did you—?"

"The pen might be significant," I said.

"Most likely it fell out of her pocket when she was struck."

"No, it—"

"Kim, can I see you a moment?" Shaper beckoned her. "Walker, keep looking."

When Shaper turned his back on me, a flush of heat rushed into my cheeks. Had I been dismissed?

"Do I remind you of your ex-wife or something?" I tapped his shoulder. "Is that why you're being abrupt with me?"

Shaper glanced over his shoulder. "Yeah, the long blond hair and the fact that you're five-eleven means you're a carbon copy."

I was five-five in my bare feet and had shoulder-length dark hair. He was attempting subtle humor in a somber world. I allowed myself to smile.

As Deputy Kim joined Shaper, I flashed on an image by Vikki's hip. She'd pushed snow away, creating an arc along the right side of her body like angel wings children made. In the middle of the wing had been a design.

"Detective Shaper," I shouted.

He pivoted.

"Vikki had drawn—carved—something. In the snow." Was I crossing the line of helpfulness? I didn't care.

"Kim, did you see anything?" Shaper asked.

"No, sir."

"About hip-high, right side. It might be wiped out because, well, I skidded to her." *Dang the slippery snow.* "And then I straddled her to give her CPR." Even without binoculars, I could see the chunks of snow that sat in a pile by Vikki's side.

To his credit, Shaper didn't scorn me. "Describe it."

"Lines. Elliptical."

"Was it someone's name?"

"No, it was like—"

"Shaper," a man yelled from a Mercedes, one of many cars slowing for a look. He ground the car to a halt and scuttled out. With his pencil mustache and needle-thin nose, he reminded me of a French Legionnaire.

Shaper said, "Deputy Kim, have one of the guys take pictures of the gate and fence." He tramped toward the mustached man while donning his jacket and gloves.

"Does he know what he's doing?" I asked Kim.

"Shaper worked Homicide in San Jose. He was one of their best."

"Why did he move to Tahoe? Did he get demoted?"

The deputy shook her head. "He wanted a change of lifestyle."

"Who's the guy he's talking to?" I asked.

"Mark Collins. The DA."

While he spoke, Shaper chopped the air like a conductor.

Karen joined us, taking a moment to do her cigarette-roll routine again. "Collins is a real jerk, but he's got a spotless record."

"Why is he here?" I asked.

"Because his office will get the case." Karen shrugged. "He's a control freak."

As if she wasn't.

"The DA prefers to see the site for himself," Kim said. "Nick doesn't mind. He believes in first impressions. Extra eyes might spot a clue someone else misses." She gave me a brief nod and went back to work.

"Well, I didn't make a great first impression," I said to Karen. "I told him I thought Vikki had carved something in the snow. With a pen."

"Was it a name?"

"That's what Shaper asked. I couldn't form a coherent response." Frustration coursed through me. The image was still hazy. "It was more of a design. Curved lines. Maybe a flower? Vikki loved flowers."

Karen put her hand on my shoulder. "I'll add it to your statement, okay?" When I didn't answer, her gaze softened. "You know what? I'm taking you home. Wait here. I'll get my car." She'd moved it to create room for the rest of the vehicles.

The moment Karen was out of sight, a perky young woman with a pixie face and short-cropped brown hair scurried toward me. She carried a tape recorder in her left hand.

"Hi, I'm Gloria Morning." She smiled, exposing straight white teeth, but quickly changed her demeanor to one of concern and gravity. "I'm a reporter from the *Tahoe Daily Tribune*. Can you tell me what went down here? Somebody died, it appears."

"Talk to Detective Sergeant Shaper."

"C'mon. Who died? You can at least tell me that."

"Vikki Carmichael." I tripped over her name. A lump caught in my throat.

"People are saying you found the body. First on the scene usually sees something important." Gloria's doe eyes squinted with concentration, her mouth pursed for a response. "Mind if I record our conversation?" She didn't wait for my approval. "Did you know her? Do they know who did it? Do they have a suspect?"

"No."

"No, you didn't know her? Or no—"

"Stop. I'm not answering your questions."

"What's your name?" Gloria asked.

"Aspen Adams." Dang. Why couldn't I keep quiet? Did I need to seal my mouth with electrical tape?

"Hey, I know you." Gloria cocked her head to one side. "Yeah, we went to Stanford together. Remember?"

I shook my head.

"You were a psych major, I was sociology. While we were waiting to do that dream study, we chatted about being Type A personalities. You work at a rehab center, don't you? You're a therapist."

"Not anymore." My three years at the Bay Area Rehabilitation Clinic, BARC, working with teens had ended painfully. My last patient's tortured face flashed before me. He was fifteen, a promising artist, but he'd been abused. To him, suicide was the only way out. Losing him nearly caused me a nervous breakdown. I moved to Lake Tahoe a week later.

"Are you okay?" Gloria asked. "You look pale."

A flurry of heat ran up my neck and into my cheeks. I'd learned to build a protective wall around my heart following my parents' deaths and an even bigger wall after my patient died. Now? With Vikki? I might as well invest in a brick factory.

Karen screeched to a halt in her Explorer and screamed from the open window, "What the blazes are you doing, Morning?" She leaped from her car and marched toward us.

"It's the first murder in Lake Tahoe in years." Gloria faced Karen with a steely resolve. "It's newsworthy, don't you think?"

Karen glared at her and said to me, "Get in the car."

"Is she your only witness, Detective Brandon?" Gloria asked.

My mouth dropped open. "I never said—"

"Do you think others will come forward?" Gloria was nothing if not persistent.

Karen snapped, "You're the reporter. You figure it out."

When I closed the passenger door, Karen said, "Shut your mouth with the press, okay? We keep a lid on this, we catch the perp."

I studied my hands, duly chastised.

"Reporter." Karen grunted and pressed on the accelerator. "She's no more a reporter than I'm a frigging stop sign." She glanced at me. "You poor kid. What a heck of a morning you've had. Let's get you some food and something hot to drink."

In truth, I still needed to puke.

Chapter 4

For the seventh time in the past hour, my breath created a circle of fog on the picture window in the living room of my cabin. On any normal day, gazing at the magnificent view of the lake through the towering trees would inspire me, but not now. Life's norms had changed.

One hour drifted into the next, with images of Vikki lying on the snow flickering and fading in my mind. I'd wanted someone to tell me her death was all a dream, a nightmare. No such luck.

When I slammed my palm on the armrest of my chair, the wood split on impact. "I've got to do something," I muttered.

It didn't matter that Detective Sergeant Shaper seemed capable. The futile attempt of the police to solve my parents' murders clouded my logic. Action was going to be the way to honor Vikki's memory. I stood up and paced the room, trying to come up with a plan. What could I do to investigate her murder without infuriating the sheriff's department? I knew her better than anyone, and I was a trained psychologist. I could get people to talk.

I turned on the radio for the twelfth time, praying for music and not the morbid babbling of reporters about Vikki's death. But reporter it was.

"So, you lived on the same street as Miss Carmichael. Tell me how close you were to her," the reporter said. Because murder was so foreign to the resort area, word of Vikki's death was spreading fast.

I snapped off the radio. Seconds later, my landline telephone rang. My aunt had insisted I have one. Sure, she could call me on my cell phone, but she wanted backup. In case. Cell reception in Lake Tahoe could be iffy. The persistent jangle was unnerving. I didn't want to answer, but the digital answering machine could be delinquent—sometimes answering, sometimes not. Reluctantly, I trudged into the kitchen and lifted the cordless receiver off its base.

"It's me. How are you doing?" Gwen Barrows, my best friend next to Vikki, had heard about the murder and had called numerous times. She'd begged me to come to her restaurant. I'd turned her down. Vikki and I had made the Homewood Tavern a hangout. In the wake of her death, I couldn't face the crowd, and food sounded disgusting. "Are you watching KINC? Some gal named Gloria Morning is quoting you."

"I thought she was a newspaper reporter."

"Not anymore. KINC snapped her up." Gwen's voice was raspy from the pack-of-cigarettes-a-day habit she'd shaken. "Turn on the television. She's saying she's got an insider exclusive. People are going to think you know something. That might put a target on your back. Be careful." Somebody yelled an order in the background. Gwen said, "Gotta go. I expect to see you."

I grumbled. I hadn't let that reporter wheedle anything out of me other than my name. After my patient's suicide and my parents' murders, reporters had pursued me nonstop. I had become adept at fending off newshounds.

I switched on the television. A picture of me I'd never seen before appeared in the upper right corner of the screen.

Gloria Morning gazed into the camera, her face animated. "Miss Adams thinks a pen found in the victim's hand is relevant, but our meeting was cut short by Detective Brandon—"

"I never said that. Liar."

I switched off the set and dialed the news station. "Give me your producer," I said to a tinny-voiced receptionist.

Six transfers and a barrage of nasty words later, the show's producer came on the line.

I introduced myself. "Gloria Morning quoted me incorrectly in her piece on the Carmichael murder. I want a retraction."

"I'm sorry, Miss Adams. Of course." The woman apologized and promised the retraction would occur at the earliest opportunity.

Yeah, right. As if I believed that.

I ended the call and plodded through the living room, dragging my fingertips across the nubby couch and the burnt sienna leather chair. My gaze rested on a pair of antique snowshoes hanging from pegs on the walls and the antlers beside them that were two generations old. I'd kept a few family artifacts.

Without warning, the fire crackled in the flagstone fireplace. I snapped to attention, nerves tingling. Gwen's words replayed in my mind: *People are going to think you know something.* Would the killer think that? Would he make me his next target?

Why didn't I have a dog? A slobbering, loving creature to calm my frayed nerves. I'd wanted to adopt one but had decided against the idea because of the erratic hours I worked. Keeping an animal penned up all day wasn't right.

Desperate to hear the soothing *lap-whoosh* of the water, I moved onto the porch. In the comforting silence of nature, I prayed that Vikki would find peace in the great beyond.

A crackle in the woods ended my devotion. Was somebody lurking there? Watching me? My heart hammered my chest. Unable to make out anything in the shadows of the trees, let alone a stalker, I hurried inside.

Something rustled in the pine needles beneath an opened window, probably nothing fiercer than a squirrel. Even so, I rushed to every door and window and twisted the locks. Once the house was secure, I sat on my bed in search of inner calm.

The screech of tires followed by a squeal of brakes and the slamming of two doors shattered the serenity.

Whoever was in the driveway was not trying to sneak up on me.

I hurried to the narrow window in the foyer and peeked through the checked curtains. "Shoot."

The catalyst for my overachieving, Type A personality was bounding up the steps to the porch. She beat on the front door with her fist.

Grudgingly, I opened it.

At five-nine and one hundred and sixty pounds, my sister Rosie was a forbidding figure. She always reminded me of a rhino ready to charge. Thirty-three years of life had not been kind to her. Inserting heroin into her veins for over half that time hadn't helped. Her hair was silver, her skin mottled. She tramped inside tugging her thirteen-year-old daughter, Candace, by the hand. "Hey, little sis." I couldn't remember Rosie ever using my given name.

Teeth clenched, I said, "What a surprise."

My least favorite memory of Rosie was when she'd accused me of coercing our parents to rewrite their will. They had skipped Rosie and me and had left everything to my unborn child, should I conceive, and Candace, who'd been one year old at the time. It wasn't much, but it was sitting in a trust earmarked for their college tuitions. Neither Rosie nor I could touch it. A bank executor had control. At the time, Rosie couldn't admit that her habit had made our parents change beneficiaries, and I couldn't let go of the suspicion that one of her drug addict friends had robbed and killed them. The meeting in the lawyer's office hadn't been pretty: curse words, papers flying, a chair smashing into the wall near my head. We'd seen each other less than a handful of times in the past twelve years.

"Not too hard finding this place," she said. "Nice digs."

Rosie had spent her teen years sneaking out of the house to feed her drug habit. When she turned eighteen, after a painful family intervention, she crawled into a rehab facility. The staff had helped her develop a bit of self-esteem and had put her to work at a company that needed a filing clerk. Unfortunately, with the steady cash, she'd found she could afford heroin again, and her habit returned full force.

"How's tricks?" she asked.

"Fine. Can I get you a glass of water?"

"Got wine?"

"Not if you're driving."

"You always were a self-righteous chick." A Salem cigarette hung from her mouth. Dirty fingers removed it while she spoke. "I need you to take Candy for a week." Rosie thought naming her daughter the slang version of her habit had been funny. To me, the idea had been crude. I refused to call the girl anything but Candace. "I have a job interview."

"That takes a week?"

"I can't be distracted."

"Bullpuckey."

"Cut me some slack. It's not like her father can take her."

Candace's father went MIA before she was born.

"Say yes," Rosie said.

I sighed. "Yes, okay."

Rosie shoved the cigarette between her lips and inhaled. She blew a long stream of smoke out her nostrils. The beast was restless. "I brought some things for her."

Candace, a willowy girl with olive skin and the Adams's traditional ski-jump nose, fidgeted like a hummingbird at a feeder, ready to fly off at a moment's notice. She was shorter than her mother, clad in nothing more than a cotton crop-top and torn jeans. Her gaze was fixed on her feet, which were tucked into a pair of shabby sandals, toes pointed inward. She clung to a frayed duffel bag.

"What happened with your last career move?" I asked. "Or were you fired from that, too?" The bitterness in my voice was hard to curb.

Rosie shifted from one foot to the next. "Not a good fit."

"Candace"—I turned to my niece—"why don't you get something to eat in the kitchen? I've got some apples. They're in a basket on the counter."

"Okay." The girl smiled, the tentative look in her pale green eyes melting away. "Do you have any orange juice?"

"Yes. Help yourself."

"Candy, make sure you give me a hug before I go."

Candace slipped through the foyer, casting a wary glance in her mother's direction, but since Rosie didn't prevent her from leaving, she continued on.

"What's the real reason you brought her here?" I asked.

My sister loped into the living room and draped herself across the leather armchair.

"You've got a new boyfriend," I said. "Is that it?"

"Caught me out." Rosie tendered a familiar grin, the signature devil-may-care gleam in her eyes. "He hates kids."

"Every guy you've dated hates kids."

"That's not true."

Being in the same room with Rosie made me itch. Indigestion bubbled up. "Doesn't Candace have a friend she can stay with?"

"She's on a year-round schedule at school. Six weeks off starting in January is crap. All her friends are out of town, and my friends—" Rosie gulped down a nasty laugh. "Well, you wouldn't want her to stay with *my* friends." She pulled off her ratty denim jacket and flung it onto the couch, determined to make herself comfortable whether she had been invited in or not. "Look, Candy's thirteen. She could get in trouble if left alone. Keep her a week. That's all I ask." She yanked her cheap T-shirt out of her raggedy jeans and stretched. "Got a beer?"

"No beer. No wine."

"Okay, don't give the flake anything to drink, even though I drove all the way up from Auburn without stopping."

"An hour and a half. Big deal." I'd chosen to become a therapist because of Rosie, clinging to the illusion that I could save somebody else since I couldn't save her. Me, savior to the world. Ha!

"You're a killjoy of a hostess."

"Who's throwing a party?" I could dish it out when necessary.

Rosie sneered. "And here I thought I was the one Mom screwed up."

"Don't blame Mom for your mistakes."

"Ooh, testy-testy."

Rosie's drug habit had been a bone of contention for years. Mom kept bailing her out even though my father and I had advocated tough love.

"Candy, baby," Rosie yelled, "Mama's out of here." She grabbed her jacket and slung it over her shoulder.

Candace tiptoed out of the kitchen. Rosie hurried to her and gave her a squeeze. "You be good." To me she said, "Take care of her. She's my precious cargo." Without a backward glance, she tramped out the door.

The chill of approaching night combined with the apprehension of a week of motherhood made me shiver.

How did Candace feel? Abandoned? Relieved? The last time we had seen each other, we had played Monopoly all afternoon. I'd offered to babysit so I could get to know her better. Little girls were good at tuning out abusive situations, but she was a teenager now. Teens could suffer in silence.

"Listen, something happened today," I said, "so if I seem a little quiet or distant, I don't want you to take it personally."

Candace chewed on her lip. "Can you tell me?"

I paused. "A friend of mine died this morning. She was . . ." I wanted to kick myself for even mentioning it but realized I needed to tell her before she heard it on the news. "She was murdered."

Candace shuddered.

"I'm pretty shaken up."

"I would be, too." Her gaze was filled with concern.

"I told you so that you wouldn't think, well, that you weren't wanted or that I was ignoring you." I put my hand on her shoulder in an effort to bolster her flagging spirit. "Hungry?"

"Um-hm," Candace whispered.

"Good. I'm taking you to a restaurant a few miles north of here, up in Tahoe Pines." I glanced down at Candace's feet, at the sandals. "Do you have some other shoes in your bag?"

"A nightgown, a toothbrush, and a pair of underwear." She stared at her feet and hid one behind the other.

"Your mom didn't pack anything else?"

"We, uh, sort of left in a hurry."

"What size shoe do you wear?"

"Eight."

"Me, too. Let's get you some tennis shoes and something warm."

We raided my wardrobe and found a bulky white chenille sweater. I grabbed jeans with no holes and held them out to Candace. She glanced in the mirror.

"They might be a little short, but they should fit otherwise," I said. "I've got boy hips."

"You do not." Candace smiled, a ray of sunshine peeking through.

Other than height, we looked similar. If I didn't know better, I'd swear the girl was my own. We had the same pale green eyes and prominent cheekbones. Even the wave, length, and auburn color of our hair were similar.

As she turned her back to remove her crop-top, I stifled a gasp. Her ribs pushed at her skin. Memories of my battle with anorexia surfaced. In my teen years, I'd lost interest in food. Anorexia, the typical ailment for a perfectionist, dominated my life, and I shed more than thirty pounds in a matter of months. If a college girlfriend hadn't stepped in and suggested counseling, I'd have died.

I moved into the bathroom to give her some privacy. Once she'd slipped into my jeans and sweater, I returned and handed her a belt.

A pair of running shoes caught her attention. She picked them up. "Are these okay?"

"Sure." The ones I'd worn when I'd found Vikki on the beach. I'd tossed everything I'd been wearing into the laundry. To wash away the ache that had gripped my soul, I'd taken a shower until the water turned cold. "I'll be ready in a few minutes. Why don't you sit in the living room and check text messages or something?"

"I don't have a cell phone."

"You don't?"

"We could only afford one for Mom."

"I'll get you one. So we can be in touch."

"Cool." Candace tiptoed out, rubbing her arms down the sleeves of the sweater.

While getting dressed, I made a decision. I would call the sheriff's department in the morning and offer my services. Knowing Vikki as well as I did, they'd appreciate my input. I fastened my hair with a silver clip, daubed on enough makeup to give myself some color, and headed to the living room.

"Aunt Aspen—"

"You can call me Aspen from now on. What's up?"

"I'm glad you said yes." Her lip trembled. Her eyes glistened with tears.

I wrapped my arms around her and whispered, "Of course I'd say yes," while my mind tried to figure out what I was going to do with a thirteen-year-old for a week.

Chapter 5

The sun set over the mountains as Candace and I drove to dinner. I glanced at her and felt my jaw tensing. I wanted to take care of her without being an enabler for Rosie's errant behavior. Would rejecting Candace do irreparable harm? She hadn't stopped tapping the passenger window of my Jeep since we'd climbed in. I rolled down my window half an inch and drank in the fresh air as it whistled through the tiny opening. How I hoped the heavenly scent of Tahoe would infuse me with patience.

"What's the name of the place we're going to?" she asked.

"Homewood Tavern."

"Do you go there a lot?"

"A couple of times a week."

"The lake is pretty."

It lay to our left. In this part of the lake the colors ranged from pale green to deep blue.

"How big is it?" Candace stopped tapping and smiled sweetly, a kid anxious to be loved.

"Twenty-eight miles long and twelve miles wide. The largest freshwater lake in the United States."

"Wow."

"It's about as long as the English Channel is wide and half again as wide as San Francisco Bay. Seventy-two miles around the shoreline and over sixteen hundred feet at the deepest point. It's the largest subalpine lake in North America."

She giggled. "You should write Wikipedia pages."

I laughed, too. "I've read a lot of books about Tahoe. I love it here."

She fidgeted in her seat to get comfortable. "Tell me more, please."

"Um, okay. Tahoe was discovered by Captain Fremont on Valentine's Day in 1844."

"Valentine's Day? Cool."

"He first gave it the name Lake Bonpland after some botanist. I'm not sure why. Around 1860 the area became known as Lake Tahoe."

She frowned. "Is Tahoe an Indian word?"

"Yes, Washoe Indian. Tahoe means big water. We're part Washoe, you know."

"How much?"

"Your mother and I are one-eighth, which makes you one-sixteenth."

"Where do Washoes live?"

"All around here, many in Dresslerville, southeast of South Lake Tahoe. They're a peaceful tribe that inhabited the Tahoe area before settlers moved here."

On the three-mile drive to Tahoe Pines, Candace continued to grill me. I navigated the unlit road with my headlights on high beam. Windshield wipers on low moved frequently enough to remove the powdery snow that was falling.

We passed Sunnyside Resort, a decades-old, natural wood hotel nestled in a glade of pines. Its popular restaurant had a long porch with an incredible view of the lake. The hotel's marina was constantly busy.

About a half mile farther down the road, we drew up in front of the Homewood Tavern, which had been constructed in the same style as Sunnyside. Within months of its opening, the Tavern was thriving.

By the looks of the parking lot, the place was packed. I was forced to find a spot along Highway 89. As I pulled to a stop, the brakes snagged. The Jeep skidded to the right.

"Shoot." A week ago I had taken the car into the repair shop for a tune-up. All the fluids had checked out. The mechanic must have overlooked something. I put the car in Park and yanked on the hand brake. I slid out and waited for Candace to catch up.

"C'mon," I said. "I'll introduce you to Gwen. Tomorrow we'll enroll you in ski school while I'm at work. You enjoy skiing, don't you?"

Apprehension filled my niece's eyes. "I've only been once."

"I have a friend who's a great teacher."

We climbed the steps and pushed through the saloon-style doors. They swung open with an irritating squeak.

"WD-40," I said to the hostess, whose skin was weathered from too much sun.

"I'll WD-40 when Gwen decides that letting in sub-twenty-degree temperatures is stupid at this time of year." She grinned.

A cacophony of cheerful talk filled the room. The place was overflowing with diners. Rock and roll music blasted from a free jukebox. A wood fire crackled in the stone fireplace. Hurricane candles at the center of each table gave the room a warm glow.

How many times had Vikki and I eaten here? How many times had we disturbed patrons with our raucous laughter? Struggling with the reality that she was dead, I faltered.

Candace gripped my arm. "Are you okay?"

"I'm fine."

Gwen was nowhere in sight, so I guided my niece through the maze of tables. As men ogled her, a protective urge to pluck their lustful eyeballs from their sockets shot through me.

"Let's check in the kitchen," I said.

The Tavern was best known for its pasta dishes and fresh-baked breads, in contrast to Sunnyside's menu, which was heavy on steaks and ribs. The dissimilarity had worked. Both places drew a huge clientele.

I led Candace into the kitchen, a chrome and white-tiled area bustling with activity. The scent of garlic permeated the room.

"Chef Timothy, this is my niece, Candace."

Timothy, a self-proclaimed glutton, stood by the stainless steel stove, his soft chin and cheeks pink from hovering over steaming pots. He tucked errant bangs beneath his chef's toque and in a voice that was as reedy as a clarinet, said, "Hello, hello, hello."

"Uh, hi." Candace looked apprehensive.

"Timothy is the heart and soul of Homewood Tavern," I assured her.

"How about you pull up a chair and I make you some of my special pasta Alfredo?" Timothy pulled butter, cream, and cheese from the oversized steel larder. "So what'll it be? I can make zesty meat sauce, too."

Candace seemed uneasy with the prospect. "Um, I'm not hungry."

I put my hand on her shoulder. "Why don't you sit with Timothy for a bit anyway? I'm going to talk with Gwen." I noted the apprehensive look in her eyes. "You'll be okay here. Timothy has a couple of daughters who are a little older than you."

"Seniors," he said. "They're looking at colleges. You thinking about college?"

"Someday." Candace plucked at the sleeves of the sweater I'd loaned her.

"C'mon. A little dinner. How about a nice white sauce?" Timothy retrieved a carton of cream. "We'll talk about school."

"Do you have anything lighter?" Candace chewed on her lower lip. "My stomach's sort of queasy."

"How about something vegetarian?" Timothy pointed to numerous bottles of herbs and a variety of fresh vegetables lying on a wood block. "Take your pick. I'm suspecting you're an angel hair girl, as pretty as you are."

Candace blushed.

"You can watch me in action." Timothy grabbed a handful of pasta and dumped it into a pot of roiling water. "Do you like to cook?"

"Um, yes. Sort of." Candace glanced at me with wide, fearful eyes.

Man, I wanted to strangle her mother.

I said, "Timothy, make me some grilled chicken and vegetables while you're at it."

"No peppers." Timothy shook his head, familiar with my tastes. He nodded toward the back door. "Gwen's outside for a smoke."

I kissed Candace on the cheek. "I'll be right through those doors."

I found Gwen standing on the porch, enjoying the last of her break. Her white shirt clung to her ample chest. Half a dozen gold chains hung down her cleavage. She rushed up and hugged me hard.

"Air, I need air," I rasped.

She released me. "Darlin', I've been crying my eyes out over Vikki."

"Me, too."

"I'm glad you're here." A vivacious redhead from North Carolina, Gwen was the kind of woman who would be struck dumb if her hands were cut off. She riveted me with her brown eyes. "Something else happened. What?"

"My sister. She's the reason I have my niece for a week."

"No warning?"

"None." I glanced toward the kitchen. "I left her with Chef Timothy."

"Wise decision. Let me buy you a drink, and you'll tell me everything."

We strode into the bar and passed a table of men well on their way to inebriation.

"Miss"—the larger of the two hailed Gwen—"couple of Heinekens."

"Miss? You don't know me too well, do you?" Gwen had been married twice. "FYI, you guys better use a tube of sunblock tomorrow. The kind with zinc." Both men resembled raccoons, with large white circles around their eyes.

I'd seen a number of scorched faces over the years. Some people didn't realize how high up Lake Tahoe was. The city was located a mile above sea level, and the top of Alpine Meadows was eleven thousand feet. The true hotdog skiers and locals knew how to take care of their skin. The tourists often came unprepared.

Gwen ducked under the hatch to the bar, poured two beers, and set them on a tray. She nabbed a waitress and pointed to the raccoon-faced men. When the waitress left, Gwen poured me a glass of pinot noir, brushed her hair over her shoulders, and fixed her gaze on me. "Tell me about this morning, you poor thing."

"It was horrible." I took a seat on a stool. A bitter taste crept up my esophagus, but I wasn't sure antacids could battle the pain and win.

"You found Vikki. Did you see anything? Any clues?" Gwen nibbled on a pretzel while glancing around the bar. "That reporter hinted—"

"I didn't tell her squat."

A waitress plunked six empty beer mugs on the bar. "Another pitcher."

Gwen filled a pitcher from the tap and slapped six new glasses on a tray. She washed the dirty ones in the sink, her movements as rhythmic as a dance—dunk, scrub, dunk, dry. When she finished, she put her wet hand over mine. "Sweet Vikki didn't deserve this."

"No kidding." The first time Vikki and Gwen had met was at my cabin for a dip in the hot tub. Vikki had imbibed way too much that night. Gwen had been ultra gentle with her, like a mother hen. She went out of her way to drive Vikki home.

"How did you find her?" Gwen asked.

I told her, battling the army of tears that threatened to overtake me.

"Who's handling the investigation?"

"Detective Sergeant Shaper." I took a sip of the wine.

"Nick?" Gwen gazed across the room. "The premium eye candy sitting in the corner booth with the blond?"

Chapter 6

I swiveled and peered in that direction. Shaper, still in his black turtleneck, was sitting in a chair to the right of the fireplace. A well-toned woman in a sleeveless red sweater rose from the table. She kissed him on the cheek and headed toward the ladies' room beyond the foyer. As if he felt my gaze, Shaper turned.

He stood and sauntered to the bar with panther-like strides. He rested his foot on the brass railing and smiled. A long line formed down his right cheek, what some might call a dimple and others might call a crevice. "Hello, Miss Adams."

"Detective," I said. "Or do you prefer Detective Sergeant?"

"Detective is fine."

"Why aren't you busy investigating?"

"Even I need to take a few hours off to eat."

"Why here?"

"Because the food's good." He leaned an elbow on the bar. "I come in here a lot."

"You do?"

Gwen's head swung back and forth as she watched us.

"Mostly Fridays," Shaper said. "I've been in on Sundays, too. I've seen you."

"You didn't mention that fact this morning."

"You didn't disclose that you'd seen me at a city council meeting."

So he'd spotted me there, as well.

Down the bar, a heavyset Latino waved his credit card at Gwen. She retrieved it and rang up his check, though her gaze remained on us.

"So, what's going on with the investigation?" I asked Shaper.

"We're going through Miss Carmichael's life with a fine-toothed comb."

Now was the time to offer my professional services, but the words wouldn't form. I ran a finger along the rim of my glass. "Do you have a suspect?"

"Not yet."

"What about Vikki's neighbor, Garrett Thompson?"

"He was with a few buddies playing poker until three a.m."

"Are you sure?"

"They've verified he was there."

I recalled how Garrett had reeked of alcohol. "If they'd been drinking, maybe they wouldn't remember—"

"He and his friends are in AA." Shaper grinned. "You aren't questioning my thoroughness, are you?"

"No, it's . . . He smelled like stale beer."

"I'll check into it." He squinted. "You don't look like you believe me."

Should I explain how the police had bungled my parents' case? The event was definitely coloring my reaction to him. Before I could, Shaper's significant other returned to their table and scanned the bar area. When she spotted him, her eyes grew dark. He nodded in her direction. Appeased, she plopped into the booth and twisted the hurricane candle.

Gwen returned and Shaper said, "Pour me a glass of zinfandel, would you, and a tall club soda with lime and extra ice?"

"Sure. I'll put it on your tab, darlin'." Gwen winked at the detective as she did with all the customers. Her flirtatious manner never scared anyone away. Quite the opposite, in fact. On any given night, more than three-quarters of the clientele were men. She filled his order and set the glasses on the bar.

Shaper picked them up. "Have a nice night, Miss Adams. And don't worry about the investigation. We're professionals."

A polite dismissal. I could handle that.

Shaper started toward his table and turned back. "One more thing. You being Miss Carmichael's best friend, do you know where we might find her parents?"

"You mean her adoptive parents?"

"She was adopted?"

"Mm-hm. She never met her birth parents, as far as I know. I told all this to Detective Brandon earlier."

Shaper shrugged. "I must've missed it when I read your statement. There's a lot of information to process."

"Vikki's parents live somewhere near Sacramento, I think."

"Do you recall her father's first name?"

"I don't. She didn't communicate with them much."

"Why not?" Shaper was as unrelenting as a prosecutor.

"She said growing up with them had been an idyllic life that she had put behind her."

Shaper set the drinks back on the bar, his gaze narrowed with suspicion. "You can outgrow something idyllic?"

The way he said it implied Vikki had kept a dirty little secret. Maybe she had. Everyone had skeletons. Vikki hadn't known everything about me, either.

"I don't know. Maybe you can."

Shaper held my gaze for a long moment, then said, "Thank you. Good night." Underlying his response was a wealth of mistrust. He tipped an imaginary hat and strolled back to his table, where he handed the glass of wine to his companion and sat down.

Gwen joined me while wiping her hands on her apron. "He's a looker, isn't he?"

"And colder than Maggie's Peak." Snow graced the mountaintop above Meeks Bay, even in the hottest months.

Gwen clucked and patted my hand. "You have a tendency to judge all men harshly."

"I do not."

"For Pete's sake, you have every right, after your ex-husband ran off with that nymphomaniac musician."

"What man could resist?" I'd discovered my auteur conductor husband prancing around the living room, his lead violinist chasing him with her bow. His dance on the wild side ended our three-year marriage. Before him, I'd called myself an idealist. Post-him, I'd become a realist.

"Shaper's different," Gwen said.

"You know him well?"

"What he's willing to share after a few beers. And what his cohorts spill behind his back."

"Is that his wife?" I asked, nodding in the direction of the woman with him.

"Her? Nah, she's just one in a string of dates from what I can tell. He seems to go for athletic types."

I glanced back at Shaper, who was smiling at something his date said.

Gwen moved away to collect a tip from the far end of the bar, waved goodbye to a patron, and resumed her elbows-on-bar position by me. "So Vikki's parents are missing in action?"

"Guess so. You'd think with all the resources law enforcement has nowadays, they could find a person's family."

"It's not as easy as it sounds." Gwen poured a glass of water and pushed it toward me.

"Until they locate her parents, there won't be a funeral." I chugged down my water. "Will Shaper be meticulous?"

Gwen nodded. "He's an A-1 cop with a pristine record. But if you're worried about him screwing up, you could initiate your own investigation. You are a PI, you know, in case you forgot."

"I'm a process server with about as much authority as a janitor." I ground my teeth together while mulling over the possibilities. "You know what? You're right. I can at least check around and ask questions. The sheriff's department doesn't hold a patent on that."

Chapter 7

On the drive home I slipped in a CD of the Eagles' greatest hits, but I didn't sing along, not even to "Peaceful Easy Feeling," my mind too cluttered with distractions. If the sheriff's department was coming up dry, I needed to solve my friend's murder. Where would I begin? What facts did I have?

"Aunt Aspen, slow down," Candace cried.

Without realizing it, I had accelerated to over fifty. The maximum on the winding road was a prudent thirty-five miles per hour. I tapped on the brake, but it didn't take. I pressed again. Nothing.

"What the—"

I tried yanking on the hand brake. Zilch.

The tires hit something—a rut. The car swerved. My headlights strafed the houses to our left and the lake to our right. Candace screamed. I couldn't risk looking at her. Ahead was a sharp curve that had mangled many a speeder.

Heart pounding, I made a sharp right into the turn.

Candace slammed into the passenger door and yelped. "Can't you stop?"

"No. The brakes—"

The Jeep hit an icy patch. I maneuvered a full circle, came out straight, and tried to get my bearings. Mariposa was ahead on our left. I whipped the Jeep onto it. At the end of the cul-de-sac was an embankment.

"Cover your face," I ordered and plowed the Jeep into the mound of snow. Pounds of dirty ice tumbled onto the hood. The car revved with nowhere to go.

Candace lowered her hands. She was pale with fright. Her teeth were chattering. "Are we—"

I switched the engine off and put my arm around her shoulders. "We're fine. Are you okay? Just scared?"

She bobbed her head.

"In the morning, I'll call the tow company." The mechanic was going to have plenty of explaining to do. "For now, let's get you home."

When we walked into my cabin fifteen minutes later, I noticed the answering machine had a few messages. Before I could check them, my cell phone vibrated. I answered.

"I've been calling you all night. Where have you been?" Karen Brandon yelled so loudly that I had to pull the phone away from my ear. "Why did you talk to Gloria Morning after I told you not to?"

"I didn't," I hissed, my nerves frayed from the drive. "Maybe one of your staff did?"

"They wouldn't—"

"Well, neither would I."

"Then how—"

"I don't know. You find out. You're the detective." I stabbed End and checked my digital answering machine messages. Seven. The most recent were left by Karen—six of them. I erased each without listening further than her name, and played the final one, recorded late last night. From Vikki. A cold sweat broke out on my face when I heard her voice.

"Aspen, it's me," Vikki said. "I'm sorry you had to leave so early for your stakeout. I wanted to tell you something, and I'm sorry I've kept it a secret until now. I don't want to call your cell phone, just in case you forgot to put it on vibrate. We'll talk tomorrow, okay? Love ya."

Tears pressed at the corners of my eyes. How come I hadn't seen the message last night? Or this morning? What kind of bad karma was that? I would've called her back. I would have been there for her.

"Aunt Aspen, are you okay?" Candace asked.

"Yes," I lied. My hands were shaking. My face felt flushed. "I'm just wound up from the brakes going out on my car. Let's get you ready for bed."

• • •

In the morning, after a protein breakfast and a hot, restorative shower, I called AAA. They towed my Jeep to Pete's Repair Shop. Candace and I rode along. After Pete determined that the brake line had sprung a leak, something that happened during the winter according to him, he apologized, saying it might take a day or two for the part to come in, and gave me a loaner Jeep—same color, same model.

Minutes later, after transferring all my gear from my Jeep into the loaner, I drove Candace to Alpine Meadows. Ever since I'd learned to ski at the age of seven, Alpine had been my favorite place to do so. The runs were groomed, the chairlifts were speedy, and the lodge was a comfortable place to hang out. Most recent memories included Vikki. The two of us had often skied a last run together and caught up over a glass of wine at the rustic bar.

Candace, who was dressed in my aqua North Face jacket, ski pants, and turtleneck, looked like every other teen on the slopes. After filling out a bunch of forms, I enrolled her in an all-day ski lesson with Zephyr, a bubbly, trustworthy teacher. I waited with Candace until her class was assembled and assured her I'd be done with work before she knew it. When I kissed her goodbye, anxiety surged inside me. She wasn't a kindergartner, but she was fragile. Seeing her sharing a tube of sunblock with a girl her age brought me a tad of comfort. She'd made a friend.

Traffic was light on the drive to the office in Incline Village. The sun gleamed in a cloudless sky. The weekend entertainment havens of the Dragon Pitch and Putt and the decades-old Brockway Cinema were idle, as were any businesses that rented boats. No one wanted to go out on the lake when temperatures hovered in the twenties.

I parked on Highway 28 and wended my way past a ranch-style house, through overgrown juniper bushes, to a white bungalow that served as the home for the Maxine Adams Detective Agency.

An arbor adorned with bare stalks of clematis vines that were months away from blooming served as the entrance to the one-room bungalow. Beneath the trellis, I batted away the dangling rubber snakes, put there to scare birds from eating the fruit off the berry bushes that crowded the path in summer.

When I walked into the cheery office, the aroma of Guatemalan coffee greeted me. None of that powdered stuff for my aunt. She served brewed coffee because the fragrance brought back memories of the anthropology expeditions she'd taken in the rain forests of South America during her twenties.

"Hello?" I called. No one was in sight. Our chatty receptionist was missing in action, and our two veteran investigators worked varied hours.

"Hi, sugar." Max waved to me from her crouched position on the floor. She was fiddling with a wire. The bungalow was equipped with state-of-the-art fire alarms and security devices. Even the windows were bulletproof. Max was the master technician.

Max—just Max, never Maxine except for the company name—rose to her full height of six feet, all three hundred pounds of flesh draped in her standard muumuu, this one crimson with large blue and yellow parrots on it. Beige Birkenstock sandals exposed painted toenails. Bloody Mary couldn't hold a candle to Max. She was a mountain of a woman with a gigantic heart and colossal wit. She claimed she'd been a mere slip of a girl during her anthropology stint, prior to marrying my uncle. However, food—sugar in particular—had taken on a fascinating allure the day she returned. Hence, *sugar* had become her standard moniker for anybody dear to her.

I said, "I need to pick your brain."

"Let's have a meet. And I'm not talking roast beef." Max always laughed at her jokes, whether I joined in or not. "Can you believe what's going on?"

Thinking she was referring to the murder, I said, "No."

"Heaven knows if we'll have the rest of the day to live with all these quakes."

"Earthquakes?"

Max pointed to the muted television to her right. Per usual, I'd ignored it as I'd come in.

"Five. All under three-point-oh, mind you, but still . . ." Max switched off the television. "Didn't you listen to the news on your way here? Sit down. I'll get us some mugs of java and a few cookies. Catch the lights."

She motioned in the direction of one of the many standing lamps. She'd furnished the place with overstuffed chairs and footstools, believing that investigators needed comfort to be able to concentrate on the puzzles that faced them. The desk in the corner was outfitted with a pair of computers that we all used.

I sat in my favorite chair, the one with a view of the arbor. "I served Mr. Lazar."

Max returned and set two cups of coffee and a plateful of homemade chocolate chip cookies on a side table. "I heard. His wife's pleased."

"You know, he's a good man." I lifted a cup of coffee and took a sip. "I suggested he join AA."

"So have a lot of people."

"I think he'll do it this time."

Max wagged a finger. "Remember, don't get wrapped up in them. They can twist wires around your heart. Now, tell me about Vikki Carmichael. I assume you want to look into her death."

"Why would you—"

"I have ears and eyes. You know, investigating murder isn't what our office specializes in. So give me a good reason why you should pursue it?"

"Because she was my friend."

"Mm-hm." Max nibbled on a cookie while staring at me, as if she were a jurist waiting for the defense attorney's summation.

"You of all people know I don't open myself up to many people, but Vikki was special . . . funny, quirky." I sighed. "She made me take risks I'd never considered before. Parasailing. Speed-skiing down double-diamond runs. She even goaded me into rappelling." I'd never forget the complete euphoria I'd felt as I propelled myself backward off the top of the mountain with only a piton to hold my weight and a rope and leather strap to protect me. I'd also never forget the sound of Vikki cackling. "She had to taste every bit of life, and yet, as gutsy as she was, I felt the need to protect her. All the time."

"She was the sister you never had."

"I've got Rosie."

Max laid her hand on mine. "Family isn't always a direct relation." She gazed at me with her all-knowing eyes. "Something's troubling you about your decision to get involved, isn't it?"

"I'm worried I'll botch things up. I'm a novice. And impulsive. And I make snap judgments, all of which were deterrents as a therapist."

"Stop beating yourself up. You have a good brain, and your previous work is a huge asset. The time has come for you to spread your wings. I'll oversee what you do. Now, share everything. Leave nothing out."

Chapter 8

I proceeded to tell her all that had occurred since I'd found Vikki's body.

When I finished, Max folded her arms. "First, you need to learn every detail of your friend's life. Her boyfriends, her family, her business transactions, her favorite food, her favorite color."

"Pink and burgundy."

"What vitamins she took, whether she was on the pill, whether she did drugs."

"No drugs. Vikki was a health nut."

"Everyone has secrets. You've got to uncover them. In the secrets lies the truth."

I flinched.

Max aimed a finger at me. "Spill."

I told her about Vikki's message and her claim to have a secret.

"You've got to thrash it into the open." Max carried the plates and cups to the kitchen. "Remember to make a case file."

Within that sacred manila folder, an investigator logged addresses, phone numbers, and notes. All of it was uploaded to a computer, as well, but an investigator was to carry the actual file everywhere with her so she had something as a reference.

I pulled a folder from a cabinet, added a label, and wrote *Vikki Carmichael* on the tab.

"Write a file memo first," Max said. "Once that's done, set up contact sheets for friends and family." She crossed the room to sing to her cats. Currently, the enormous calicos were nestled on the area by the bay window where Max had set up a scratching post and mounds of pillows.

After I completed the initial file memo, I went online and found the white pages for government departments. I scanned the listings. Since I'd joined the agency, I'd never had to find someone other than the primary—the person we needed to serve with papers—whose location my aunt provided.

"Max, help. How do I find Vikki's family? I don't know their names."

"Try Facebook or LinkedIn," a man said as he strode into the office.

I spun around and smiled. "Hi, Dan."

"Hey, gorgeous." Dan Wilkins swaggered toward me, but I knew his swagger was all bravado. He was as down-to-earth as they came. "Lunchtime." His curly beard and mustache tickled my face as he kissed my cheek. "You've got to eat." He swooped strands of his tousled hair off his face. "The roads are clear of snow. How about a bike ride and picnic?"

"I can't."

During the course of our friendship, Dan and I had participated in a variety of adventures: hiking, biking, and skiing. Over a year ago, however, we crossed into uncharted territory and made love—he'd lost his sister; I'd consoled him; one thing had led to another. Though the sex had been pleasant, there weren't any fireworks, and the uneasiness afterward felt awkward. The next day, risking the end of our relationship, I asked him to turn back the clock. He agreed.

I said, "My friend Vikki—"

"I heard. I'm so sorry. You poor kid."

"I'm going to investigate."

Dan cut a quick look at Max. She nodded.

"Are you in town for a while?" I asked. Dan was a journalist for *Sportsmen of the World* magazine, most recently covering kayaking in Australia.

"A few days. How about dinner tonight?"

"Can't. My niece is staying with me."

Max opened her mouth but didn't say anything.

"She's a teenager now and quite sweet," I said to Dan. "I dropped her off at Alpine for a full-day ski lesson." I rubbed my temples and drew in a deep breath. "When she leaves, I'll call you, okay?"

Dan got as far as the door and turned back. "I almost forgot. I thought you'd like to have this." He withdrew a photograph from his pocket.

In the picture, Vikki, clad in a hot pink ski outfit and a gold chain with a charm that glimmered in the sunlight, was standing with her fellow avalanche crew volunteers.

Tears filled my eyes. That was Vikki. Even in a disaster, she was sparkly. "She looks like cotton candy, doesn't she?" I tapped the photo. "See this necklace? She said this was a magic wand that would fix all her problems."

"What problems?" Dan asked.

"The usual. Boyfriend woes, money troubles." I kissed Dan on the cheek. "Thanks for bringing this. I didn't have a recent picture."

For the next hour, I searched online for all Carmichaels that lived in the vicinity of Sacramento. More than three thousand existed. I recalled that Vikki's father's name started with a *G* or *J*, so I limited the search to Carmichaels with either letter as the first initial. That resulted in a list of over seven hundred.

Two hours later, having slogged through one hundred—none of which were a match—and knowing I couldn't plow through the remainder before I needed to pick up Candace, I gave up and drove to Alpine Meadows. The sudden discipline of scheduling my life around another person was daunting, yet I was looking forward to seeing her.

I found her standing beneath the breezeway gabbing with a few other teens.

"Hi, Candace, how'd it go today?" I asked.

"It was so cool." Candace pointed to the friends on either side of her, the girl gawky, the boy handsome beyond his right to be. "Aunt Aspen, this is Waverly and Justin."

"Nice to meet you." I signaled for Candace to get her rear in gear. "We need to buy you a parka that fits."

Candace followed in my tracks, kicking up snow, her mood carefree, and her skin glowing with color, even though she had worn sunblock.

We headed to the Tahoe Outdoorsman, a sports store catering to every kind of recreation that Tahoe offered. The lone salesperson was discounting winter items. I threaded my way through myriad clothing racks, with Candace a few steps behind me searching for the right parka. In January the selection could be limited, depleted by the onslaught of post-Christmas bargain buyers. We decided on a yellow parka, which did nothing for Candace's skin tone, but she loved it.

Standing at the register, Candace asked, "Is going to college important?"

"Absolutely. Getting a good education opens doors. I earned my degree in psychology."

"Oh, that's right. Mom said you were a shrink."

Rosie must have enjoyed using that snide term, considering her track record with therapists. I could hear the sarcasm oozing out of her.

"I was more of a counselor to troubled teens."

Candace tilted her head. "So how come you became a private eye? I mean, the job is dangerous, right?"

The salesgirl set aside her other chore and began to ring up our purchase, doing so with the passion of a dead trout.

I turned to Candace. "First, I'm not a full-fledged PI yet. I work in an investigation office, and I serve legal papers. And second, I don't put myself in dangerous situations. Most investigators don't tackle things head-on, like with guns and fists. They're more inquisitive."

Candace wrinkled her nose, not understanding.

"They ask questions," I said, "and try to ascertain what a suspect is thinking. We decode nonverbal signals." Max's recruitment handbook words tumbled from my mouth.

"So you don't get into fights?"

"I do my best not to."

"Where did you meet your friend Dan?" Candace asked.

The one-hundred-and-eighty-degree turn in conversation jolted me. "Dan?"

"Yeah. He introduced himself to me at Alpine today." She jutted her hand. "'Hi, I'm Dan, a friend of your aunt's.' He said he has a season pass and thought he'd take a few runs. He's nice."

Had he gone there to check her out? Was he worried she was a danger to me? He and I would need to have a chat about boundaries.

The clerk handed Candace her purchase and said to me, "Are you sure you don't want one, too?"

"Yeah, Aunt Aspen, you need a new one," Candace said. "This one's looking pretty tired."

"I've got another at home. Thanks."

On our way to the car, I remembered I didn't have a second parka at home. I'd left it last night at the house Vikki was house-sitting. I stopped in my tracks. *Vikki.* Throughout the day, images of her lying in the snow had plagued me. She hadn't been wearing a parka or even a light jacket. Only the burgundy sweater. The temperature had been about twenty degrees. She should have donned something warmer. Had the murderer taken it, or had Vikki gone to the shore thinking she'd be there for less than a few minutes?

No obvious struggle. No skid marks.

In her voice-mail message, she said she'd kept a secret from me. Maybe she'd met someone new. Maybe they'd looked at the stars.

And things went south.

Chapter 9

When we walked into the cabin, I told Candace about my missing parka and said I wanted to fetch it. I didn't tell her that while I was at Vikki's, I wanted to see if I could figure out who killed her. If she'd met somebody after me, maybe her calendar would hold a clue.

"I'm cool if you go." Candace nudged me toward the door. The scent of chamomile shampoo lingered in her hair.

"I'll be gone a half hour. Then I'll pick you up and we'll head to a bookstore, okay?" Thinking about ways to amuse her was a challenge.

She nodded.

"No loud parties."

"As if." Candace's laughter reminded me of the tinkling of wind chimes.

"There are some oatmeal cookies in the cupboard if you need a snack. I wrote my cell phone number on the pad by the answering machine."

"Go." She shoved me onto the porch and slammed the door. The lock clicked tight.

Even though I was concerned about leaving her alone with a mere deck of cards as her companion, I headed for Vikki's. About six months ago, she'd given me an extra key to the place, in case of emergencies. I decided to exercise the option.

Unfortunately, fate thwarted me from my mission. At least a dozen cars were parked outside the well-lit A-frame. A Placer County Sheriff's Office vehicle stood in front. Hours had passed since Vikki had been killed. Why were they here now? Maybe the owner had barred them from searching the place without a warrant.

Some officers were taking photographs on the road. If the goal was to get tire track imprints, it was too late. Snowplows had eliminated any of those. The area across the two-lane highway nearer the lake would be devoid of tracks, too, but detectives scuttled about.

The fragrance of wet pine mixed with diesel emissions from a passing delivery truck permeated the air. The sun had just set. A mustard-colored moon was rising over the mountains. The moon's glow illuminated the waves lapping the shore.

Along the path that led to the front porch, Vikki's handiwork was evident everywhere: a pair of garden angels, a pot filled with artificial pansies, a gold plaque greeting visitors with a prayer. The owner had allowed her to decorate as she'd pleased.

At the door, an officer carrying a box of various tumblers and wineglasses passed by me. Another officer, a heavyset guy I recognized from the crime scene, stepped across the threshold to block my entrance. "Sorry, ma'am, you can't enter."

The rustic A-frame wasn't big. Every room except one was visible from the doorway. A few of the sheriff's department staff were rummaging through Vikki's CDs and DVDs as well as the kitchen cabinets and bedroom closets. Personal items had been tossed onto chairs, tables, and couches. Vikki would cringe at the mess. The photographs she'd taken and hung in frames on the walls looked intact.

"What's going on?" I asked, my voice at dog-whistle pitch. "If I'm not mistaken, the murder occurred at the edge of the lake. Who's in charge?"

"I am, Miss Adams." Nick Shaper emerged from the bathroom to the left. He joined me on the porch and closed the door.

"Detective, why are you tearing Vikki's place apart?"

"We're doing a routine search. Why are you here?"

"To get a parka I left." Frustration peppered my tone. The fact that the detective was doing his job properly didn't placate me. "It's royal blue."

"I can't let you have it quite yet."

"Why not?"

"Procedure." He wore a black turtleneck again. Did the man have any other color in his wardrobe?

I cocked my head and folded my arms, unwilling to budge. "Have you spoken to the owner of this place?"

"Yes."

"Does he have an alibi?"

"Why would he want to kill Miss Carmichael?"

"He wouldn't. I didn't mean—"

"Was she late on the rent?"

"She didn't pay rent."

"Did they have some other arrangement?"

"No. He'd met Vikki at Alpine Meadows and wanted to help out. She said he was gracious that way. He lent a hand to all sorts of young people on limited means. Vikki was thrilled to win his trust."

Shaper pursed his lips, a gesture that was sensual while at the same time disapproving. I didn't appreciate the disapproving half. "For your information, he was in open-heart surgery from six p.m. until six a.m. Are you done with your inquisition?"

"I wasn't—" I paused, wishing I could take back the last minute of time. "I'm sorry."

Shaper popped a piece of chewing gum into his mouth and stuffed the wrapper into his jeans pocket.

The crisp air cut through my sweater. I yearned for the North Face parka I'd left at home. "Vikki wasn't wearing a jacket."

"Yes, I'd noticed."

"Maybe she went to look at the stars with a friend. Someone she knew. Someone she felt comfortable with."

"Someone who put an arm around her to keep her warm. Got it. I'm not an idiot, Miss Adams." Shaper tucked his gum away inside his cheek. "The acquaintance or lover angle has occurred to me."

"That's not what I meant. I don't think you're—" I huffed. Had Shaper been let go from his previous job because of a slipup on his part, hence his twisting around my comment?

He shifted his weight. "Why do you think the killer was a man?"

"I don't know. I assumed—"

"You know better than to assume."

The door opened, and Deputy Kim poked her head out. "Nick, you need to take a look at something."

Chapter 10

"Good night, Miss Adams." Shaper walked inside, leaving the door ajar.

A set of keys marked with tags hung on a hook by the door. I reached in and lifted it with my fingertip. One tag read *Gate to Beach.*

Shaper strode to me and removed the keys from my hand, his gaze hard. "Those are evidence."

Leaving the door ajar had been an oversight, not an invitation. Darn.

"Whoever had access to these keys is a suspect," I said.

"Right now everyone's a suspect."

"Am I?"

"When I read your statement, I didn't think so. Now . . ."

What could lead him to suspect me? I wondered until I remembered the officer carrying the beverage glasses. "You found my fingerprints on a wineglass. Wait. No, you wouldn't know they were my fingerprints yet, would you?" I glared at Shaper. "My cookbook. For stir-fry. You found it in the kitchen. With the dedication from my mother inside the cover." That had to be what was bugging him. "I admitted I was here last night. Do you honestly think I got so angry at the way Vikki was dicing onions that I took her to the beach and clobbered her to death? She was my friend."

Shaper pulled a handkerchief from his back pocket and offered it to me. "Have you seen a doctor about the tears?"

"I'm not going to cry," I said, though I could feel moisture pressing at the corners of my eyes.

"You might be suffering post-traumatic stress disorder."

"I'm not." When I'd first started working with abused kids, I'd done extensive research on PTSD. After witnessing a violent act, a person may undergo feelings of disorientation. I hadn't. The memories that witnesses recalled could be vague and unreliable. Mine weren't. I would never forget Vikki's lifeless form on the snow. "I've cried a little. That's to be expected when your best friend dies."

"How did you and Miss Carmichael meet?"

His questions didn't follow logically. Was he trying to keep me off balance?

"It's in my statement. You read it."

"You met at Alpine Meadows. How long ago?"

"A year ago December."

"I've never made a best friend in that short a time."

"Women are different from men. We invest ourselves a lot sooner." I blew out a stream of frustration. "Vikki and I connected on a number of levels. We had a lot in common."

"Like what?"

"We were both foodies. We liked songs by Beyonce, Rihanna, and Madonna, as well as classics by Elvis and the Eagles and Sinatra. We couldn't get enough of looking at the stars. She knew every constellation." I sighed.

"Where were you the night she died?" Shaper asked.

"That's also in my statement, but I'll tell you again. I ate dinner with Vikki around eight, then I went to a job around nine thirty."

"Which job?"

"I was working a case in Incline until midnight. I had to serve a restraining order."

"Any witnesses?"

"Yes. The neighbor spotted me when he took out the garbage. Around ten thirty, I served Mr. Lazar with the order. We talked for a while."

He looked dubious. "You talked?"

"He was an alcoholic who wanted to quit. After I served him, he asked me to sit with him for a spell. To help him get past the desire." I didn't give Shaper the play-by-play, but Lazar had opened up about his children. Told me their names. Their hobbies. "I drove home. I washed my face, drank a glass of water, and got into bed around one."

"By yourself?"

"Yes." The brazenness of the question irked me.

"What's Mr. Lazar's cell phone number?"

Though I'd put that in my statement, I recited it. I'd called the man so many times, his number was emblazoned on my brain. "Did I change any of my statement?"

"Not that I can tell."

So he didn't need glasses. "Are you through with me?"

"For now. Where are you off to next?"

Before it dawned on me how invasive that question was, I said, "Home. To my niece. She's visiting for a week. Got a problem with that?"

"Nope. Don't hesitate to call if you think of anything else."

"Oh, you bet." I headed down the path and turned back. "By the way, I've been hired to investigate this case." It was a small lie. "My boss will be the lead detective so I'm legit."

When I reached the Jeep, Shaper was still observing me from the doorway. Kim tagged him on the shoulder. He turned, albeit reluctantly.

On the drive home, stars blazed against the pitch-black expanse, yet neither they nor the doleful strains of Rihanna's "Stay" could calm my rattled nerves. I ranted and raved. Vikki's house was being ripped to shreds, and I was powerless to help her.

By the time I picked up Candace to go to the bookstore, I'd composed myself. Or so I thought. When I led the way into Lakeside Books, one of many shops in a building that abutted the lake, I bumped into a colorful display announcing a book signing at seven and then, on my way to the information desk, I plowed into an easel with yet another announcement.

"Good coordination, Aspen," I mumbled.

Candace giggled. I gave her the stink eye.

"Where can the teen section be found?" I asked the information hostess.

The woman pointed toward an area strung with boisterous posters and bright yellow signs saying *Don't vegetate. Read.*

Together Candace and I searched the shelves. We selected half a dozen books. And a prepaid cell phone. After paying, as I was giving Candace a lesson on how the cell phone worked, a woman called my name.

Karen Brandon strode toward me, looking robust in a brown suede jacket with upturned collar, a tan shirt beneath, her long legs even leggier in tight jeans tucked into flat-heeled hiking boots. As she drew nearer, I could see her gaze was roiling with anger. "What's this about you going to Vikki's place?"

"I—"

"I told you to keep your nose out of things. Nick said you were spouting theories."

"I went to get my parka. While there, it dawned on me that Vikki wasn't wearing one."

"Yeah, so?"

"The temperature was in the twenties. She should have put one on. I mentioned it to Detective Sergeant Shaper."

Karen batted the Clive Cussler book she was carrying against her leg. "Nick said you've been hired to investigate."

I nodded.

"By whom? Yourself?"

Caught.

She scoffed. "That's what I figured. Look, Aspen, this is way out of your league. Give it up."

"Vikki was my best friend. No, she was more than that. She was family. She deserves special consideration."

Candace cleared her throat. "Aunt Aspen, may I look around?"

"I'm sorry for being rude." I gestured. "Karen, this is my niece, Candace. Candace, this is Detective Brandon."

"Hi," Candace murmured. "Now may I?"

"Sure"—I handed her the bag of books we'd purchased—"but stay where I can see you."

After she left, Karen touched my shoulder. "This is a knee-jerk reaction because the police botched your parents' murders."

"Isn't it true that if you don't catch the killer in the first forty-eight hours, he's as good as gone?"

"Our crew is thorough. Nick Shaper will solve this. You don't need—"

"Yes, I do."

Karen eased off. "May I buy you a cup of coffee?"

Adjoining the bookstore was View of the Lake Bistro, a charming café. I glanced at Candace.

"Both of you," Karen said.

I fetched Candace, and we made our way to a table. The decor was simple with blue gingham tablecloths and drapes, tiny white vases on each table, and miniature paintings by local artists for sale on the walls. Soft rock emanated from a radio sitting on the glass counter. The owner, a zaftig woman with a joyful personality, asked for our order as we stepped inside. In seconds she brought over two black coffees and a diet Coke.

Karen removed her jacket. Beneath, she was wearing a short-sleeved golf shirt. I shivered looking at her. With the cool air coming in every time someone entered or exited, my sweater and turtleneck were barely enough to keep me warm.

Candace whispered, "Aunt Aspen, the girl I met at ski school is over there. Can I say hello?"

"Sure."

Candace hurried out of her chair.

"So what's with Shaper?" I asked. "Has he got a fragile ego? He seemed, I don't know, on guard."

Karen poured a dollop of cream into her coffee, added three sugars, and stirred. "He's got some personal history that's causing him grief."

I didn't want to know the guy's life story, but I was curious about why he had been so brusque with me. "Like what?"

"Two years ago, his wife claimed spousal abuse. He's not an abuser, but she alleges that he is." Karen shifted in her chair. "Truth? She lied. She was with her boyfriend, Nick's boss, who I guess could get a little rough. To make Nick's life hell, his wife came up with the story that Nick was the one laying into her." Karen's biceps bulged as she tapped her short fingernails against the mug. "She even recorded the times and dates when she'd gone to the hospital with bruises."

"Are you sure he didn't hurt her? He's pretty intense."

"Just because a man's wound tight doesn't mean he would abuse a woman. People used to think my father was abusive. He wasn't." Karen sipped her coffee and continued. "Nick was ostracized by his peers. He couldn't get people, especially women, to work with him."

"Did you have misgivings?"

"At first, but I'm willing to give people the benefit of the doubt. Nick's a good guy. I trust him with my life."

"Did his ex-wife clean him out?"

"They're not exes yet. They're in the middle of divorce proceedings. She's still in San Jose. Nick had lots of friends who would vouch for his character, but he couldn't verify where he was all those nights she claimed he hit her."

"Why not?"

Karen folded her hands in front of her. She had that questioning look of whether she could trust me. After a moment, she said, "He has a sister who needs care. He was with her."

I waited. There was more.

"She's an alcoholic and suffered blackouts and memory lapses."

"So she couldn't corroborate his whereabouts."

"Exactly."

"How is his sister doing now that he's moved here?"

"She's clean and sober and living with him."

That was a commitment I hadn't expected.

Karen brushed her bangs off her forehead. "I've met her. She's nice. She's working at Safeway." Abruptly, she left the table with her mug, crossed to where some warming trays kept pots of coffee for refills, and replenished her supply. Once she returned to the table, she repeated her cream and sugar routine. Responding to my curious glance, she said, "The sweeter the better."

"Back to Vikki. I was wondering if her former boyfriend—"

"What former boyfriend?" Karen asked.

"I never met him. She could be private about a lot of things. She didn't want me judging the guy too soon. Billy something. Starts with a *T.* He worked in South Lake Tahoe. At a casino, I think. She broke up with him two months ago. What if he showed up, convinced her to take a walk, and—"

"Stop, Aspen." Karen heaved a sigh. "You don't know if he killed her. You don't even know if a *man* killed her. You have to stop speculating. Leave it to the professionals."

"Will you track him down?"

"We will when we can figure out his contact information. As it turns out, your pal couldn't write a coherent, legible sentence." Karen pursed her lips. "All her personal data reads as if it's in code. All initials or scribbles."

"That means you've gone through her datebook." Vikki carried it with her always. She'd confided that she had a terrible brain for numbers so she wrote every little detail in that black book. Funny how those memories stuck in my head. "Maybe I could help you decipher it. As a therapist—"

"We have experts going through it."

"As a therapist, I reviewed lots of teenagers' journals. I can read almost any kind of scrawl."

"No. Thanks." Karen set cash on the table. "Look, to be honest, I don't need you snooping around making me look bad."

"How could my investigation make you look bad?"

"It just does."

I didn't understand her self-esteem issue, so I backed off. "If you don't find her parents, I'd like to do a funeral service for her."

"Got it." Karen stood. "I've got to go. Don't forget your books." Candace had set the bag on her chair. "By the way, I wouldn't leave that niece of yours alone at the house. With too much time on their hands, teenage girls get into a boatload of trouble." She left without a backward glance.

I grumbled. Why did Karen think she knew how to raise a kid better than I did? She'd never been married. She had no children. Perhaps she made the parting shot because I'd stuck my nose into her business. Maybe she thought by riling me, I'd back off.

She didn't know me very well.

Chapter 11

An hour after Candace and I returned home, I knocked on the guest room door. No response. She hadn't answered when I'd yelled that dinner would be ready in a half hour. I found her lying on the bed. Her skin was gray. Perspiration beaded on her upper lip.

"Sweetie, what's wrong?"

"I get headaches. I'm fine."

Quickly I brewed some tea and returned. She struggled to sit up. After she took a few sips, the color returned to her cheeks.

"Do these happen often?" I asked. "Do you wear glasses?"

"No."

"When was the last time you saw a doctor?"

"I can't remember."

Had Rosie neglected all of her parental duties? I touched Candace's forehead and sensed a mild temperature. Not enough to worry about.

"I'm making spaghetti. Hungry?"

"Starved." Her face lit up.

Maybe that was where her headaches were stemming from. "Didn't they feed you at ski school?"

Candace shook her head.

"I gave you lunch money. I'm going to flog Zephyr with a ski pole when I see her."

"She tried to make me eat," Candace said, quick to come to her defense. "I wasn't hungry then." Thoughts of her suffering from anorexia plagued me again. Was that why she got headaches? Or was stress the reason?

"Are you okay spending the week with me, or do you want to go home?" I asked.

"Stay."

"Well, one of my rules is you have to eat."

"Okay," she said in a tiny voice.

I kissed her cheek. "I asked Gwen to join us. Hope you don't mind." I ambled into the kitchen, pulled vegetables from the crisper, set them on the cutting board, and put on a large pot of water to boil. Candace slogged into the living room and switched on the television.

A few minutes later, she sneaked up behind me. I whirled around, the chopping knife in my hand pointed right at her.

"I didn't do it." She raised her hands in mock fear.

I set the blade down. "Sorry." I was on edge. For good reason. A killer was loose in Lake Tahoe, and the sheriff's department wasn't any closer to identifying the guilty party. I hated to think Vikki's killer might get off scot-free. "Headache gone?"

"Yeah."

"Good. Give me a hand."

After heating some oil in the frying pan, I tossed in the onion I'd chopped and pitched in some ground beef and tomato sauce. I added a couple of tablespoons of tomato paste, a generous teaspoon of oregano, a teaspoon of crushed garlic, and stirred again. The fragrance made me salivate.

"Start by pulling the leaves off the broccoli stems," I said.

Candace sorted the vegetables into piles, broccoli on the left, snow peas in the middle, and zucchini on the right, as if she were arranging them alphabetically to be read instead of eaten.

"You sure have lots of spices," she said, referring to the rack of glass jars that sat on a ledge above the stove.

"My mom loved seasonings." I ground the pepper mill over the steaming sauce.

"I wish I'd gotten to know Grandma better."

"I do, too." I offered Candace a knife. "Want to dice the veggies?"

Without asking for guidance, Candace arranged the zucchini sideways on the cutting board and chopped as fast as a chef, her knuckles bent. If one slice wasn't the same size as the one before, she went back and trimmed it.

I must have looked at her oddly because she said, "I watch cooking shows, and I practice on celery."

"I knew you hadn't learned that from your mother."

Rosie was a miserable cook. The notion of putting something into her body that wasn't fast food or drugs would never occur to her. Her daughter had skill. Perhaps I could nurture that ability.

"Do you get the chance to mess around in the kitchen at home? I mean, cook real meals?"

"When there's food in the refrigerator, which isn't often." She offered the truth with no embarrassment. "But that's okay because I'd get fat if there was. I like to eat too much."

The front door opened. "Hello?" Gwen sauntered in. "I've got wine." She waved a bottle of Chianti.

During dinner, we listened to my iTunes playlist Soft Rock Hits. Because Gwen had joined us, getting Candace to talk was difficult. She didn't eat more than a bird. After the meal, she went to her room, and Gwen and I nestled into the armchairs by the fire with mugs of coffee.

". . . then I took his keys," Gwen continued with the story she'd started at the dinner table about a drunk guy at the bar.

"You are one tough cookie," I teased.

"You bet your sweet booty I am." She took a sip of her coffee. "This is good. Do you want a job making java at the Tavern? Mine stinks."

"You need to buy better beans."

"I'm cheap. Shoot me."

We sat in silence for a moment, the licks of flame in the fire mesmerizing, the whisper of a gentle breeze grazing the pines outside calming.

"I bumped into Karen at the bookstore," I said. "She thinks she knows better than I do how to care for Candace."

Gwen chuckled. "That Karen. She's good at pushing buttons."

Somebody knocked on the door. I wasn't expecting anyone else. I looked through the peephole and saw the reporter, Gloria Morning. I opened it up and glared at her.

"Got a minute?" she asked.

"You have a lot of gall, Miss Morning. No, I don't have a minute, and I want you to stop pestering me." I started to shut the door.

She slid her foot inside to prevent it from closing. "You saw something at the murder site. You know you did."

"I have nothing to say to you. Good night."

"Aw, c'mon, we Stanford grads have to stick together."

I leaned forward, my gaze as dark as I could muster. "Look, we may have gone to the same school, but we're nothing alike. I would never use somebody the way you did."

"Use somebody?"

"You lied on television. Leave me alone."

"You're trained to see things others don't. When you're ready to talk, call me." Gloria held out a white business card. I didn't take it. She flicked it inside. "I don't care what time it is." She strode to her Chevy SUV and drove off.

I picked up the business card and tossed it onto the kitchen counter with the other paperwork that needed to get filed, and headed back to Gwen.

"Man, that woman," I groaned.

"What'd she say?" Gwen set her mug on the coffee table.

"She thinks I saw something at the crime scene."

"Did you?"

"No." Tears pressed at the corners of my eyes. Picturing Vikki's body was agonizing. I shook the tension from my shoulders.

"Which brings us back to where we started. Karen. At the bookstore."

"She warned me to keep an eye on Candace. She said young girls have too much time on their hands."

"Of course she did." Gwen grinned. "Karen was a devil-child herself. Don't tell me you don't know her history? She's told everyone."

I frowned. Why did some friends tell each other everything and others revealed their history in bits and pieces? One night after book club, I'd brought Karen to the Tavern. Now Karen was a regular customer. For some reason, it irritated me that Gwen knew more about her than I did.

"She had an affair with a married man."

"Someone in Tahoe?"

"No. When she was a teenager. Back in Rocklin." She'd grown up in a suburb near Sacramento. "Karen got into her cups one night at the Tavern. Out it all gushed." Gwen finished off her coffee. "She got her heart broken, which explains why she goes through men like an ice machine, crushing and spitting them out with glee."

"Just because one kid makes a bad choice doesn't mean another will," I said in defense of my niece.

"I'm not sure Karen was ever a kid, know what I mean?"

I laughed.

"You know, I have a grown daughter," Gwen said.

"You what?" I couldn't hide the astonishment in my voice. Did everyone I knew have secrets? "Why is this the first I've heard of it? How old is she?"

"Twenty-eight."

"C'mon." I snapped my fingers. "Show me a picture."

"Don't have any."

"How can you not carry pictures?"

"My wallet was stolen last year." Gwen waved her hand. "Poof. Every picture, gone."

"You must have some on your cell phone."

"Nope. They got destroyed when I accidentally dropped the phone in the lake."

I was dying to know how the gene pool had played out. Was the girl as pretty as her mother? Did she have the same coloring? The same sense of humor? "Where does she live?" I asked.

"Sacramento, last I heard." Gwen grimaced and shifted on the couch. "I did it wrong. I had her too young." Gwen was somewhere in her early forties. She must have been a teenager when she'd conceived.

Never having had sex before the age of twenty and refusing to have sex without benefit of protection, I didn't know how it felt to make a major life mistake. Well, not that kind, anyway. Given the choice now, I'd prefer to take a few more gambles. Eat ice cream for a year. Have sex on a whim. Dance naked in the moonlight. At thirty years old, I was willing to suffer the consequences.

"My parents were against the guy," Gwen said.

"What's your daughter's name?"

"Gabriella. I wanted something that sounded romantic. Something Italian and sexy. Gwen Barrows is such a boring name. But Gabriella . . ." Gwen made a big loopy movement with her hand. "She hates her name. She hates me."

Was hatred a rite of passage for daughters? If I had a daughter, would she hate me? I'd loved my mother.

"In truth, I embarrass her," Gwen said. "And to think that I dropped out of high school and learned to bartend so I could support her."

"You've done well by that."

"I don't know where else I could have made five hundred bucks a week except, you know . . ." She chuckled. "And that was out. I remember going to bartending classes, carrying Gabriella in a papoose sack on my back, tossing gin and tonics and squeezing limes until my fingers hurt, and then crashing on a mattress I'd bought at the Salvation Army store."

"I couldn't have done what you did."

"Those were not the days. Gabby . . ." Gwen pulled her shirt out of her jeans and shook the tails. "You want to talk about a devil-child? There wasn't a time when she didn't say no to me. She was obstinate from the day she was born. A girl for adventure, that's what she was." Gwen leaned in. "You can pick out those girls a mile away. The wild hair, the look of a wanderer in their eyes. You've seen them." Gwen aimed a thumb at herself. "The apple didn't fall far from the tree. I was the same way. I wanted to sail around the world, but stupid me, I got knocked up. Talk about your major ball and chain."

"Didn't you enjoy raising her?"

"Don't get me wrong. I adore my daughter, even if she won't talk to me." Gwen's voice filled with bitterness. "That boyfriend of hers coerced her to leave the nest years ago. He put all sorts of notions in her head about how terrible life was at home. Men. Can't live with them, and you can't kill them and get away with it." Gwen licked her lips. "I'm sorry. My mouth's on fast-forward tonight." She glanced toward the hallway. "Candace sure is quiet."

"Solitude is a teen's rite of passage to independence." Those words had been inscribed on a sign at the rehab center. I put another log on the fire and realized the wicker basket was empty. "I'll be right back. I'm going to get some wood from outside."

"Don't bother." Gwen got to her feet. "It's time to hit the hay. You sleep tight. And if you want to talk about Vikki, day or night, you call me, hear?"

I walked her to her car, and we hugged goodbye. When she backed her aging Capri onto the road, I yelled, "Lights."

She switched on her headlamps and zoomed away. As I turned to go inside, out of the corner of my eye I detected a bent figure in the shadows by the woodpile.

My heart pounded. "Hey, you!"

The figure startled and darted around the back of the house.

I grabbed a piece of wood, intending to run after him, but stopped. Was I insane? Candace was inside. Alone. I raced into the house, locked the door, and sped to her room. She was sound asleep, lying on her side tucked into a fetal position.

Pulse revving, I hurried to the dining room and peeked through a window. I didn't see movement. Whoever was out there had probably been a neighbor, embarrassed to admit he was pilfering firewood.

I returned to Candace's room, pulled the covers around her shoulders, and kissed her forehead. She smelled of fresh soap and almond lotion.

She stirred. "Hi," she murmured. "Will you go skiing with me tomorrow?"

"Sure." I'd barely spent any time with her. I wanted to get to know her, and I wanted her to feel welcome. "In the afternoon. After I put in a couple hours at work."

"Cool." Candace stretched to her full length and rolled onto her stomach. "Good night."

Edgy after seeing the trespasser, I tossed in my bed. Images of Vikki on the shore replayed in my mind like a movie trailer: her hair fanned out, the angel wings in the snow, the grooves in the ice that resembled a flower or an ancient Celtic design. Who had killed her? Why?

I fell asleep vowing to find answers. Tomorrow, I would search for Vikki's parents, and then, after spending time bonding with Candace, dig deeper.

• • •

I slept fitfully but awoke to a crisp, cloudless day. Tufts of snow that yesterday had clung to the branches of the pines had melted and turned into sparkling icicles. Sunlight cascaded through the icy darts and shot rays of golden light across the road.

During my morning run, I revisited Shaper's question: was I suffering from post-traumatic stress disorder? Should I call a shrink? No, I hadn't imagined the shadowy figure by the woodpile. I was fine. Tense, but fine.

The three miles passed quickly. I jogged down the driveway and checked the perimeter of the house as a precaution.

Underneath the front porch something glinted. I knelt down and found a metal can—barbecue lighter fluid. Empty. I inhaled. A noxious odor emanated from the woodpile. I investigated and discovered that the logs had been drenched. Had the trespasser done this? Had he meant to torch the house? No way. It must have been a teenager. Emptying the fluid on the wood was meant as a practical joke. There had been a rash of pranks in the neighborhood in the past year.

But then I remembered the brakes on my car rupturing, and fear gripped me. I flashed on Gwen saying that the killer, thanks to Gloria Morning's report, might think I knew something. Had my friendship with Vikki made the murderer come looking for me?

I hurried inside and dialed Karen, but she didn't answer her cell phone. I called the sheriff's North Lake Tahoe Station and reached a clerk. Karen wasn't in. I left a message with both my home and cell phone numbers and briefly described the incident.

When I hung up, my aunt Max's words came back to me. *In the secrets lies the truth.* I knew what I had to do. I needed to review Vikki's datebook.

Chapter 12

After a hearty breakfast, Candace and I dressed for skiing. Then I drove her to Alpine Meadows. As we neared, the mountain rose up before us. The dramatic crags of silver-black rock jutted into the sky. Magnificent drifts of pine trees dotted the steep slopes, each dusted with fresh snow. Because the ski runs opened at nine, the area was already bustling. Parked cars filled the lots that lined the road. Weekend skiers tramped up the slight incline.

Candace pointed toward the main skiing bowl beyond the chalet. "That is so cool. All the chairlifts look like mini escalators and then they disappear."

"And if you ride them, you get a day pass into heaven."

She grinned.

Minutes later, I dropped her at a morning private lesson with Zephyr and reminded her that she had to eat lunch. I would return in the afternoon *to bond.*

At the office, with no subpoenas to serve, Max opted to utilize my talents another way. She gave me the task of pulling all the completed files from the cabinets and adding a file history closure statement to each.

After I finished the task, I resumed my investigation where I'd left off—searching for Vikki's parents. Two hours later, I was as stymied as before. None of the two hundred Carmichaels I'd contacted had known Vikki.

On the way back to Alpine Meadows, my forehead felt as if it was strapped with steel bands. I opened the window to let the crisp mountain air in and dialed Karen again. When she still didn't answer, I left a more cryptic message. "I want to see Vikki's datebook." No *please.* No *thank you.* I hoped she would be agreeable.

I met Candace by the ski school check-in counter. She looked radiant.

We trudged up the hill and got in the long line for Summit Chair, the high-speed quad chair that was the main lift to the top of the mountain. Knowing we had at least a five-minute wait before we boarded, I fetched my cell phone to see if Karen had returned my call. She hadn't. "Dang."

"Everything okay?" Candace asked, her forehead pinched.

"Just dandy." I pocketed the phone and zipped my parka. "Have you got a crush on anyone at school?"

"Sort of." Candace was opening up. A comfort zone was being reached.

"Who?"

"A guy who plays soccer."

"Cute?"

"Very. Except he doesn't pay any attention to me."

We chatted about Soccer Guy for a minute or two. He was a good student, wore braces, and lived with his dad and stepmother. Although he often sent Candace email messages via one of her girlfriend's computers, he declared he didn't like her a bit.

"I wish I had bigger breasts," Candace blurted.

I cringed. "Why?"

"Because boys like them."

"Most of them outgrow that."

"Do you have a crush on Dan?" Candace asked, holding her hand above her eyes to block the sun. "He's nice."

"Yes, he is, but he's just a friend." I stressed the last word.

Candace scrunched up her nose. "He seems real smart."

Smart, good-looking, and adventuresome. Why wasn't I head over heels for him? Today, I decided, was not the day to ponder life's big questions.

To my right a skier yelled, "Shaper, catch you after." The guy *schussed* past the lift line and made a skilled stop by the chalet.

I searched the hill and spotted the object of the skier's shout. Detective Sergeant Shaper, looking fit and trim in black wind pants, parka, sunglasses, and snow-dusted black cowboy hat, had pulled to a stop by a little girl who had fallen near the bottom of the slalom run. What was he doing here? Why wasn't he out tracking down Vikki's murderer?

Candace poked me to advance in the line, but I was too busy watching Shaper. If not for him, skiers zipping down the chute would have wiped the girl out. After he removed her from harm's way, she tore off toward the Hotwheels chairlift. Shaper, on the other hand, joined the line in which we were standing.

Discreetly, I moved my sunglasses from the top of my head and put them on.

Too late. Shaper caught sight of me and waved. "Good afternoon, Miss Adams. You look nice."

"What the heck are you doing here?" I blurted, not registering the compliment.

"Skiing. Don't worry, I'm on the case."

"It doesn't look like it."

"Looks can be deceiving." Shaper removed his hat and batted the snow from it. "The office said you called. What's on your mind?"

"I didn't call you."

"Detective Brandon. Me. What's the difference?" The line inched forward. Shaper talked around the people between us. "What's this about lighter fluid?" Through his sunglasses, I couldn't tell if his gaze was amused or stern.

"Nothing. Already handled." Now, in the calm of day, I didn't want to sound paranoid.

"By the way, I talked to Mr. Lazar." Shaper smiled a cockeyed grin.

Something fluttered in my stomach. If I could've batted the feeling away, I would've.

"He corroborated your whereabouts but said you left him at midnight. That leaves an hour unaccounted for. The coroner figures Miss Carmichael's death occurred between ten and one. You claim you arrived home at one. If you can clear up your whereabouts, I can cross your name off the list."

"I stopped to pick up some things at the grocery store. Milk, eggs, juice. I tossed the receipt but I used a credit card. Do I need a lawyer?"

"I don't think so." He smiled again.

Was he baiting me or was severe paranoia worming its way into my psyche?

"Shouldn't you be interrogating genuine suspects?" I asked, which was what I planned to do when the bonding with Candace was over.

"You run, don't you?"

"Yes."

"Well, I ski. An hour every day whether there are blizzards or ice storms."

"You're like the postal service."

"Clears my mind."

"What do you do during the summer?" I asked and regretted the question. I wasn't interested in his routine.

"I usually take a long walk off a short pier. Happy?"

The chairlift operator said, "Ma'am?"

Candace nudged me. "It's our turn to load."

I scooted ahead and glanced over my shoulder for the oncoming chair.

"By the way, I heard you asked Karen about Miss Carmichael's datebook," Shaper called. "You want to take a look at it?"

Before I could respond, the chair scooped up our two riding partners and us. Our skis scraped the icy base and we whooshed forward.

"Who was that?" Candace asked.

I whispered, "The guy in charge of solving my friend's murder."

"He's cute."

Cute and possibly cooperative. A potent pair.

• • •

Following an afternoon of avoiding snowboarders and instructing Candace on her wedge turns, I was exhausted and hungry. We kicked off our skis and headed in. A light snack on the chalet patio would do wonders for my flagging spirit, provided we could find an available picnic table. We strode into the expansive chalet, a structure that had been rebuilt in the 1980s after an avalanche wiped out the smaller building. Metal beams secured the high ceilings. Multiple picture windows offered a view of the mountain. Loud rock music blared from the bar area.

Skiers had queued up by the numerous food stations to select meals from the assortment of choices. Every picnic-style table in the place was packed with children and adults, jackets and hats off, most faces beaming with excitement.

Candace said, "The ladies' room line is twenty people long."

"Give it a while, if you can."

A half hour later, I carried a tray loaded with our lunch outside—pizza for her, yogurt for me—and found two spaces at one of the picnic tables.

"Aspen, what a surprise." Dan approached, a pair of ski goggles looped over his right bicep, a snow-covered red knit cap in hand.

"Apparently you're working hard," I joked.

"Somebody's got to do it."

"Tough life being a journalist."

"Hi, Dan," Candace said.

"Mr. Wilkins." The words zinged out of my mouth, as if my parents had taken over my body.

"She can call me Dan," he countered. "Hi, Candace. Listen, Aspen, I have to work, but can we talk for a sec?" He jerked his head to the right and headed toward the breezeway.

I told Candace to stay put and followed him. "What's up?" I stifled a smile. Sneaky spy behavior didn't suit him.

"I didn't want to talk about Vikki at the table. I don't know how much you've divulged to Candace."

"I appreciate that."

"You're aware that Vikki helped the ski patrol when she wasn't working the lifts, right? Well, a couple of them are asking about her." Dan leaned against the railing. "Maybe you could learn something from them since, you know, you're investigating."

"Has the sheriff's department questioned them?"

"Not to my knowledge. Your presence might put them at ease."

Unless one of them was guilty.

Chapter 13

While I met with Vikki's coworkers, Candace was more than happy to hang out on the patio, especially after seeing Justin—the good-looking kid from the day before—carrying a plate of pizza. She waved to him. He joined her.

The ski patrol office was situated near the First Aid room, a location that on weekends could become crowded with people suffering from ski pole punctures or worse.

Joey Blain, a hotshot snowboarder sporting a bandage across his cheek, fiery tattoos, and a triplet of sword-shaped earrings in his right ear, was exiting as I reached for the door handle. He scrubbed his bleached hair with one hand then slipped on his baseball cap.

"Hi, Joey," I said. "Having a good day?"

"Rad." Joey offered a thumbs-up. "Yo"—he replaced his dopey grin with a frown—"sorry to hear about Vikki. Dude, that blows." Not waiting for a response, he inserted earbuds into his ears and strode off.

As I slipped into the safety patrol room, a chorus of hellos rang out from a few men and women I recognized. Some of them were what I called weekend warriors. They drove up from the Bay Area or Sacramento locales on weekends. A few were well into their sixties and seventies.

Across the room, Dan was sitting at a round table with a pair of young women who seemed to be attending to his every word. I joined them.

"Ladies"—Dan rose to introduce me to Vikki's friends—"for those of you who haven't had the pleasure, this is Aspen Adams."

Words of sympathy poured out of the women.

"She had a good heart," mumbled the toothy blond with braces. She had a Swedish accent.

"I don't know what I'll do without seeing her smile," said the one with a lustrous black ponytail. "She—" The woman burst into sobs.

"Don't mind Sara," the other one said. "She wears her heart on her sleeve."

Sara's dramatics surprised me. Her beauty was enough to garner plenty of attention.

"Sit, Aspen." Dan pulled the chair out for me. "You ladies talk. I've got to meet that guy over there." At a table across the room sat a man who looked like he could catch a grizzly bear with his teeth. "He's taken over three thousand people off this mountain in a stretcher."

As I settled into the chair and unzipped my parka, the women introduced themselves. The toothy girl was Malika. After a few minutes, they grew more comfortable with me and questions gushed out of them: "You found her?" "Was it awful?" "Who did it?"

Their questions continued for quite a while and then the conversation turned personal.

"She was so full of life," Sara said.

"Her smile could light up any room." Malika wiped a tear off her cheek.

Their declarations came across as honest, so why hadn't Vikki ever introduced me to them? Why had she kept various parts of her life separate? That was unfair, I told myself. I kept my friends separate, too. Vikki. My cooking club. I was the only reason Gwen knew Karen and Vikki.

"Once, Vikki revealed she wanted to be an artist." Malika's eyes sparkled with the memory. "That's why she took all those photographs."

Vikki had been deft with a camera.

"How about that time Vikki took over the kids' ski classes because what's-her-name got sick with the flu?" Sara said. "The kids loved Vikki."

"Who are you kidding?" Malika snorted. "What's-her-name didn't have the flu. She found out she was pregnant."

"Right." Sara snapped her fingers. "I forgot. FYI, did you hear she's keeping it? She's not married."

"Aspen doesn't want to hear about her," Malika said.

Sara stroked her ponytail. "Remember those happy faces Vikki would make?" She addressed me. "Two weeks ago, I'd needed a smile. My boyfriend had dumped me. Vikki drew happy faces on my cheeks. Geez, I laughed so hard."

"She was very religious," Malika said. "One of the faithful, that's what she called herself."

"She sure was." Sara nodded. "She went to the meetings every Sunday, snow blizzard or high winds."

"What was the name of the church?" I asked.

"The Source of Serenity."

"Never heard of it."

An uncomfortable notion niggled the edges of my mind. Had a cult lured Vikki? Had she wanted out and one of the faithful led her to the lake's shore?

"They meet at the top of the mountain." Sara pointed at the window. "By Roundhouse."

Roundhouse was one of the intermediate chairlifts. At the top was a flat area with a tremendous view of Lake Tahoe. On Sundays, a variety of organizations were allowed to hold services there.

"Do you know why she went to that church?" I asked.

Sara said, "She met the guy that created the church on the slopes like almost two years ago. March, I think. And wham, she became a regular. She said he was very nice. He's the reason she started working here. He thought she'd find this job more fulfilling than her other job."

"Would you recognize him?" I asked.

"Never met him," the women said in unison.

"Do you know if Vikki saw him socially?" I asked, intent on finding out about the men in her life.

"Uh-uh. He was old. She was into Billy," Malika offered. "Billy was a stud."

"If you prefer thin, brooding types." Sara shrugged.

"Do you know his last name?" I asked.

Again, they shook their heads.

"There was also a creep that hung around." Sara aimed a finger at Malika. "You know the one I mean. The thickset guy with the nose."

"I forgot about him." Malika shuddered. "I haven't seen him for a while."

"How old?" I asked.

"Late twenties," Sara said.

"An ex-boyfriend?" I asked.

"No way." Malika seemed sure.

"Was he a skier or a snowboarder?"

"I doubt he ever exercised," Sara said. "He was always wearing a Pendleton shirt and jeans and boots. Not snow boots. Regular ones. He drove a truck. Double cabin. Bright blue." She looked to Malika to confirm her assessment. "Maybe he was a mechanic here."

I shifted in my chair. "Where can I find Billy?"

"Don't have a clue," Sara said. "I think he works at some club or casino."

So Vikki had kept Billy separate from everyone, not just me. Across the room, Dan snapped his notebook shut.

"Will there be a funeral for Vikki?" Malika asked.

"When the family schedules one, I'll let you know." I stood and thanked them.

They said quick goodbyes and headed outside, their break over.

Dan joined me. "Well?"

"Have you heard of a group called the Source of Serenity?" I asked.

"I have. They meet here and also hold services in a church across the state line, north of Incline Village. I skied with the pastor once. Ed something. He tried to get me to attend, but I declined."

Declined was his polite way of saying he gave the guy an earful of his anti-religious rhetoric. He claimed that being raised by a zealous Baptist grandmother had nothing to do with his current beliefs or lack of same, but I didn't buy it.

"Is he a nice guy?" I asked.

"Sure, if we talked skiing, snow conditions, and avalanche control." Dan grinned.

"What did he look like?"

"Receding hairline, fifty, fairly fit. I don't see him as a murderer."

"Many didn't see Ted Bundy as a murderer, either."

Dan pecked my cheek and headed for the door. "Call me when you're free for dinner."

As I exited the building and returned to Candace, I couldn't help wondering about the Source of Serenity.

• • •

In the car on the way home, I glanced at Candace and winced. Her sweet face was the color of strawberries. I'd applied sunblock, but it hadn't protected her fair skin.

She didn't seem to mind. She gushed about the wonderful moments she'd spent with Justin, who happened to live in Auburn and enjoyed the same music she did and was so *way cool*. Poor Soccer Guy would never know how quickly he'd lost Candace's heart.

When we arrived at the cabin, I told her to put aloe cream on her face. As she headed for the guest room, I added notes about my conversation with Vikki's coworkers to her file. Afterward, although no light was blinking, I checked for messages on the answering machine.

A familiar response rang out: *You have one message.*

"Spastic machine," I muttered, vowing to buy a new one.

"Aspen," the recording began. "It's Gloria Morning. Please contact me. I know you think—"

I stabbed Erase and snarled, "You have no idea what I think."

Once I'd finished bringing my case file up to date, I set it aside and called Candace to help with dinner. I handed her romaine lettuce and said, "Chop off the end and tear six leaves into pieces." I coated a frying pan with olive oil, sprinkled in crushed rosemary, and tossed in chunks of chicken doused with cornstarch. I stirred continuously to prevent the poultry from sticking to the bottom.

"So what did you learn from Vikki's friends?" she asked.

"I found out I'm nosy, but then we knew that already, didn't we?"

Both of us laughed. I told her a bit about the Source of Serenity.

"I've never been to church," she said.

That was no surprise. Her mother had shunned it at an early age.

"So when will that detective give you the datebook?" she asked.

"Good question." Would Shaper share it? He didn't have to.

I brushed a hair off my face and grabbed a container of premade risotto—I loved it so much that I made a batch every weekend to nibble on throughout the week. I put two heaping spoonfuls into the pan with the poultry, pulled off a garlic clove, minced it with fervor, and pitched it into the pan. The savory aroma made my mouth water.

Candace held up the lettuce pieces for inspection. "Are these okay?"

"Perfect." I regretted my choice of words. Perfection was the goal that a typical anorexic tried to achieve. I vowed from that point on to remove the word from my vocabulary. Noting that Candace glowed under the praise, I made another vow to broach the subject of her diet soon. First, I wanted her to feel loved and confident. She seemed to be eating. Different environment, different habits?

"Did Vikki have a boyfriend?" Candace asked.

The question caught me off guard. "Yes. Why?"

"All the time, you hear about guys going off on their girlfriends. On the news. Online. Maybe he killed her. One of my mom's boyfriends—" She bit off her words.

"Don't worry. I know she's had a few." More like dozens.

"He was arrested for beating a girlfriend."

I flinched, hating to think of everything Rosie was exposing Candace to.

"He never hit Mom or me," she added. "He's in jail now."

"Good to know."

Candace washed her hands. "Can I call Waverly, you know, the girl from skiing?"

"Sure."

She skipped out.

After dinner, knowing I couldn't find the boyfriend without a peek at Vikki's datebook, I decided to look up the Source of Serenity on the Internet. Its main office was located in Incline Village. Evening services were held at nine p.m. nightly.

Eager to put one line of inquiry to rest, I contacted Gwen and asked for the name of a responsible woman who could stay with Candace while I visited the Source of Serenity. No way was I letting my niece stay alone. Not after the incident with the woodpile.

"Come on, Aunt Aspen, a sitter stinks," Candace complained when I told her I'd found someone. "I can take care of myself."

"Uh-uh. Not with the pranks in the neighborhood and the break-ins. And don't forget there's still a murderer loose."

Tahoe. Once a safe haven. Never more.

Within fifteen minutes, a large woman with a sweet face walked in. She was a registered nurse who knew self-defense, which bolstered my confidence, and assured me that Candace was in good hands. By the time I reached the door, she and Candace were scrolling through TV channels.

Chapter 14

At the far end of Incline Village, I pulled into a parking lot that had been cleared of snow. Tucked in the back of a quaint set of novelty shops stood a square blue building. On the door someone had painted a huge orange sun and beneath that in italics *The Source of Serenity*.

I strode into the entry, which was tile inlaid with a mosaic sun. The scent of oranges wafted from an incense burner. *Good morning, sunshine.*

"Hello? Anybody here?" I called. It was too early for the evening service crowd.

A simple desk, two rattan chairs, and a settee were arranged at odd angles in the foyer. A pair of potted palm trees stood on either side of the archway that led to the rest of the building. A security camera was mounted above each palm.

I peered down the hallway looking for signs of movement. A recording of Beethoven's *Eroica* symphony was playing in one of the rooms.

Undeterred by the cameras, I slipped along the hallway and, opening doors, peeked into the rooms. The first was lined with mirrors. The walls in the second were inscribed with New Age slogans. An upright piano stood in the corner. A third room was crammed with plants. A fourth was painted blue and lined with aquariums teeming with tetra.

When I opened the door to the fifth room, my breath caught in my chest. The walls were papered with a series of front pages from newspapers boasting age-old headlines such as *SDS Survivors, 200 Commit Suicide*, and *Mass Graves Found.*

"May I help you?" a man asked, the timbre of his voice deep and soothing.

I spun around and took a moment to absorb the vision. He reminded me of an aging cocktail lounge singer. Elderly women might consider him striking. I didn't. His cowboy-style shirt, which was studded with silver brads and oyster shell buttons, was too flashy, and his jeans were too tight for a man his age.

"Are you unable to speak?" he asked.

"Are you the pastor here?"

"Yes, I am. Reverend Brock. Everyone calls me Ed." He raised his chin, looking like he was trying to remove any folds on his neck. He smoothed his thick hair. I suspected it was a toupee.

"Reverend." I jutted a hand. "Aspen Adams."

"A pleasure."

When he gripped my hand, I experienced warmth followed by a sensation of sliminess.

I yanked my hand away. "This is an interesting room."

"We keep it so our flock will not be swayed by the devil's enticement. *Blessed be the Lord, my rock, who trains my hands for war and my fingers for battle.* Psalms 144, Verse 1." Brock closed the door. "What brings you here?"

"I'm searching for . . ." I hesitated. "For inner peace." It wasn't a total lie. If I could find Vikki's killer, I'd be completely at peace.

"Jeremiah 15, Verse 19: *The Lord says, 'If you return to Me, I will restore you so you can continue to serve me.'*" Brock held out his arm, palm up, to lead me away from the headline room and back to the foyer. "Come sit with me, have a cup of chamomile tea, and tell me what ails you."

"No tea, thanks." I followed him, noting the graceful way he glided forward. His hair hung past his collar, a tad sloppy yet comfortable, giving him the air of a regular guy.

"Nice place."

"It's home."

On our way, I paused at the room where the symphony was playing. The door was ajar. Within, an athletic woman in her mid to late thirties, wearing a yellow sleeveless sweater and neon-green stretch pants, was slotting folders into a file drawer. In between insertions, she conducted an imaginary orchestra. The desk in the room was cluttered with telephones, water glasses, containers of ballpoint pens, and piles of pamphlets.

Brock swiveled and smiled at my fascination. "My assistant adores Beethoven." He grasped the doorknob and slid the door shut. In the foyer, he gestured for me to sit in a rattan chair.

I did and crossed my legs. The chair squeaked under my weight.

The reverend moved the admission placard on the desk and leaned against the fragile table, his palms gripping the edge. "Inner peace," he murmured. "We have a meeting tonight to help many find the same. It begins in an hour. Perhaps you'll stay?"

"Perhaps."

"There will be at least a dozen similar to yourself."

"How many attend?"

"We have over two hundred faithful in the Tahoe area. We have sister organizations in other parts of California as well as Nevada and Oregon." Brock smoothed the top of his hair. It jiggled, confirming my suspicion—a toupee. "Now, why don't you tell me why you're really here?"

"I'm doing research about cults." Not too far from the truth. I could sleep with my conscience.

"We are a church, not a cult. Let's get that distinction straight." His voice held an edge. "We dedicate ourselves to the Lord through prayer, song, and meditation."

"Okay."

"We preach the goodness of the spirit, the unity of humanity, and the promise of eternal life. *So must the Son of God be lifted up, that whoever believes in Him may have eternal life.* John 3, Verse 15."

"So you adhere to the teachings of the Bible?"

"Absolutely."

How many cults had started that way, only to be diverted from their mission because of the egos of their leaders?

Brock pushed away from the table, and I, believing I had been dismissed, rose. Brock waved at me. "Sit. I'll be right back."

He hurried down the hall and returned with his assistant. Her skin was the color of whipped caramel. Her blue eyes were mesmerizing. With her right hand, she flipped her long braid over her shoulder then tugged the hem of her sweater over her stretch pants. In her other hand she clutched some pamphlets.

I stood to greet her.

"Lily would like to give you some reading material." Brock nudged the woman toward me. The booklets tumbled out of her hand. Brock chuckled. "You'd never know she was an all-around athlete in college and came in sixteenth in the U.S. Olympic trials for the biathlon. How long ago was that, Lily? Eighteen years? She's been with us for three months."

Lily scooped up the papers with ease and handed them to me. "In this, you'll find our mission statement."

I scanned the first pamphlet. The material seemed pretty straightforward and steeped in the basic Protestant tradition. What made this group different from the others? What had lured Vikki to it? Why not go to a church closer to home? Why drive the extra forty-five minutes, in good traffic, to Incline or get suited up to ride to the top of the mountain at Alpine Meadows on a non-work day?

Brock said, "If you'll read through the next pamphlet, you'll learn our secret."

I opened "The Parallel Book of Love."

Brock said, "Source of Serenity is a group that doesn't subscribe to organized religion. We are people who have turned away from the typical churches that practice in tithing and donating goods and services. Simply believing is enough. A person's soul is saved by faith."

I flipped to another page.

"Read the quote from Acts."

I read where he indicated: *"There is salvation in no one else, for there is no other name under heaven . . ."* I closed the pamphlet and slipped the literature into my purse.

"Are we good?" he asked.

"There is another reason I'm here. A friend of mine, Vikki Carmichael—"

Lily covered her mouth; tears sprang to her eyes.

Brock lowered his head. "Dear Vikki. We heard she was killed. What a shame."

"I'm investigating her murder."

Brock raised his head. "Are you from the sheriff's department?"

"I'm a private investigator."

"I assume, seeing as Vikki was one of the flock, that you as well as the sheriff's department will want to know where I was Wednesday night. I was here leading a Bible study. We've been reviewing the book of Ephesians. We convened from nine until eleven."

According to Shaper, the killer had struck between ten and one.

Plenty of time for the reverend to drive to the west side of the lake, but I wasn't going to press him. Not yet.

"I was hoping you might know people who were close to her."

"Excuse me. You said you were her friend. Don't you know who they are?"

"I don't know everybody. For example, I don't know any of the people who visit your church."

"We are not in the habit of divulging secrets of the faithful."

Secrets. The word caught me off guard. Vikki had wanted to share a secret. "I'm not asking you to break any confidences. I'm asking for names of people with whom she might have associated."

"Well, let's see, there was—"

"Billy, of course." Lily sniffed and wiped her nose with the back of her finger.

"Her boyfriend," I said. "Do you know his last name?"

"Tennyson."

"Do you know where I can find him?"

"At the Emerald Casino. He works at the cabaret. That's where they met."

Vikki had told me she'd been a dancer before working at Alpine Meadows. I'd never asked her where she'd worked.

"The cabaret," Brock muttered. Disapproval passed across his face.

Lily rushed to say, "Reverend Brock didn't appreciate Vikki being involved in such a career. He felt it was beneath her. After joining the congregation, he convinced her that she could do better. As for Billy"—Lily worried her hands—"Reverend Brock advised him to move into another position, too, but he wouldn't. He's a lighting technician."

"Is he one of the faithful?" I asked.

"He was."

An overly theatrical sigh escaped from Brock's lungs. Aha, Billy was a renegade. A deserter. Maybe he would be able to tell me more about the actual business of the church.

"Thank you for your help." I headed for the door but turned back. "One last thing. Did Vikki ever mention where her family lived?"

"Never," Brock said.

As I drove home, I continued to think about the reverend. Where had he come from and what credentials did he have to create a church? Was he ordained? And what about Lily? She'd looked dumbstruck at the mention of Vikki's name. She was new to the church but seemed devoted. Had Vikki known something that could expose the church as a scam?

Chapter 15

"Max, are you here?" I barged through the agency door, tossed the case file on a desk, and slung my parka on a chair. The pungent aroma of pepperoni pizza permeated the room. Even though my appetite was nil, my salivary glands went into overdrive. "Max?"

"And a fine good evening to you, too, sugar." The temperature was sixty-four degrees in the cottage, yet she wore a sleeveless muumuu and brown weave Birkenstocks, confirming my belief that my aunt had Eskimo blood in her. She carried a box of pizza to the kitchen table and patted the chair beside her. "Hungry?"

"No, but thanks." I poured myself a cup of coffee—Colombian laced with hazelnuts—and joined my aunt at the table. "Have you heard of the Source of Serenity?"

"It's a religious group in Incline."

"I don't trust the reverend. I want to research where he came from and what he did before."

"Did you bother to ask him?" Max always preferred the direct approach. "Perhaps he'd tell you." When I didn't respond, the lines around her mouth became deep furrows. "All right. This is different than locating an address. First, we go to USSearch.com, a website filled with general information. If the man has a record, it'll show up. The site will also give us his addresses for the past ten years, and so on."

Following her instructions, I sat at the computer and attempted to pull up the site. The Internet did not respond. While it whirred searching for a signal, I read through the Source of Serenity literature Lily had handed me, most of which seemed benign on the face of it. One of the pamphlets consisted of more than twenty pages. Entire passages were devoted to teaching the faithful how to become a full spiritual being. When I was in college, I had seen circulars with far more subversive language. No warnings for cults prickled my antennae.

I set the literature aside and checked the computer. Still no response from the website. Frustration coursed through me. I decided to contact Billy Tennyson instead.

"Max, I'm going to follow a lead. Would you keep trying to get on this website and research Brock for me?"

"I will, but"—Max waved a finger at me—"I want you to be sure you're taking proper precautions to insure your safety."

"I am."

"A murderer is different than a bail jumper. Don't operate on emotion—"

"Operate on fact. Got it." I gave her a squeeze and whispered, "Thanks."

Max grabbed my shoulders. "May I suggest, once again, that you carry a gun?"

"No." We'd had the conversation before. A canister of pepper spray was all I'd pack.

As I slipped out the door, Max yelled, "Remember, the truth is not always what you see."

• • •

On the drive to South Lake Tahoe, I checked in with the sitter. She assured me all was well. She and Candace were watching reruns of *The Brady Bunch.* I hung up wondering if the poor kid wished she could have a normal family like that.

Though smaller in scope, South Lake Tahoe reminded me of Las Vegas with its high-rise hotels, glittery lights, and colorful people. Some parts of it were seedy while others demanded one have a lot of cash on hand. The best part of the area, as far as I was concerned, was Heavenly Valley ski resort. A gondola ride took people to the summit. Beyond that, there were dozens of runs, from easy to black diamond. At the top of the mountain, you could see all the way across the lake to where I'd spent many childhood summers.

The skies were clear. A gibbous moon gleamed overhead. The stars were not as bright in South Lake Tahoe as in Tahoe City. Too many neon lights.

About a half mile past the expensive section of town, I spotted the Emerald Casino. The exterior needed a fresh coat of paint. Its neon sign looked tired. The sign for the Gemstone Cabaret, an adjunct of the casino, was in better shape.

Because of the reverend's disdain for Vikki's choice of career, I'd assumed the club would be the kind with girls gyrating against poles and receiving dollars in their thongs for the effort. My first steps onto the plush green carpet made me breathe easier. The establishment was clean and begging to be considered upscale. There was the odor of smoke and the stale smell of liquor, but that was to be expected. Slot machines were in abundance. Rows of huge potted plants created aisles. The ceilings were shiny green and adorned with gold-rimmed lights. To my right, a green coffee shop was half filled with diners.

In the center of the casino, gold chrome railings protected an area designed for high-stakes poker. Five armed men stood guard while a handful of wealthy men and women played.

Around the golden corral stood crescent-shaped felt tables, each filled with blackjack players. As I strode through the area, the raucous sound of bells and whistles started to blare. Someone had hit the jackpot.

The Gemstone Cabaret was located at the far end of the establishment. Green leather booths circled the room. The murals on the walls featured the Gold Rush. A semicircular stage about fifteen feet wide and six feet deep stood opposite the entrance. Mylar fringe curtains flanked either side. Stage lights jutted from the apron. At the hostess's desk, a leggy young woman with lustrous blond hair was poring over the reservations list.

I approached. "Where can I find the manager?"

She pointed to the right. "You can't miss him. He's the overweight ex-boxer wearing the tux. His name is Rocky Yeats."

The man in question, late twenties, black hair swept off his forehead and held there with gel, stood at the bar among a group of men. "Watch this." He bobbed his head, plucked a shrimp off a plate with his teeth, and swallowed it whole. "How about that?"

I drew near and cleared my throat. "Mr. Yeats, could I have a word with you?"

He turned and rubbed his bulbous fighter's nose. He eyed me head to toe. Was this the guy the ski patrolwomen had called a creep? "Here for the job?" He spoke with a New York accent. "Yeah, okay, you've got full lips. Hair's a good color, right length. Shoulders are a little broad, but you're—"

"I didn't come for the job."

"Too bad. You could see good money. What can I do for you then?"

"My name's Aspen Adams. I'd like to ask a few questions about Vikki Carmichael."

"Aw, Vikki. I saw the news. Too bad, huh?" He bowed his head in a moment of silent something. "She hasn't been around here in months. Man, she could move." Rocky ran his fingers over his lacquered hair. "I hated losing her to that nine-to-five job at the idiotic ski resort."

"You visited her there, didn't you?"

Loud music blared through speakers. Lights snapped on to my right, illuminating the stage. Three women with long platinum hair, clad in scanty clothing and ultra-high heels, slinked toward the middle of the stage. Each carried a fold-up chair.

The tune, a rap version of "Gentlemen Prefer Blondes," reverberated off the walls as the trio began their routine.

"Did you visit Vikki at Alpine, Mr. Yeats?" I repeated.

"Me? Nah."

Why lie? Visiting a former employee wasn't a crime.

Rocky nodded toward the dancers. "See them? Vikki was as good as Tess, the washed-up ballerina in the middle. Best I've got, though at forty-seven she's pushing it."

Tess twirled and blew a kiss to a man sitting at a table near the apron.

"She was a ballerina?"

Rocky chuckled. "Nah, that's what we call her because she puts on airs." He fiddled with the French cuffs of his shirt, uncomfortable with direct eye contact. "You a cop?"

"I'm doing research."

"Research, as in you're a reporter?"

"I'm a PI."

"Who hired you, her folks?"

"A private party. Look, Mr. Yeats—"

"Rocky."

"How well did you know Vikki?"

"Pretty good. She danced here for two years. She was making boffo money. But she up and left." He straightened his collar, looked around the room to make sure his patrons were enjoying themselves. "Stupid, if you ask me. I mean, the ability to dance is a gift, right?" He splayed his hands in an attempt to win my agreement.

"Does Billy Tennyson still work here?"

"Yeah."

"Is he good at his job?"

"Good enough."

"May I talk with him?"

"He's on his break."

"Tell me about him."

"The dope wants to work in films, you know, backstage stuff. What do they call them, gaffers? But he hasn't saved enough money to get to Hollywood yet. If you ask me, he never will." He waved his hand. "He's always dreaming."

The music stopped and the audience applauded. A few yelled come-ons, but the women ignored them and exited the stage.

Tess sashayed toward us. "Rocky, were you two talking about me?" She yanked the black wig off her head, revealing spiky blond hair beneath. In hard contrast, her skin was peach-toned and freckled. "Care to introduce me?" She cocked her head in my direction and smiled. Either an orthodontist had made a mint on her teeth or she had good dental genes.

Rocky puffed out his chest. "Tess Marks, um . . ." He looked at me.

"Aspen Adams." I extended my hand.

She had a strong grip, a direct gaze, and stood six inches taller than me. The shoes helped. "Pleased to meet you. Got a question for me?"

"No, she doesn't." Rocky nudged her. "Get back to your dressing room and change for your next number."

"Yeah, yeah." Tess strutted away.

Rocky smoothed his hair. "Where were we?"

"You were telling me Billy wanted to make it in Hollywood."

He worked his tongue inside his mouth. "He didn't hurt Vikki, if that's what you want to know. Yeah, he took it hard when she broke it off—"

A side door opened. In strolled a young man with ash blond hair and riveting cobalt eyes.

Chapter 16

"Billy," Rocky said. "Get over here."

Billy obeyed. "What do you want?" He was handsome yet edgy in a bad-boy way. I could see why Vikki had fallen for him.

"This woman is investigating Vikki's murder. You should talk to her."

Billy wadded up a pack of Marlboros and sky-hooked it into a nearby trashcan. "Who says I should?" He tore open a fresh pack of Marlboros while eyeing me.

"Vikki was my friend," I said.

A deep pain settled behind Billy's gaze. He sighed. "Yeah, okay. Fire away."

"You need me, you come get me." Rocky rejoined his companions at the bar.

Billy caressed his stubby non-beard. Was he capable of murder? I didn't see him lifting a rock and slamming it into Vikki's head, but I was a novice.

"Can we sit someplace?" I asked. "I'll buy you a soda."

"We've got a machine in the back for employees. Follow me."

We stepped over the electrical cords and headed into the semidarkness toward a vending machine that advertised Pepsi. I paid for two sodas and handed one to Billy.

He leaned against a column that supported a catwalk. His biceps bulged under his shirt as he raised his soda can and licked the perspiration off the sides.

I remained mute, having learned as a therapist that an individual would initiate a conversation if the other person stayed silent.

True to the theory, Billy began to talk while pulling on a rope that raised and lowered a grouping of klieg lights. "Me and Vikki were going together for a couple of years. Then she, like, ended it. She was a great chick."

Okay, so she hadn't fallen for him because of his perfect diction and vocabulary. Maybe he had a good sense of humor. I continued to sip my soda, my gaze acknowledging that I'd heard him.

"She was getting all religious."

"You're not keen on religion?"

"I went with her to those meetings until I realized it was . . ." Billy chugged his soda, squished the aluminum, and tossed it into a trashcan.

To my left, Tess cleared her throat. "Hey, Mr. Macho, three bulbs burst stage right." She had donned a thigh-length silk kimono. It flapped open, revealing a lacy garter belt and smoky gray stockings. A tattoo of a coiled snake peeked out from beneath one of the garter straps.

"I'm on it," Billy said.

"Better be." She winked at him and disappeared.

"Go on," I said. "Until you realized it was what?"

"Not my thing." Billy shrugged. "Vikki loved all the pageantry. The music and the singing and all." He tapped the pack of Marlboros. A cigarette jutted out. He offered it to me.

I declined.

"Vikki and me, we were great together. Like, she understood my goals."

"You want to be a gaffer in Hollywood."

"Sure do. She knew how much it meant to me. She said she'd go anywhere with me. Then all that religious stuff split us in two." A hank of hair fell onto Billy's forehead, further cementing the edgy bad-boy image. He slipped the cigarette between his lips but didn't light it. "Can't smoke inside."

"You want to go outside?"

"Nah, I'm okay. So after a few months of the preacher telling her crap, like her dancing wasn't okay, and her buying into it, I'd had enough."

"You had or she had?"

He kicked a loose nail in the floor with the toe of his hiking boot until it came out, retrieved it, and tossed it into the trashcan. "Vikki was hot when she danced."

I'd bet she was, but I wasn't going there. "Tell me more about the Source of Serenity."

"All those meetings. Meditate on this, meditate on that." He slapped the wall hard. "What a load of bull."

My first opinion of him was changing. I couldn't decide which irked me more, his lack of tears or his anger at being dumped.

"Vikki was private about your relationship," I said.

"Yeah, it was just me and her. The two of us against the world."

"You hated that she broke it off."

"Man, yeah. She was the best. She had a great laugh." An impish look crossed his face. "She said her mother would've been so mad if she'd found out about us."

"You never met her family?"

"Nah. She said they were, like, real strict. They don't have phones or electrical equipment in their house. Plus they lived too far away. They were from somewhere near Auburn, I think."

Funny, I could've sworn that Vikki said she'd grown up near Sacramento. Auburn wasn't that far away, but it wasn't considered a Sacramento locale. Also, she had never mentioned that her parents were strict. Was Billy making everything up on the fly?

"Billy, do you recall her father's name?"

"Jerome."

Jerome, of course.

The music in the cabaret started up again, this time a disco version of "Diamonds Are a Girl's Best Friend."

"Who picks the music here?" I asked.

"Rocky." Billy leaned forward and whispered, "If you haven't figured it out, he's obsessed with Marilyn Monroe."

The three previously platinum-haired women, now sporting short curly bobs, scooted past us.

Tess backed up, adjusted her faux-diamond-studded collar, and tugged at the bodice of her pink teddy. "Ahem. Handsome, going to light this show or not?"

"Tell Benny to cover for me," Billy said.

She gave him a nasty look and traipsed off.

"I have a few more questions," I said.

"Shoot."

"Tell me what ticked you off about the Source of Serenity other than its meditation practices."

Billy cocked his head. "They wanted money, like, from everyone."

"That's not what their brochure says."

"Yeah, they spout that garbage that says no tithing. No one wants to be in for a dime anymore. Most of us barely make enough to cover rent. But the SOS"—he bracketed the letters in the air—"what a scam. They wanted me and Vikki to give everything we had. They didn't say that out loud, but Rev said, 'The more you give, the more you live.' "

I'd seen that phrase in the literature but had taken it to mean doing acts of kindness. How naïve was I?

"Me"—he snatched out the unlit cigarette and squished it under his boot heel—"I said no thank you. But Vikki gave up dancing and handed over a bundle."

I gaped. "How much?"

"A couple thousand. Not enough for a down payment on that fancy Mercedes the preacher drives, but still."

If the church's purpose was to amass wealth, then why had Brock encouraged Vikki to give up dancing for a minimum wage job at Alpine Meadows? She hadn't earned much as a water-ski instructor, either.

"Just so you know, Vikki didn't exactly trust the church, but she trusted Brock. Not sure why, but I didn't question her. She had good instincts."

Just not good enough instincts to stay off the beach the night she died.

"Last question," I said. "Where were you between ten p.m. and one a.m. the night she was killed?"

"Wednesday, right?" He nodded to assure himself of the date. "I was with my brother. We went out drinking. It was my night off."

"He can vouch for you until one a.m.?"

"Yeah. Every minute of it."

Of course he could. He was family.

The music ended and two of the dancers bustled by, their pink outfits fluttering. Billy gazed after them.

Tess followed and pulled up beside us. "When you're done with him, Miss Adams, I need to talk—"

"Tess." Rocky barreled around the corner. "The minute the show's over, you take the costumes to the cleaners."

"Why do I get double duty?"

"Because you messed up the routine."

Tess growled and disappeared into the dressing room.

Rocky yelled, "You don't like it, find another place to work."

The bolt on the door snapped shut. He grumbled and tramped away.

I glanced at Billy. "Cleaners?"

He hitched a thumb. "Twenty-four-hour place down the road. Caters to the smaller casinos that don't have in-house laundries. We take turns dropping off the load."

The idea of contacting all the places that Vikki frequented was daunting. Her life before working at Alpine Meadows had been riddled with people I'd never met. Could I cover the territory? I had to. What if someone from the laundry, and not Rocky Yeats, was the guy who had visited Vikki at Alpine?

"What's it called?" I asked.

"South Lake Tahoe Laundry. Very original. A passel of Eastern Europeans make a mint on all of us. Wish I had their business." Billy rotated his head to loosen knots in his neck. "I've got to catch the next set and fix those bulbs. Anything else?"

"What did you do before this job?"

"Odds and ends. I got my GED then went to trade school for movies and stuff." He pounded his fist on the wall. "Man, Vikki was supposed to go with me to Hollywood. We had a plan." His shoulders shuddered and slouched. Tears threatened to burst from his eyes.

Mr. Cool was dissolving. Or he was a good actor.

"How I wanted to get her out of this hole. She was so smart. Always reading and writing. Always trying to better herself. Man, she loved going to the library. Frank supplied her with lots of books."

"Frank?" I bristled with frustration. "Who's Frank?"

"Frank Novak."

Had he vied for Vikki's affection, too?

"He's the book geek at the library in Tahoe City. Everybody knows Frank."

Not me. I bought my books or swapped with my book club friends.

"You won't find him there tonight," Billy said. "The place is closed. Weird hours. Budgets are thin, you know?"

"Billy, you done gabbing?" Rocky pulled back the stage curtain. "I need your help." He squinted at me. Did I detect anger in his eyes?

"Sorry, ma'am, but he's got to get a move on or quit." He snapped the curtain closed.

To Billy I said, "Thank you for your time."

"You bet. Let me know if you find out anything about who killed my girl." He disappeared as the opening bars of "Happy Birthday" emanated from the bar area.

The three dancers, wearing blond Marilyn Monroe–type wigs, hurried past me and stepped into a cardboard cake that the other stagehand had moved into place behind the curtain.

Even though I was done with Billy, I recalled Tess asking to chat with me. I'd noted the urgency in her eyes. She had something to reveal. I waited on a stool in the shadows. More than halfway into the women's song, Rocky stole past. His body language screamed that he was up to no good. After looking right and left, he slipped into the ladies' dressing room. I tiptoed to the door and peeked inside. The guy was fondling the discarded pink teddies. Gross.

Outside the dressing room, I spotted an unframed picture of Rocky posing with Vikki and the rest of the dancers. It was stuck to the wall with tape. I snatched it and tucked it into my purse. As I returned to my chair, the music stopped and applause ensued.

I returned to the darkness to process what I'd seen. Lots of people had quirks. That didn't make them killers. But Rocky's proclivity added to my sense of unease about him. Maybe he'd made a pass at Vikki and she'd snubbed him, so he killed her in a fit of rage. What was his alibi?

One of the dancers approached me, Marilyn wig in hand. She fluffed her natural curls. "You the detective?"

I nodded.

"Tess said she'd touch base later. She had to get to the cleaners pronto."

I hurried to the dressing room and glanced in the hamper outside it. Empty. Apparently Tess had taken Rocky's threat to heart.

As the dancer sashayed away, she said, "I almost forgot. Tess said the thing she was going to tell you was nothing anyway."

What some people assumed was nothing could be everything. If Tess didn't touch base with me in the next day or so, I'd contact her.

Chapter 17

On my way through the Emerald Casino, I stopped when a familiar voice rang out above the din.

"I saw you, cheater. You pulled a card from the bottom." Karen Brandon stood at one of the blackjack tables. She pounded her fist on the felt top. Chips jumped with each impact. The dealer looked as stoic as a Buckingham Palace guard. "Don't lie to me," Karen continued. "You're trying to rob me of a thousand bucks. I want a fair deal." Her words slurred together. Even from a distance, her eyes appeared dull and watery, her blond hair a mass of tangles. She wore a silk shirt opened one button too low, exposing a lacy, hot-pink bra. "You owe me."

Two security guards appeared and flanked the dealer. A third approached Karen and gripped her arm.

"Unhand me," she shouted. "Do you know who I am? Where's the manager?"

I drew closer and spotted four ten-dollar chips on top of a bill. That hefty a tip signified the waitress had served a lot of liquor. Karen's head listed to the side. She snapped it back to attention.

I sidled up to my friend and the guard and whispered, "I know her." He released her and I touched her wrist. "Karen, it's Aspen. Want to get a cup of coffee with me?"

At first she batted me away, but when she was able to register who I was, she settled down. "This dealer is trying to cheat me."

"They can't," I said. "The shoe prohibits it."

In front of the dealer was a four-deck card caddy that allowed only the top card to be slid off. It made cheating impossible.

"They've got ways."

"No, there're cameras everywhere." I pointed overhead. "Security's a high priority."

A five-hundred-dollar chip sat on the table, her bet for the current hand, which included four cards faceup—a four, two threes, and a two. A fifth card lay facedown.

"May I?" I reached out to take a peek. Karen grabbed my wrist, but after a moment's hesitation, released me. I turned the card over. A two of diamonds. Her total was fourteen. The dealer had twenty showing—a four, a six, and a jack. He'd beaten her fair and square.

Tears slipped from Karen's eyes. I took hold of her arm and grabbed her purse. The security guy seemed content to let me take the lead. I guided Karen to the parking lot in front of the hotel and helped her into my Jeep.

"We'll retrieve your car tomorrow," I said.

"I took Uber."

That was a good indication that she'd known she would be drinking too much.

Within seconds, Karen was snoring. I secured her seat belt, popped into the driver's seat, and didn't think twice. I headed for South Lake Tahoe Laundry.

• • •

A bell chimed as I strode into the facility.

"Be right with you," a woman yelled.

The aroma of freshly pressed clothes took me back to college nights sitting on top of the dryer while I pored over test material. Bright fluorescent lights gleamed overhead. The place was not more than twenty feet wide, with huge oval tracks holding garments on hangers. Sequins or spangles decorated many of the outfits. Three pink teddies and other Gemstone costumes lay on the counter. Tess had come and gone.

In the back, a thickset woman draped plastic wrap over a series of dresses, while a slim younger woman transferred the wrapped items to the oval rack.

After a moment, the younger scurried forward, her smile sweet and eager. "Telephone number, please."

"No. I'm not picking up. I need to ask if you know her." I held up the photo I'd snatched and pointed to Vikki.

The woman looked at the picture and smiled. "Yes. Emerald Casino." She nodded. "Miss Carmichael. Very nice. She hasn't been in for months."

"She died."

The woman gasped.

"How many people work here?"

She glanced toward the back. "Me and my mother."

"Who works here on other days?"

She looked up to the ceiling while calculating. "My sister and grandmother. My two cousins. Six in all."

An authentic family business. "Are any cousins male?"

"Yes."

I glanced at Karen in the Jeep. She was still out cold.

"Does one of them drive a truck?" I asked.

"Yes."

My pulse kicked up a notch. Maybe I was closer to learning the identity of the creep who had stalked Vikki at Alpine Meadows. "What kind of truck?"

"Dirt," she said. "When he's not driving our delivery truck, he works construction. He dumps dirt."

Not a bright blue double-cabin. Strikeout.

Frustrated, I thanked her for her time and returned to the Jeep. On the drive north around the lake, I wondered if the library in Tahoe City might be open even though Billy said the place kept irregular hours. Near Brookline, Karen mumbled something but she didn't waken.

I put my cell phone on speaker, and hands-free, asked Siri to connect me to the library. I reached a recording that provided the schedule: the facility wasn't open on Saturdays or most Mondays, although one Monday a month the place was open in the evenings. The rest of the schedule was so erratic I ended the call.

As I drove past Chinquapin, an area closer to Tahoe City, Karen stirred. "What the heck? Where am I?"

"In my car. I'm taking you home."

She swiveled in her seat. "Where were you? You weren't there."

"What are you talking about?"

"I called your house. You left your niece alone. How could you?"

"No, I didn't." I shot her a defiant look. "There's a sitter with her."

"No, there's not. The sitter left."

"What?" I called home.

After a few rings, Candace answered.

"Candace, it's me," I said, trying to keep my voice calm. "I'm with Detective Brandon. She said the nurse I'd hired to stay with you left. Is that true?"

"Yes."

"Why did she leave?"

"Because her sister was in a car accident." Candace's voice was faint. "I told her it was okay."

"Sweetheart, we talked about this—"

"I checked all the doors and windows."

My insides twisted in a knot. How dare the nurse not call me. Granted, she'd left for an emergency, but what if—

"I'm fine," Candace said. "I'm in bed."

I tamped down my anger. "Okay, I'll be home in a half hour. Call me if you need—"

The connection cut off. I glanced at the readout: *Roaming.*

"Shoot." I tossed the phone into the cup holder.

Karen cackled. "Guess we won't be having the nurse back again."

"Shut up."

"Don't get touchy because you failed as the new mama."

Nerves jangling, I almost slapped her.

After a long silence, Karen said, "I'm sorry. I'm a jerk. I have no business telling you how to handle your niece."

The white center line flickered on the dark road. My eyes worked hard to stay open. I needed sleep.

"I was returning your call," she added. "You left me a voice mail."

I'd messaged her about the stranger and the lighter fluid on the woodpile and my desire to see Vikki's datebook. That seemed eons ago. Now was not the time to discuss any of it. "When did you start gulping down Jack Daniel's?"

"Sometime between goodbye and good riddance."

"What're you talking about?"

"My boyfriend dumped me." I'd never met Karen's latest flame. She'd said he was perfect for her because he didn't expect her to be Susie Homemaker.

"What happened?"

Karen finger-combed her bleached hair, which didn't help much. "His wife showed up."

"You didn't say he was married."

"I didn't know." Tears leaked down her cheeks. She brushed them with the back of her hand. "Boy, can I ever pick them."

I wouldn't get into that debate. At one of our first meetings, she'd revealed she had a bad track record. I'd never pried.

"I think I'll send him a Dear John email. Maybe I'll copy wifey-poo." Karen smacked her lips. "I need some water. Got any?"

I always kept bottles of water in the car. I reached over the seat and grabbed one. Karen cracked it open and drank hungrily.

"I've been searching other leads on your pal's murder, by the way," she said. "I don't want you to think I'm letting that one slip away."

"Fill me in."

"I heard a couple of her ski buddies were loose cannons." Karen took a swig of water. "You ski at Alpine a lot. Do you know a guy named Joey Blain?"

"A snowboarder with a penchant for loud music."

"He has a record—petty theft. I'm interrogating him in the morning. He dated her."

If he'd dated Vikki, it couldn't have been for more than a few dates. She'd commented on how guys that used words like *dude* and *bro* irritated her. And yet she'd dated Billy, whose vocabulary was limited at best.

"Got any aspirin?" Karen asked.

"In the glove compartment."

She opened the hatch and grabbed a bottle of Tylenol, popped three into her hand, and swallowed them down with the rest of the water.

"I met Vikki's boyfriend," I said.

Karen glared at me. "Did you now?"

"Yeah. Billy Tennyson. He's good-looking in an edgy way. He works tech at the Gemstone Cabaret."

"The Gemstone? Attached to the Emerald?"

"Yep." I didn't add that if she'd been sober she might have run into him. "Vikki used to dance there."

"How'd you find him?"

I told her about my visit to the Source of Serenity. "It's a church. There are some pamphlets inside there." I pointed to the case file beneath her feet. "Pull them out."

Karen picked up the folder and flipped through my notes before removing the brochures.

"Vikki was a member," I went on. "Billy says they're big on asking for donations."

"Don't tell me you suspect some kind of religious angle in Vikki's murder." Karen looked less than convinced.

"No, but Reverend Brock is a little cagey."

"Brock?"

"Ed Brock. He's the guy who founded the Source. His picture's inside."

Karen whipped one of the brochures open and took a look.

"You or your team should go to one of the services," I suggested. "Get to know the members of the flock. Not that you care, but if you want my gut feeling on the boyfriend—"

"Your gut feeling?" She moaned, disdain oozing out of her.

I held my ground. "I'm not sure he killed her."

"One day as a full-fledged PI and suddenly you're a profiler?" Karen's gaze turned lethal.

"Four years of college and two years of a master's degree plus four additional years in the field gives me some—"

"Watch out!"

A deer darted in front of the car. I slammed on the brakes and swerved right. Karen screamed and gripped the dashboard.

After I straightened out the wheels and my heart was beating normally again, I said, "I've met a lot of kids over the years. I knew right away which ones were going to go bad and which ones had a chance."

"Do you know why you're not working with those kids now?" Karen asked. Her tone had a bite to it. "Because knowing they couldn't escape their destinies tore you up inside. The kid that committed suicide—"

"Stop."

"Face it, Aspen, kids—people—mess up all the time. This Billy Tennyson probably killed your friend, and he's going to get away with it because you—"

"Now hold on—"

"No, you hold on. What happens if you go to bat for him and he walks?" Karen pointed a finger at me, her hand shaking with intensity. "You, my friend, are a bleeding heart with no instinct for the truth."

Her words stung worse than if she had punched me in the gut. After my patient's suicide, my self-esteem had gone down the tubes. A few months ago, I'd found my way out of that hole. Barely.

I muttered, "With friends like you—"

"Why are you wasting your life in Tahoe, huh?" Karen smacked her hand on her thigh. "You're a doormat for your older sister, and you're doing menial work for a two-bit investigation agency."

"It's not two-bit."

"Before you know it, you'll get in trouble because you're bored."

"Are we talking about me or you? You're the one who was as drunk as a skunk. All because a boyfriend dumped you. Get real."

"His rejection took me back to—" She stopped short.

"To what?" I turned up Pine Lane and pulled in front of Karen's cabin. The porch light was on.

"I was a junior in high school," Karen started.

I set the parking brake. Was I going to hear the history that Gwen had hinted about? "What did you do? Steal a car? Take a joyride? Is your record sealed?"

"You wouldn't understand." Karen opened the car door. A cold blast of air and dusting of fresh snow flew inside. With her back to me, legs dangling out the door, she whispered, "Never trust a man who swears he's had a vasectomy."

"You got pregnant?"

"And had an abortion."

"I'm sorry."

Karen climbed out and pivoted. "I'm sorry, too. I had no right to say what I did a minute ago, but I was angry. If you do my job for me, I come across as inept. You know how hard I've been working to make the grade." She gripped the edge of the door. "Promise me you won't tell Nick Shaper about tonight." The fear on her face was real. "I've got it under control."

"Promise."

"One more thing, keep me apprised of what you're doing, okay?"

"You aren't ordering me to stop?"

"I know you won't."

I offered a reassuring smile. "Are you going to be okay?"

"Yeah, it's nothing a gallon of water, a bottle of aspirin, and a good night's sleep won't cure." Karen slammed the car door and trudged up the path.

All the way to Homewood, her accusation haunted me. Was she right? Had I run away from my career because I couldn't handle the truth?

Chapter 18

The moment I got home, I checked on Candace. She was sound asleep, clutching a pillow to her stomach. I kissed her forehead and slogged to bed. For an hour, I wrestled with the covers. After a while, I gave up and turned on the lamp, hating that self-doubt was stripping away my confidence. I grabbed a book—I kept a steady supply on the nightstand for sleepless nights—and opened it to page one.

A squeak in the hallway made me freeze. My door opened. I bolted upright, heart pounding.

Candace slinked inside, a sliver of moonlight illuminating her face. My heart rate subsided. "Aunt Aspen, I had a bad dream."

"Climb in." I tossed open the burgundy quilt, and she scurried beneath it.

"Mom won't tell me about Grandma and Grandpa and their parents. Will you? Staying here, seeing all the Indian things they collected, I can't stop thinking about them."

Thrilled to have something other than my failure to dwell on, I said, "Sure."

My gaze landed on some of the items in question: a pair of snowshoes used by my great-grandmother to hike into the Tahoe Basin area, a pair of moccasins, a walking stick my grandfather had carved, and the one I had shaped when I was ten.

"Let's begin with my great-grandmother. She was full-blooded Washoe."

Candace snuggled down. "What was her name?"

"Blue Sky."

"What did she look like?"

"She was quite beautiful, with long black hair and skin the color of cashews. She wouldn't let anyone take a photograph, but I've seen drawings of her."

"Was she nice?"

"I never met her. From what I hear, she was gentle and loved nature. She made beautiful jewelry and painted, too." A beautiful string of turquoise that she'd made was in the top drawer of my dresser. "My father said that every artistic bent in our otherwise left-brain family came from her."

Candace smiled.

"Blue Sky married my great-grandfather, Jonathan Adams. He was a San Franciscan involved in the lumber business and had been on an exploratory mission in Tahoe when they met. She was working at a novelty shop. They married in less than three weeks and remained married for sixty years, until she died."

"Wow."

I loved whenever she said *wow*. It sounded so fresh and innocent.

"He moved her to San Francisco to live with him, but she pined for Tahoe, so he invested in some property, and they vacationed here every summer. They had a little cabin in the mountains."

"This one?"

"No, not this one. Farther up. Toward Rubicon Springs. Great-grandfather was a tough son of an Irishman, but he adored Blue Sky. They had one son, Jonathan the Second. He in turn had three sons, Jonathan the Third, Matthew, and my father, James."

"Grandpa Jim."

"Right. As it turned out, my father loved Tahoe more than his brothers did. He told me lots of stories about Blue Sky. I guess she shared tales of her people with him."

Candace nestled closer. As I stroked her hair, I remembered Vikki asking me the same questions. Curious. Trying to connect. What had Max said? *Family isn't always a direct relation.*

Candace poked me. "More."

"Great-grandfather and Blue Sky became involved with some of the most established families in the community. Duane Bliss, who built the Tahoe Tavern—one of the first hotels in Tahoe, located about a half mile south of Tahoe City—was one of their friends. He opened the Tahoe Tavern in 1907. He added a casino that housed a bowling alley, a novelty shop, and a barbershop. It had a ballroom on the second floor."

"One-stop shopping." She giggled.

"Something like that. My great-grandfather told whale-tales about the fights he'd witnessed in the casino."

"What're whale-tales?"

"Big whopper stories with a few lies sprinkled in. The Butlers, relatives of Henry Comstock, took over the casino operation in the 1920s and turned the ballroom into a movie theater."

"It sounds so exciting."

"Yeah, it does, but it wasn't. It was lawless."

"So if this cabin didn't belong to your great-grandfather, then it belonged to Grandpa Jim?"

"No, this one's all mine. My dad bought a quarter-acre lot on the beach at Rubicon Bay and built a house from scratch. What a beauty it was. He spent every summer enhancing it. Blue flagstone. Strips of pine. The cabin was a mere nine hundred square feet, but there were twelve beds. Sadly, my father had to sell it because his business was struggling." I'd cried the night my mother told me it had been sold. Beachfront property, even the smallest lot, was valued upward of a million dollars now. No way I could ever buy it back.

Candace sat up, her cheeks flushed. "Tell me about the snowshoes."

I reached up and touched them. "After Grandpa Jim built the Rubicon house, he collected all these things. In his grandmother's honor. When he was little, she would have snowshoe races with him."

"Doesn't the snow go through the holes?"

"They're tricky. I'll show you sometime."

"How did Grandma and Grandpa meet?"

"During the summer, at a place called Meeks Bay, not far from here. It was a resort area then, not a trailer camp like it is today. Mom had a summer job at the Trading Post. A very cool job."

"What's this?" Candace tapped the circle of wood webbed with string that hung above my bed.

"That's called a dream catcher." Knitted into the string was a gold charm. Five blue feathers hung from the bottom. When I was eight, my father had taught me how to make a hoop. At the same time, I was learning to read pictographs of the Washoe Indians. "The dancing figure on the medallion is the one who carries my dreams to heaven," I said to Candace. "I hang it over the bed to protect me from nightmares."

"Are you superstitious?"

"Nope, but it gives me the feeling that my ancestors are watching over me."

Candace leaned against the pillow and sighed. "Why did Mom have me if she didn't want me?"

Icy fingers of dread clawed my throat. Though I'd expected the question to arise, I'd vowed to never divulge the ugly truth that while the baby continued to grow in her womb, Rosie had stormed around the house wailing about her stupidity. Along the way, she'd come to terms with the fact that she couldn't go through with an abortion.

I gazed at the lovely girl beside me, took her hand in mine, and blatantly lied. "She wanted you, sweetheart. Even if she's not good at expressing it, she loves you. You know what? I'm taking you on a snowshoe hike tomorrow."

"You mean it?"

"Yes. We'll go where there are no houses."

Candace threw her arms around me and squeezed hard. "But what about the investigation?"

"I've told the sheriff's people everything I know. They'll be thrilled to have me out of their hair for a day. Now, it's time to go to sleep. Hunker down."

She nestled beside me, and we lay in silence, hands intertwined, until she dozed off.

With her dainty snoring as background music, I reviewed the day's conversations. Had Billy truly loved Vikki? Could he have killed her in a fit of rage? Had Rocky lusted for Vikki and been rejected? And what about the slick Reverend Brock? Where did he fit in?

As I drifted into a murky dream world, Rocky's face merged with Billy's and Brock's. Nightmares weren't far away.

Chapter 19

"Another chilly day," the announcer on the radio said. I'd tuned to the channel that broadcast up-to-date ski reports. "For all of you ski buffs, we're looking at a foot of fresh powder by the week's end, although it might rain at the base."

Through the open bathroom window floated the chiming tones of church bells. I splashed my face with icy water and headed out to jog. Along Highway 89, early churchgoers were wrapped in coats and ski jackets. The tiny Episcopal Church parking lot had four cars in it. Methodists were meeting in the Homewood Lodge. A Unitarian congregation was gathering under the trees near Sunnyside.

My parents had raised me Presbyterian and, in uncomplicated doses over the years, had given me a reason to have faith. Following their deaths, my faith wavered. In the twelve years since then, I had read a lot of books on the possibility of an afterlife. I rediscovered my faith, but an institution like a church that required constant attendance was not where I found my inspiration. In the mountains, under the canopy of glorious pines and vast skies, was where I felt at peace. My daily runs and moments spent skiing on the slopes or swimming in the icy waters of the lake were the moments when I experienced an overwhelming divine presence. Vikki's discovery of religion at the top of Alpine Meadows made sense.

Vikki . . .

My feet slapped the wet pavement, moist from melting snow. The peppery aroma of pines stirred my memory. On the morning I'd found her body, the temperature had been crisp. The full moon had set, and the sun had started to rise.

First on the scene usually sees something important, Gloria Morning had said.

I cleared my mind and, doing a visualization exercise I'd learned in psychology class, formed a mental picture of Vikki lying in the snow, her hair fanned out like the rays of the sun. Something bothered me about the image. I started again.

Vikki on her back, her hair fanned out. No jacket. Her arms—

I slowed to a trot. One arm was above her head. In the hand by her side she was holding a pen, its cap on. No ink had seeped out. Using the pen, Vikki had carved something in the snow. A design. I was certain of it. As if conjuring up Vikki's handiwork, I started seeing smiley faces. In clouds overhead. On the fogged windows of cabins. In the puffs of exhaust coming out of cars. Vikki had loved to doodle. What had she drawn in the snow?

Think, Aspen. Arced lines. Smiles sideways. Like a pictograph in an ancient cave.

Adrenaline pumped through me. I inhaled a big gulp of air, held it for a count of four, and blew it out hard. I needed to let my mind rest. The image would come to me, in time.

The moment I arrived home I phoned Karen to check on her. She didn't answer, so I left a message.

In the bathroom, I grabbed a clean towel and wiped sweat off my neck and face. I downed a glass of water and poured myself another.

"Candace," I shouted as I walked along the hall toward the guest room. "Rise and shine, girl. Let's get a move on."

"Aunt Max called for you," she said through the closed door. We'd agreed that calling her Great-aunt Max was a mouthful.

"Is she at the office?"

"Yep. Plus another woman called."

I was popular.

"A reporter."

I grumbled but resisted calling Gloria Morning to tell her to bug off. After all, her words had stimulated my memory.

"Be ready to leave in fifteen minutes." I headed to the kitchen to touch base with my aunt.

After the first ring, she picked up. "Maxine Adams Detective Agency."

"It's me."

"Hey, sugar, I have some info for you." I could hear her clicking away on a keyboard. "Ed Brock was a big-time dentist in the Gilroy area. He has an ex-wife who lives in Los Angeles and two grown daughters, ages twenty-seven and twenty-eight. After the divorce, he earned a theological degree from West Valley Theology and led ministries on college campuses. Three and a half years ago, he sold everything, including his dental practice, and moved to Lake Tahoe."

"How did you find this out?" I was pretty certain USSearch.com wouldn't reveal that kind of detail.

"I talked to his realtor."

I was impressed. "Does he have any felonies, any convictions?"

"Clean as a whistle."

I thanked her and brought her up to date on my meetings with Rocky Yeats and Billy Tennyson, then I asked for a day off and ended the call. I wanted to call Karen again and find out if she'd gone to the Source of Serenity this morning, but I decided to hold off. After hearing Brock's history, I wasn't placing him high on the murder suspect list. Why would he kill Vikki? To what end? To steal her meager wealth? I put my notes for him into the file, to be recalled at a later date if necessary.

• • •

Candace and I drove the back road. The sky was a gorgeous peacock blue. Climbing higher into the mountains, leaving the last of the houses and two-lane streets, we proceeded up a narrow snow-plowed road. I rolled down the windows and crisp clean air rushed in. In four-wheel-drive mode, we moved up the lane. Once we reached an area designated for cars, we parked and strapped on our snowshoes.

"These look like tennis rackets," Candace said, standing in place and lifting one foot then the other to get the feel.

"As you walk, do exactly what you're doing. Pick your foot up and place the snowshoe ahead. Don't try to slide it like a ski."

Candace struggled for the first fifty steps, the snowshoes slipping out from under her. Snow spurted up through the holes. Traction was impossible. A short while later, she mastered the technique and tramped ahead of me, her face filled with exhilaration.

"No backcountry skill is more important in winter than the ability to find your way home," I said as we wove through the magnificent forest. "There are no trails to guide us in the winter, so you stick close to me."

"I will."

We followed the stream that led west. A mist of icy powder

fluttered down from the trees and onto our faces. The scent of pine was pungent. The hush was only disturbed by the whoosh of a light wind and the babble of the stream. Prickly manzanita and mountain whitethorn were growing wild along the banks.

"Watch out for stickers," I said.

Near the signpost that indicated the mileage up and down the mountain, we passed a prayer group. They were sitting on logs and rocks. We plodded past, trying not to disturb their devotion.

A half hour into our hike, Candace began to tell me stories about her friends and school. "Do you come here a lot?" she asked when she'd run out of topics.

"I've hiked here at least twenty times. This place has a cool history. Back in the early 1900s, a hotel promised the Fountain of Youth to travelers if they drank the water from the springs. Hordes of pilgrims—"

"Like on the *Mayflower*?"

"No, pilgrim means someone new to an area. An adventurer." I smiled. "Anyway, many ventured up the mountain on horseback and on foot in search of immortality. However, the promise was bogus, tourists disappeared, and the hotel folded."

"That's sad."

"Not really. The land is once again pure wilderness."

"Did you ever drink the water?"

"Of course, and though I never felt younger, I was always refreshed."

An hour later, we reached a clearing that was thick with a fresh blanket of snow. A jackrabbit dashed out of the bushes. Seconds later, a red-tailed hawk swooped down and lifted the animal by the nape of its neck. Candace gasped. Nature, displaying the struggle for survival, could be shocking.

Farther along, we saw a doe standing on a knoll near its fawn.

"Ooh, look." Candace pointed.

I nodded, delighted by my niece's enchantment. "Hungry?"

"Not yet."

After another hour, we turned back. When we reached the wooden mileage signpost, Candace said, "Feed me."

Even though we were less than a half hour from the end of our journey, I agreed. We drew near the edge of the stream and found a nest of boulders to sit on. Candace unlaced her snowshoes, and I broke out our power snacks: homemade trail mix loaded with cashews and golden raisins, a couple of bottles of Gatorade, and two banana muffins—my weakness.

While Candace munched on the goodies, I retrieved a broken bough from a sugar pine and stripped the twigs off of it, leaving three prongs of branches at the base. I pulled out my Swiss Army knife, a tool my father had demanded I carry at all times, and began to smooth the rough edges of the bough with a blade, making a walking stick about three feet in length. The rhythmic movement of scraping the bumps from the wood relaxed me.

"Being out here is nice," Candace said.

"Mm-hm."

Exercise was a natural beauty enhancer. Candace's cheeks were flushed and her eyes were sparkling.

Far off in the distance, a gunshot resounded.

"What was that?" Candace asked.

"Probably poachers. The game wardens don't patrol enough."

"Do you think he killed that deer we saw?"

"I hope not."

Her eyes filled with sorrow. "Do you miss your friend?" she asked, the question obviously prompted by the loss of the deer.

"Very much."

"Is your investigation going okay?"

"Finding the truth takes time." I had been hoping for a mental breakthrough while hiking, but the memory I was groping for remained beyond my grasp. "Finish up, and let's hit the road."

Candace donned the snowshoes and stuffed her baggie of goodies into the backpack. I could tell her legs were aching, so I handed her the walking stick. "Use this if you need to."

"Thanks." She leaned over to tie her straps and found what must have been a decade-old soda can. She sat up, frowning. "What slobs people can be."

I smiled, loving the moment. She was an eco-nut in the making.

"Think it still has fizz?" With one tug, Candace tore off the pop-top.

"Don't you dare drink it."

"I couldn't if I wanted to. It's empty. Evaporated." Grinning maniacally, she wielded the pop-top at me. "Beware the Cla-a-aw."

"Ha! I've seen that movie."

"Watch as I destroy this vile creature." She flexed the can back and forth trying to split it in two.

"Careful with that. It'll have sharp edges."

"Mom hates when I do this. She says the sound is irritating." She emitted a cackle of delight as she continued to thrash the can. Mission accomplished, she pawed the air with the pieces. "Take heart. I will defend us if a bear comes our way."

"Candace, I'm the first to say imagination is good for the soul, but those cans wouldn't stop a dog, let alone a—"

Another gunshot rang out. I felt the whiz of a bullet speed past my face. It struck a pine across the stream. I lunged for Candace and yanked her behind a log. Her untied snowshoes fell off her feet. I peered over my shoulder. The bullet had hit the tree at eye level.

"Is the d-deer hunter shooting at us?" she stammered.

I thought of the woodpile doused with lighter fluid and flashed on my brakes rupturing. Was someone after me? Us? I urged myself to remain calm and replayed the incident. The shot had sounded more like a *spit* than a *crack*. The shooter had to be far away. For now.

Peeking over the log, I looked for movement. Nothing. I removed my snowshoes, grabbed Candace's pair, and whispered, "Follow me. We'll escape along the water."

The moment I stood, another shot rang out and another bullet whizzed past. A tree branch fell off a nearby dead tree.

Candace screamed.

Pulse pounding, I tugged her through the bushes. Over my shoulder, at a distance, I spotted a glint of metal and someone in camouflage slipping through the trees. The shooter must have been using a scope.

"This way," I whispered and pressed forward. Thorns ripped our clothing. I guided Candace into the stream while praying for help to appear.

"It's cold," she whispered.

"In the water we won't leave footprints."

We ran for at least five minutes. When I heard voices singing, I steered Candace in that direction.

An assembly of more than twenty adults and a few teens were tramping down the snowy trail toward the parking area. We cut into the middle of the line. I peered around them looking for our pursuer. No figure was in sight. Had our joining the group scared him off?

Once inside the Jeep, I switched on the ignition and heater. Candace was clutching her torso and looking like she might puke. I patted her knee to reassure her.

"Why was the poacher shooting at us?" she asked in a small voice.

"I'm not sure."

I didn't call Karen Brandon yet because I didn't want to say out loud what I knew to be true. The shooter wasn't a poacher.

Chapter 20

Skittish about the security of my cabin when we arrived home, I checked the perimeter before going in. Once inside I scoured every closet and dark corner for an intruder. No one.

I told Candace to take a hot shower while I tore off my gloves and hat and dialed Karen.

When she answered, I said, "Somebody shot at me."

"Where?"

I told her. When she suggested it was a poacher, I said, "The bullets came too close. One hit a couple of feet from my head. I don't look like a deer."

"I'll check it out. Can you be more specific about where you were?"

"Near the mileage signpost by the stream. Candace and I were sitting on some boulders having a snack."

"I'm on it." One of the reasons Karen had quit smoking was because she loved skiing and hiking, two sports that required plenty of lung capacity.

"We were hiking in snowshoes so you might see our tracks. We escaped through the stream." I hated the fear in my voice. "Do you think whoever murdered Vikki is trying to kill me because I've been asking questions?" I filled Karen in about the lighter fluid on the woodpile and the punctured brake line.

"Why didn't you tell me about the woodpile before?"

"I left you a message. You didn't call me back. Last night when we hooked up, you were—"

"Under the weather." She clicked her tongue. "And the brakes? Why didn't you ask me to have one of my guys check those out?"

"I didn't think anything of it at first. My mechanic assured me it happens a lot in the winter. He's got my Jeep. He's waiting for a new brake line to come in."

"I'll have Deputy Walker follow up." I could hear her writing down the information. "Listen, I'm going to the Tavern for dinner later. Why don't you and Candace join me? You could use a little R and R."

After agreeing, I tiptoed into my niece's room and tapped on the bathroom door. "Candace, we're going to the Tavern. Grab something to wear from my closet." I returned to the kitchen and glanced at the answering machine, which wasn't blinking. Even so, I pressed Play out of habit: *You have one message.*

Stupid machine.

My sister's voice was raspy. "Hey, little sis, it's me. The guy dumped me. So I'm coming to get Candy tomorrow."

Candace appeared at my side, a towel around her wet hair, a robe cinched at her waist. The blood had drained from her face; her jaw hung slack.

"Early," Rosie added. Without another word, she disconnected.

The gas heater kicked on with a whoosh. I turned to Candace. "Want to go home?"

"Not yet."

"Even though today was scary?"

She shook her head.

"Want me to call her back?"

She nodded.

"Dry your hair. We're leaving for dinner in a half hour."

When I heard the slam of the bathroom door, I called my sister on her cell phone. She didn't answer. The call rolled into voice mail.

"Hi, it's Aspen. Got your message. I've got all sorts of things planned with Candace. You know, aunt-niece bonding stuff. Why don't you come up next week, as planned? Take some time for yourself. Let me know you got this message."

Candace came out, her hair brushed straight but still wet. She was wearing my jeans and a T-shirt and didn't look much older than ten. "Can I stay home tonight?"

"Why?"

"Don't get me wrong. Chef Timothy is a wonderful cook." She chewed on her lip. "I'm not feeling very good."

Was her uneasiness due to her mother's phone call or our near-death experience?

"I don't want to force you to do anything. It's okay to stay home, but you have to promise to eat the dinner I make, and I'm getting someone to stay with you."

"No. Don't. I'll be fine. I'll keep all the doors locked, and I'll watch movies."

"Uh-uh. Sorry."

I called Karen and begged off.

"I'm not taking no for an answer, Aspen." Karen said she'd assign Deputy Walker the job of camping out on the porch of my cabin. "C'mon. Join me. Your niece will be more than safe. You don't even need to tell her he's coming."

Of course I'd tell her.

"Say yes," Karen coaxed. "You have to unwind."

Though uneasiness gnawed my insides, I agreed.

• • •

An hour later, Deputy Walker showed up. I introduced him to Candace. Tentatively, she invited him inside. He offered to remain outside; Candace seemed relieved.

Confident my niece would be safe, I went to see Karen. By the time I arrived at the Homewood Tavern, it was teeming with customers. A fire crackled in the fireplace. Elvis's classic "Blue Suede Shoes"—Vikki's favorite of his songs—played on the jukebox. I found a seat at the bar and looked around for Karen.

Gwen, who was tending, approached with a towel and an empty wineglass in her hand. "What would have happened if there had been three wise *women* instead of three wise men?"

"They would have asked directions, arrived on time, helped deliver the baby, cleaned the stable, made a casserole, and brought practical gifts." I recited the punch line the same way Vikki had. The bittersweet memory pained me.

"Vikki had a great sense of humor, didn't she? Gonna miss her." Gwen knuckled the bar. "What'll it be, red or white?"

"Red."

"You got it." She grabbed a bottle of cabernet from the shelf behind her and poured six ounces into a wineglass. "Okay, spill. You've been snooping, and I want to know what you found out."

I filled her in on Billy Tennyson and on my gut feelings about

Rocky Yeats. I mentioned that I had been to the Source of Serenity and had questioned the reverend.

She aimed a finger at me. "I know just who you mean. He was on TV one time. Good-looking guy."

I told her my recollection about Vikki and the pen and the carving.

"Like an ice sculpture?"

"Nothing that elaborate. A design." I gestured to my right side. "By her thigh."

"If only she'd written the killer's name. Someone from the sheriff's office saw the design, right?"

"No." I groaned. "I slipped and destroyed it."

Gwen swept her thick mane of hair over her shoulder and leaned forward on both elbows. "This is much more interesting than my jokes."

"If we're telling jokes, I've got a good one." Karen slid onto a stool and slapped her palm on the counter. "Whiskey, bartender."

Gwen said, "Aspen was telling me her latest discoveries about the murder."

"So she told you about being shot at today?"

"No, she did *not*." Gwen glowered at me as if I had kept the greatest secret for last. I hadn't wanted to discuss the incident until I got a clearer picture from Karen. "But she will." Gwen stomped off to pour a whiskey. I wasn't worried. Her peeve would blow over soon.

"Change that to an Irish coffee, will you?" Karen yelled after her.

"We're out of cream," Gwen hollered back.

"Skip the cream. Double the whiskey." Karen raised an eyebrow. "Testy, isn't she?"

"A tad. Did your team find anything?"

"I went up myself." Karen combed her messy hair with her fingers. "I located the area, but I couldn't find any bullets or shells. I made a perimeter search and didn't see any snowshoe prints, either. About a half mile away, I met up with a hunter. He was stewed and admitted to firing off a few shots. I slapped him with a fine."

"What about the woodpile and the brake line incident?"

Karen shook her head. "Before heading to your house, Deputy Walker visited the mechanic. The hose had a tear in it, consistent with a rock flying off the pavement and shredding it. As for the woodpile, I think it was a prank. Tahoe City has seen an influx of rowdy teenagers. Your neighborhood's no exception."

Something bothered me, but I couldn't bring it to the surface.

"By the way, Deputy Kim met that boyfriend of Vikki's," Karen said. "She thinks he's the one who killed her, but then Kim doesn't know a hole from a doughnut."

"Am I detecting interdepartmental jealousy?"

"She's never worked a homicide before." Karen waved a hand. "Even so, I'll ask her to check out whether the boyfriend owns a rifle. Maybe he's the one who shot at you."

I pictured Billy with his anguished demeanor and bulging biceps. He was like the boy all the girls adored and every parent feared. Devious and alluring but not vicious. I didn't see him as a shooter.

"Shaper thinks he might be the killer, too," Karen continued, "and he hasn't even met him."

I sipped my wine. "Is Detective Shaper mad that I located Billy first?"

Gwen placed an Irish coffee sans cream in front of Karen, gave me the evil eye, and slipped away.

"Any help is okay by him," Karen said. "He likes to think of himself as a team player. Now, if we disagree with Shaper and Kim, and we dump the idea of the boyfriend, who else do we have?" She drank some of her Irish coffee and set it down.

Reverend Brock, Rocky Yeats, and any number of people who might have passed through Vikki's life, I wanted to shout to the rafters, but I squelched the impulse.

I said, "Did you happen to check out the Source of Serenity?"

"The Source of What?"

"Serenity. I told you about it last night."

"Right. Yeah, we're on it." Karen tapped her fingernails on the copper-lined bar. The action reverberated like raindrops pelting a tin roof. "Have you come up with anything else?"

"Vikki had a friend who worked at the library, or at least that's what Billy said. Library hours are pretty sketchy, though, so I haven't pinned him down. His name's Frank."

"Novak?"

"Yes." Was I the only person in town who didn't know him?

"Frank's the king of book titles. I think he memorized the Dewey decimal system when he was five." Karen cleaned mascara from under her eyes and scanned the bar. Was she hoping to score a date?

"Tell me about this Frank guy," I said.

"Sixties and pale, like he's lived in a cave all his life. You don't think—" Karen shook her head. "No. Frank's weird, but he's no killer. How do I know? Because the first time I met him he didn't hit on me, so I checked him out. No priors. No anything. He keeps to himself, drives a beat-up Cavalier, and eats at the pizzeria every Sunday night. He lives in a little house on Huntington."

Many of the streets in Tahoe had been named after well-known businessmen and socialites who had frequented the resort at the turn of the century. Huntington was a cul-de-sac of five houses. One of the agency's clients lived there. I knew it well. I had the sudden urge to leave the restaurant and knock on Frank Novak's door.

Karen moaned. "Oh, crap. Not now."

Chapter 21

"What's wrong?" I asked and peered where Karen was staring.

"My boss just walked in. It's like he's got GPS on me." She breathed into her palm. "Ugh. I'm going to the loo. Back in a minute."

Nick Shaper sauntered to the bar, his strides long and easy. "Hello, Miss Adams."

"Detective."

Dressed in a white cowboy hat, white turtleneck, white jacket, and blue jeans, he looked like the epitome of the good guy in a B movie. He removed his hat, set it on the stool, and put both hands on the counter. Was he with a date or riding solo?

From the far end, Gwen hollered, "Hiya, Nick."

He nodded to her before pulling a black datebook from his pocket. "Your friend's appointment calendar." He placed it on the bar and tapped the cover. "This is what you wanted, right?"

"Yes." I recognized the torn binding and reached for it.

"Yeah. No." He pulled it to one side. "The DA says I can't give it to you."

"Are you kidding?" I bit back a curse word and, exercising all the calm I could muster, said, "Did you find somebody who could decipher Vikki's writing?"

"We did. Even with her help, we're stuck with initials Miss Carmichael wrote around the day she died: *MM*, *EB*, *LL*. Do those mean anything to you?"

"No, can't say as they do, although I'd bet my house that EB stands for Ed Brock."

"Who?"

"A preacher. As for your DA—"

"Shaper," a man called from the other side of the room.

Shaper turned and, recognizing the guy, said, "Excuse me a minute." He crossed to greet him.

I gazed at the datebook and scanned the bar. No Karen. No Shaper. Would it hurt if I perused the contents? Before I could talk myself out of it, I flipped it open to January. *MM*, *EB*, and *LL* were all in there. On separate lines were different, disconnected dates. The remainder of Vikki's handwriting did, indeed, resemble hieroglyphics, plus there were lots of squiggles and curls down the sides, the kinds of doodles I'd drawn when bored in school. I spotted a *BT* and *AA*. *BT* had to be Billy. *AA* was probably me because the initials were written in for six o'clock on Wednesday—the last time I'd seen her. She'd entered *MM* at nine o'clock. Why hadn't she mentioned having another appointment that night?

While Shaper continued to talk to his friend—was he intentionally giving me time to peruse the datebook?—I flipped to the contacts section. Billy was listed under *B* with his work phone and work address. No last name noted. Under *F*, subheading *Library*, I found Frank. My own was under *F*, subheading *Friends*. Nothing was listed under *M*.

Shaper said goodbye to his pal and pivoted. I closed the datebook and pulled my wineglass closer.

"Where were we?" Shaper said as he neared. He glanced at the datebook and back at me.

I did my best not to let on that I'd taken a peek. "I was going to tell you that your DA is a pill."

Shaper smiled. "I won't disagree. Look, rest assured we're doing everything we can to find your friend's killer. We've been more than thorough. We've gone through telephone records, receipts, ledgers, and bank accounts."

"Did Vikki have a will?"

"Not as far as we could find."

"Have you reviewed all the evidence personally?"

"We share responsibilities." He drummed his fingers on the bar. Had I touched a nerve?

"How much did Vikki have in her savings? You can tell me that, can't you?"

"Karen Brandon says it's less than a thousand."

Billy claimed Vikki had donated a couple of thousand to the Source of Serenity, so collecting another grand was not the compelling reason for Ed Brock to wish her dead.

"We've had interviews with all the immediate neighbors," Shaper added. "Employees at Alpine Meadows have been more than eager to answer questions."

I'd bet Sara had opened the waterworks for Shaper.

I said, "Karen said Deputy Kim believes Billy Tennyson is the killer."

"I've reviewed Kim's report. I agree with her on most points, and his alibi is weak. Most brothers would lie for another brother."

"I don't think he has the guts. He's the type of guy who would have cried for days after Vikki broke up with him."

Shaper scowled.

"Okay, maybe he didn't sob, but he's passionate. Needy." The loving glow I'd noted in Billy's eyes had been genuine.

Shaper folded his arms across his chest. "Is this insight stemming from your expertise as a therapist?"

"As a matter of fact, it is. During my time working with troubled teens, I met a number of young men similar to Billy, rough around the edges. None of the ones I dealt with committed murder."

He tilted his head. "Maybe none got caught."

"Misdemeanors were the norm. Most of the kids were timid and scarred for life." I rubbed my neck trying to remove the knots. "They were more apt to hurt themselves than hurt somebody else. Despite his bravado, Billy's that kind of guy."

"I see."

No, he didn't. Few did.

I took a sip of wine and set the glass down. "Isn't it true that Joey Blain, a guy Vikki knew at Alpine, is a suspect?"

"We have a running list."

"What about me?" My voice sounded thin. Tight.

Shaper grinned. "I don't think you wear a size ten boot, do you?"

I pounced on the information. "So you figured out the type of shoe. What was it?"

He paused, a smirk pulling at the side of his mouth, his gaze teasing. How long could I hold off before I ripped his eyeballs out?

"A standard Timberland boot size ten," he said.

"Could you determine the style?"

"Trekker, which means just about any guy in Tahoe could be the murderer." Shaper chuckled. "Perhaps if I could narrow the field to whether they were black or brown I'd have a fifty-fifty chance."

I took his teasing in stride. He had given me information that I doubted the DA wanted me to have.

Karen returned, slipped onto the stool next to Shaper, and tapped him on the arm. "Hi, boss, what's up?"

"Detective Brandon." He patted his pockets, searching for something.

"Yoo-hoo, Gwen." Karen waved her hand. "Get Detective Sergeant Shaper an Amstel Light, on me."

I watched with curiosity as Karen's trepidation about talking with Nick Shaper turned into flirtation. She laid her hand on his upper arm and nudged her stool a little closer. Though Shaper didn't seem to mind, he didn't seem interested, either. In fact, he was still rummaging through his pockets.

"Aspen, would you please ask Gwen if she has any fresh pretzels?" Karen pushed the half-eaten bowl toward me and hitched her head in that direction.

I could take a hint. I picked up the bowl and my wineglass and moved down the bar.

Gwen said, "Refill?"

"I could use some food, too. Karen wants pretzels."

Gwen delivered a beer to Shaper and a bowl of snacks to Karen and returned. She topped off my wine and set a bowl of pretzels in front of me. "Now, tell me about getting shot."

I gave her a sixty-second recap. She was shocked. Worried. She asked about Candace. I assured her she was fine; Deputy Walker was at my cabin.

"What's got your attention?" Gwen craned her neck, staring in the direction I was.

"Nothing."

Gwen faked a sneeze to cover a word that sounded like *liar* and laughed.

"It's Karen. At one moment, she's as tough as nails. The next, she's sugar and spice. She asked me to join her for dinner, and now—"

Gwen laughed. "Do you blame her? Nick reminds me of my first husband. Handsome and smart. Like nectar for bees." She fanned herself. "Mm-mm. I couldn't get enough of that man. You like Nick. I can tell."

"I have no interest in Detective Sergeant Shaper."

"C'mon. Admit it."

Not willing to give her the benefit of an answer, I switched topics. "Tell me about your second husband."

"I'd rather not. My third was much more fun."

"Third? Hold it. You told me you'd been married twice."

"That's because I've done my darnedest to erase number two from my memory bank." Gwen straightened her shirt collar as a flush of red crept up her neck. "Each time I was more stupid than the last, if that's possible. Fell for the same line: *Baby, you mean the world to me,* which translates to: *Let's do it.*" A cloud of failure suffused her face. "I'll tell you this. Most men are good-for-nothings who don't stand a chance if women ever figure out how to run the world." She shimmied her shoulders. "I'm taking a break."

"When you come back, bring me food. I'll take anything."

As she hurried from the bar, I glanced at Shaper. Not that it mattered, but I was pleased to see he'd slid his chair away from Karen's.

When Gwen didn't return in five minutes, I decided to pass on food and opted to find Frank Novak. My hasty departure had nothing to do with Karen hitting on Nick Shaper. Nothing.

Chapter 22

I drove up Huntington Lane, a narrow street lined with snow-dusted cars, and pulled to a halt in front of a white cottage. A burgundy Cavalier stood in the driveway. Smoke billowed from the chimney. Juniper bushes grew along the front of the house.

As I walked up the pathway and reached for the doorbell, my cell phone rang. I pulled it out, saw Candace's number, and answered.

"Aunt Aspen?" Candace sounded weak. "Please come home. I'm sick."

"Where's the deputy?"

"Out front."

I breathed easier. She wasn't alone. She must have been embarrassed to reach out to him. I told her I'd be right there—Frank Novak could wait—and dashed for the car. I drove as fast as I could without breaking the sound barrier.

When I arrived home, I screeched to a halt and my stomach knotted. A black Wrangler stood in the driveway—Walker had arrived in a Subaru—and a person was rocking in the wooden chair my grandfather had made. As I leaped from my car, I realized the person was Nick Shaper and I breathed easier.

"Good evening, Miss Adams." He struck a match and doused it. Not smoking. Biding time.

I darted up the stairs to the front door. "Where's Deputy Walker?"

"He just left. I spelled him."

I thrust the key into the front door lock, but it jammed.

"Allow me." Shaper took the key from my hand and unlocked the door. "Why was my deputy here anyway? What's going on?"

I gave the door a shove and heard Candace retching. I raced down the hall.

Without an invitation, Shaper trailed me. "You left the Tavern so abruptly, I wasn't able to give these to you." He brandished a packet of photographs. "They're of you and Miss Carmichael. I'd stowed them in my car. They're copies—"

"Not now." I barged into the bathroom. Candace was kneeling on the floor, her hands gripping the sides of the toilet bowl. "Get me a wet towel, Detective."

Shaper dropped the pictures on the bathroom counter, soaked a green hand towel in the sink, and handed it to me. While I tended to Candace, he wet another one and mopped the floor.

"*Shh*. It's okay, sweetie." I stroked her back. "I'm here." I looked up at Shaper. His gaze was filled with concern. "You can go now. Thanks for the help."

He frowned and slipped out the door.

Ten minutes later, I guided Candace to her bed. Because she was shivering, I covered her with an extra blanket and took her temperature, which was close to normal.

"Do you want to tell me what happened?" I wiped the hair off her forehead.

"I don't know." She was lying. "I'm very tired."

"Okay, let's talk about it in the morning. I want you to rest tonight. Call me if you need anything. I'll be in the kitchen." I tiptoed out of the room, leaving the door ajar. When I reached the kitchen, I was startled to find Shaper familiarizing himself with the books on the shelves in the adjoining living room. "What are you still doing here?"

"I made a pot of coffee. Want some?"

Kneejerk responses sped through my mind. I jammed my lips together. The guy had, after all, helped me clean up vomit. After a long moment, I said, "That would be nice."

Shaper left the room and returned with two Tahoe-themed mugs of coffee. "I figured you drink it black. Black coffee makes women beautiful, my grandmother used to say."

"Beautiful? As if. I must look a sight."

He handed me the mug. I held it between my hands, letting the warmth comfort me.

"Does your niece have the flu?" he asked.

"I don't think so. No temperature."

Shaper set his mug on the coffee table and returned to fingering through my books. He seemed to be on a quest. "Did she eat something bad?"

"Before I left, I fed her pasta with vegetables sautéed in olive oil."

"Garlic?"

"No." I tilted my head. "Why are you exploring my books? What's so fascinating?"

"You."

The answer took me aback.

Shaper grabbed one of the books, sat on the arm of the couch, and began to flip through it. "Have you read all these?"

I nodded.

"I'm impressed. Bonhoeffer. Freud. Kant. I'm guessing you took a religious overview class in college."

"More than one."

"Pretty heavy stuff." Shaper turned to the last page. "Does it make sense?"

"A lot of it does. You've never read any of them?"

"I'm just a law enforcer, ma'am."

How did he know the books contained religious stuff, then, *hmm*?

"I earned my degree in administration of justice, went to two years of law school, grew disenchanted with the law, per se, all the mumbo-jumbo, and decided to become part of the system."

My library was filled with works by authors such as Ogilvie, Peck, and Provinem. I cherished the broad spectrum.

Shaper looked at me more intensely than anyone had in a long time. I appreciated his interest and hated it all at the same time. My heart began to pound.

When I found my voice, I said, "Did Karen inform you about the shooter?"

"What shooter?" He returned the book to the shelf.

"I was in the woods hiking with Candace, and someone took a couple shots at us. One bullet hit a tree, the second knocked a branch down."

"When?"

"Earlier. That's why Deputy Walker was camped out here."

"No wonder Candace is feeling sick. Why didn't you tell me before?"

"Because I'd told Karen."

That seemed to irk him, but he shrugged it off. Did he want me to contact him instead of her? "She sent Walker over so you and she could have a drink?" His words came out clipped and judgmental.

I didn't answer.

"Any idea who shot at you?" he asked.

"No."

"You don't think it was an accident."

I nodded. "Call it gut instinct."

He didn't mock me, as I'd expected him to, so I found the courage to mention the lighter fluid incident and the ruptured brake line.

"Karen sent Walker to the mechanic, who determined a rock had ripped a hole in the hose." I sipped my coffee. "Karen says I'm wrong about the shooter, too. She ran into a hunter who admitted to popping off a few rounds."

Shaper retrieved his coffee mug and moved closer to me. "You're holding something back."

"No, I'm not."

"Why did you want Miss Carmichael's datebook?"

"Because I want to help. I can't sit back and—" I chewed my lip.

"Watch us botch up the investigation? We won't. *I* won't."

"My parents . . ." My nerves tingled with raw energy. The memory of my parents' deaths was always at the edges of my mind. "They were murdered. The police never found their killer."

"I'm sorry," Shaper said, his voice low and gentle. "Would you feel better if I looked into the incident in the woods? You know, an extra set of eyes?"

"I'm sure Karen was thorough."

Shaper reached out and touched the collar of my shirt. I backed up a step.

His cheeks warmed. Apparently, he hadn't realized how intimate the gesture had been. "It was twisted," he mumbled in explanation and then set the mug on the coffee table and strolled to the door. "Don't forget the photos in the bathroom." He opened the door, tipped an imaginary hat and said with a wink so slight that I would've missed it had I been looking anywhere other than his face, "Take care, Miss Adams."

The headlights on the Wrangler lit up, and he took off down the road.

I checked the locks on the doors and windows, and feeling a bit ridiculous, pulled the can of pepper spray from my purse. I placed it on the end table by the sofa as an intense loneliness consumed me. To keep it at bay, I nestled into the corner of the couch, clutched a pillow to my stomach, and tried to make sense of the initials and scribbles I'd seen in Vikki's datebook.

When I couldn't, I rose to check on Candace. I found her fast asleep, tucked in a fetal position. I grabbed the photographs Shaper had brought over, went to my room, and tossed the packet on the bed. A few of them fell out of the envelope. The top photo was of Gwen, Vikki, and me sitting in my hot tub a week ago. Vikki had used the self-timer app on her cell phone to take it. She'd nearly broken her ankle hopping into the water in time. In the glow of the porch light, her chestnut-red hair matched Gwen's. Her smile was way too big and her gaze a little out of focus. She'd had too much to drink. We all had.

I crossed to the window and glanced at the hot tub, now protected with a brown waterproof cover. One night in late summer, I'd introduced Gwen to Vikki. Though they were fifteen years apart, they'd bonded like soul sisters. They told the same kinds of jokes and drank the same brand of scotch. Both would climb into the hot tub with jewelry on, something I'd never do.

I fingered through the rest of the photos and returned to the first. What was bothering me about it?

Vikki's earrings. She'd removed them before she'd climbed into the hot tub. "To appease you," she'd joked.

I hurried into my bathroom and retrieved the dangly gold earrings from the dish on my sink. I'd take them to Vikki's place tomorrow. Her things should be in order if her family came to claim her body.

Her family.

Why hadn't someone from the sheriff's department connected with them yet?

Retreating to my makeshift office in the dining room, I double-clicked the Internet icon. I pulled up USSearch.com and typed in the name *Jerome Carmichael.* A message blinked that a city was required. I opened a second page on the Internet showing a map of California. One by one, I ran through the list of cities between Sacramento and Auburn.

Two hours later, my eyes bleary with fatigue, I came up with a match.

Jerome Carmichael, age 67, retired hardware salesman. With an address in Nevada City. No phone was listed for him, so I decided I would visit first thing in the morning.

After shutting down the computer, I double-checked every lock in the house. Later, lying in bed, even though I was trained in self-defense and had a can of pepper spray at the ready on my nightstand, I felt the overwhelming fear of being helpless.

Chapter 23

"Are we there yet?" Candace wriggled in the passenger seat. Her color was better. She had eaten a breakfast of eggs and toast.

My biggest concern was that she hadn't spoken until now. We'd been driving for over an hour. The Carmichaels lived less than ninety minutes from Tahoe City. I'd made multiple attempts at conversation but nothing had worked. Not Justin. Not Soccer Guy.

"Just a few more minutes," I said.

She wrestled with her jacket and her jeans. "Aunt Aspen? I heard you talking to Detective Sergeant Shaper last night."

I blanched. Shaper and I had discussed the shooter and the other incidents. It hadn't dawned on me to check whether Candace had been listening in. "Please, sweetie, don't worry. Detective Brandon went up to the springs and determined the shooter was a hunter who'd had one too many beers. It was an accident."

"No, it's not that. It's . . ." She chewed a fingernail. "I don't want you to die."

I laid my hand on her shoulder. "I won't. I promise."

She mustered a smile.

"Why don't you navigate for me?" I said. "Nevada City should be coming up. Press the GPS on the dash and read the upcoming turns."

Fifteen minutes later, after passing two miles of wooded area without seeing another neighbor, we located the Carmichaels' home. Vikki had never mentioned that she'd lived in such a remote place. By her account, I had expected a pretty farm with a white picket fence.

A shiver ran down my spine at the sight of the ramshackle place. Shutters were hanging loose. Half of the shingles on the roof were dilapidated. A beaten-up Ford truck stood in the gravel driveway. Rickety birdhouses hung on posts and tree branches. On the front steps, a pair of chickens nibbled at their already-chewed feathers. If I'd seen a three-legged dog with no tail, I wouldn't have been surprised. Had Vikki painted a portrait of an idyllic life to bury the memory of a bare-bones existence?

I parked the car, and Candace and I climbed out. A power-driven saw blared to our right. We headed in that direction.

In an opened garage separate from the house stood a hunched man, the skin on his face leathery from sun. He wore a heavy Pendleton jacket and a hunter's cap with the flaps turned up. A plank of wood stretched across two wooden sawhorses. A pile of splinter shavings lay at his feet. Hanging around the garage on dozens of hooks were a variety of handmade birdhouses. Little ones, big ones, some with porches, others with shutters. None good enough to sell.

"Mr. Carmichael?" I shouted as I approached. "I'm Aspen Adams."

The older man switched off the power and, with the saw in hand, brushed a hank of white hair off his face. "What do you want?"

"Nice birdhouse."

"I have the best collection in Nevada City."

"I can see you do. Is your wife here?"

"If you're a salesman, you can take a hike. We ain't got no money to buy anything." He returned to his sawing.

I drew nearer. "I'm not here to sell a thing, sir. It's about your daughter Vikki."

He snapped off the power to the saw again. "Who'd you say you were?"

"A friend of your daughter's."

"She ain't here." His jaw clenched tight.

"Please, is your wife around? There's something I need to tell you both. I'd rather tell you together."

He seemed to sense the immediacy in my voice and put the saw down. "Velda!" he yelled and darted toward the back of the house.

Candace and I followed him, running to keep up.

Before he had opened the screen door, a woman in a dirty floral dress, long pink sweater, and tattered pink slippers appeared. Wisps of brown hair trickled out of her bun. As she pushed the door open, her hand poked a hole in the webbing. "What is it, Jerome?"

"Velda, this gal wants to tell us something about Vikki."

The woman planted her hands on her broad hips and eyed me. "Come in. The girl, too."

Candace strode in before me. "Nice place," she said.

Mrs. Carmichael—Velda—beamed with appreciation as she led us into the kitchen. "Sit down. I'll get some tea. We'll talk once I've poured." She bustled about, straightening this, nudging that.

The walls were in dire need of paint. Clean dishes had been slotted into a draining rack on the side of the sink. A perky vase full of winter pansies sat on the windowsill.

Velda set a chipped sugar bowl on an old Formica table that was nicked and banded with silver. "Sit."

We obeyed. Air oozed from the plastic chair cushions.

While the four of us waited for the teapot to whistle, I scanned the room. A desk to my right was stacked with old J. C. Penney catalogues as well as ancient *National Geographic* magazines. On a recessed, three-tiered bookshelf stood a dozen cookbooks that looked pristine and untouched. One was still wrapped in cellophane shrink-wrap.

Vikki had fed me another lie. She'd said her mother was a brilliant cook.

After the tea was poured and placed on the table, Mr. Carmichael—Jerome—said, "Say what you have to say." A man of many words.

"Sir, I'm afraid that your daughter—" I regrouped. "Vikki died a few days ago."

Velda inhaled and covered her chest with her hand. Jerome shook his head and made a clucking sound. Tears would've been appropriate. Questions of *how*, *where* and *why*, too. Had they been responsible for her death?

"Sir, when was the last time you saw your daughter?"

"Two, three years ago. We don't travel much. She lived in Lake Tahoe. That's quite a ways."

A handful of maps were wedged between the cookbooks. If they didn't travel, why have maps? For the same reason they had cookbooks—everybody did.

"What'd she die of?" he asked in between sips of tea. "Pneumonia or something?"

"No, sir, she was killed."

"By a drunk driver?"

"No, sir. She was murdered."

Velda clutched her throat. Jerome's eyes rolled back in his head. Was he going to have a stroke? In unison they said, "Lordie."

Candace looked at them and back at me. She didn't seem disturbed by their display. She seemed interested, like a clinical psychologist. How often had she seen her mother overwhelmed by emotions or besieged by drugs?

After a few more moments, Jerome dabbed tears from his cheeks. "We loved that girl, but living here wasn't good enough for her. She went to college and never came back."

Thanks to student loans, Vikki had earned a degree in marketing, but when she got a job in the field, she'd hated it. Three years later, she migrated to Lake Tahoe.

"We loved her as our own," Velda said. "Same as all the others."

"Others?" I asked.

"We adopted four children."

I had photos of my mother and father in my kitchen, in my living room, and in my bedroom. Where were the memories of their children?

"Do they live nearby?" I asked.

"No." Velda wrung her hands together.

"Ma'am." Candace patted the woman's arm. "This must be very hard for you. Could you tell my aunt where your other children are so she could talk to them?"

Velda looked up at my niece. The tears abated. "We never see any of them. They don't come by. They don't write."

Had something weird gone on in this house?

"Lynanne, she's the oldest. In her late thirties now. She left the day Vikki turned six. They hardly knew one another." Velda clamped her hands around her mug of tea. "She said she needed to find herself. Can you imagine? Needing to find yourself at sixteen? I think she went to Lake Tahoe, too."

I made a mental note to search for Lynanne Carmichael, though if she lived in Tahoe, I couldn't understand why she wouldn't have contacted the sheriff's office. The news about Vikki had been on every news station.

"We treated Lynanne good. I think she was angry that we brought the boys into our home. Two-year-old twins." Velda *tsked* like her husband had. "Jerome tried to teach Lynanne to build and hunt and live in the wilds, but she didn't enjoy it. She said she wanted girl things. We didn't understand."

"I build birdhouses," Jerome said.

I nodded. "What are the boys' names?"

"What does it matter? Both of them were good-for-nothings. When we got them, they were as tainted as aged copper. They ran off at sixteen, too. They weren't keen on hunting or building birdhouses." She glared at her husband.

Jerome hung his head in shame. By his wife's tone, he was the reason the children had fled, and he'd always be blamed.

"They moved to North Carolina, last I heard," Velda added.

"And Vikki?" I prompted.

"She loved to dance, that girl," Velda said.

Jerome looked up. "It wasn't my fault she left. I told her she could dance. I let her do anything she wanted. She said we were too isolated. She needed friends." He shrugged. "Who needs friends when you got nature all around?"

"She wanted to dance," Velda repeated.

So she ended up in Lake Tahoe as a showgirl.

"How was she killed?" Velda asked.

"Someone beat her with a rock. The sheriff's department is investigating."

Velda shuddered. Candace clasped the woman's hand.

"Do you want to have a funeral service for her?" I asked.

"No," Jerome said. "When she left, she said goodbye for good. We won't fuss over her."

What had these people done to make their children run away? Simply asking them to enjoy wilderness didn't seem enough of a reason. Sure, they were different, but they didn't strike me as cruel. Perhaps I wasn't seeing the whole picture.

"We never hurt her, mind you," Velda said, as if reading my mind. "We're similar creatures, Jerome and me. Those children weren't nothing like us."

"But you loved them," Candace said.

"Yes, we did." Velda put a napkin to her nose and blew hard.

"Ma'am." I didn't know how to broach the next subject, but I was anxious to know the answer. "Do you think the birth parents would want to know about her death?"

Velda shot a look at her husband.

Chapter 24

When Jerome didn't return Velda's gaze, she continued. "We don't know who the parents are. We did it all through a lawyer. You see, I couldn't conceive. I had a few miscarriages. Each time it happened, we adopted."

"Who was the lawyer?" I asked.

Velda stood up and shuffled to the desk loaded with catalogues. She opened the drawer and pulled out a pile of envelopes, yellowed with age. She thrust them at me. "Mervyn Tendall. He's in Auburn."

I opened the top envelope, copied the telephone number and address from the first communication, and shoved the letter back inside. Without saying a word, Velda slipped into another room. She rummaged around for something. A minute later, she returned carrying a blue Bible with gilt edges and another book that appeared to be a high school yearbook. She held them out to me.

"I always hoped she'd come back for these."

When I took them, the Bible fell open. An inscription had been scribbled on the inside cover: *To GVB, Mama loves you.*

I said, "What do these initials stand for?"

"Don't know. The Bible came with the child."

"What was Vikki's birth name?"

"I don't know that, either. We were told her name was Victoria by the lawyer. She was two months old." Velda sniffed. "I preferred Vikki."

I stood and extended my hand to shake.

Velda squeezed it so hard I winced.

After a brief exchange of condolences, Candace and I climbed into the Jeep. I handed her the books. As I backed out, the tires skidding on gravel, she flipped the yearbook open and scanned the pages. In seconds she found Vikki's photograph among the seniors.

"Gee, she was pretty," Candace whispered. "Look."

I glanced over and slammed on the brakes when I saw the picture next to Vikki's. "Read that name."

"Richard Yeats."

Richard. Rocky. With his lacquered black hair and his fighter's nose.

I whipped the car around, screeched to a halt by the Carmichaels' house, and leaped out. Velda was feeding the chickens. I thrust the yearbook at her and pointed to Rocky's face. "Do you know this boy?"

"Of course. Richard. Such a sweet young man. He moved here from New York some fifteen years ago, I think." She clapped her hands together to get rid of the rest of the seed. "He wanted to be Vikki's boyfriend so bad. He'd come around in his truck and ask her on dates, but she never said yes."

"Did Richard ever threaten her?"

"My, no. He was as gentle as a lamb. He did chores for me. He was a hard worker."

"What kind of chores?"

"Cutting firewood and killing the chickens for supper. All I can cook is chicken. I burn water." She chuckled. "Richard loved my roasted chicken."

"Thank you, ma'am. I appreciate your time."

Velda looked over her shoulder and back at me. She put her calloused hand on my arm and whispered, "Make sure you give her a good burial."

• • •

Mervyn Tendall's Victorian-style home was painted ice blue with white shutters. The evergreen hedges had been trimmed. The mat on the porch read *Welcome*. Though Christmas had been over for weeks, decorative snowflakes and Santa's elves clung to the windows. A holly wreath hung on the door.

I rang the doorbell.

The woman who answered was trim and elegant, white hair pinned back. Her brown wool pants matched her cashmere sweater. I could hear the sounds of children echoing from a room at the back of the house. They were playing a rousing game of tag.

"May I help you?" she asked.

I handed her my business card. "Ma'am, I'm Aspen Adams. I work for the Maxine Adams Detective Agency in Incline, Nevada. And this is Candace. My niece. I'm looking for Mervyn Tendall."

The woman's face paled. Her body shuddered. She slung a shaky arm across her chest. "My husband died a month ago. He had a heart attack."

"I'm so sorry. I didn't mean to intrude. We can come back another—"

"No. Stay. What is this about?"

"Your husband handled an adoption case that I'm interested in. From twenty-eight years ago."

"Grandma, help."

Two young girls with golden curls darted out, grabbed Mrs. Tendall's legs, and whirled around her.

"My rowdy granddaughters." She beamed.

I nodded in acknowledgment.

"Girls, go back in the den. I'm busy now."

Giggling, they dashed off.

I said, "I hate to bother you, but would you have Mr. Tendall's files?"

The woman's eyes pooled with tears, her sorrow and loss evident. "I'm sorry. They're stored away, and I'm afraid they would be difficult to go through. He indexed them by decade. He was the worst record keeper this side of the Sierras, but he was quite good at what he did."

His success was evident by the size and mint condition of the house.

"I don't mind spending some time. Where's the storage facility?"

"They're here." She pointed upward. "In the attic."

"If you wouldn't mind, I'd like to have a look."

She glanced at my card again, back at Candace, and nodded. "If you want, your daughter could play with the children until you're through."

"This is my niece."

"Forgive my mistake. You look so similar."

"I'd like to stay with you," Candace whispered.

"Sure." I threw an arm around her shoulders and led her inside.

Mrs. Tendall led us through the well-furnished house up two flights of stairs and into the attic. "My husband might have kept everything he touched, but he preferred things neat," she said as an apology.

Sunlight filtered through clean windows, not a cobweb in sight. Legal boxes occupied every square inch.

"Some deal with divorces, some with adoptions, and some with bankruptcy," she said. "He had so many clients." As she left to go downstairs, she added, "Take your time."

I looked at the myriad boxes marked *1990s* and groaned. There had to be at least fifty. If I spent twenty-four hours every day for two weeks, I wouldn't be able to sort through all of them. On the off chance I'd get lucky, I opened the closest box. To my dismay, Tendall hadn't labeled the files with anything more than a name. None of them were broken down into adoption, divorce, or bankruptcy.

Candace said, "May I help?"

"Dig in."

After an hour, we had browsed through a dozen boxes and come up dry. "This is fruitless. I haven't found one file that begins with a *C*, let alone with the name Carmichael." Though I wasn't the kind to abandon a project, I wanted to get going with the rest of the investigation. "The birth parents will never know," I muttered. "Since they didn't care enough to follow up on Vikki's life, why should I bother trying to locate them? Let's get out of here."

I thanked Mrs. Tendall and let her know I'd failed.

When we reached the car, I said, "Zephyr told me some of the kids you skied with do group activities on Monday afternoons. I think today is bowling. Want to join them?"

"Sounds cool."

Way cool, I thought.

We stopped at McDonald's on the return trip. Candace ordered a Big Mac. I opted for a salad.

As we neared Tahoe City, I said, "I'm going to make a quick stop." I turned up the road to Alpine Meadows on the off chance one of the ski patrolwomen would be there. Malika, the Swedish girl with braces, was on duty by herself.

I showed her the yearbook picture of Richard Yeats as well as the photograph of Rocky with the showgirls at the Gemstone Cabaret. "Is this the guy who was hanging around Vikki?"

She shivered. "That's him all right."

That was all I wanted to know. Rocky skyrocketed up my suspect list. I called the Gemstone Cabaret and asked for him. If I confronted him with others around, maybe he'd crack. Unfortunately, he wasn't in; he'd gone ice fishing.

Keeping my promise to share everything I learned with Karen Brandon, I called her, but I reached her voice mail. Quickly, I related the information about Vikki's parents and Rocky Yeats. If the sheriff's department could solve Vikki's murder sooner than I could, fine by me. I didn't need to be the first one to cross the finish line.

Chapter 25

The moment we drove into the parking lot by Incline Bowl and Candace spotted Justin among the group of teens, her self-consciousness returned. "I shouldn't have eaten that Big Mac. I look fat."

"You do not. You look beautiful." I handed her some money. "Go have a good time."

As she emerged from the car, Justin hurried to greet her. The smile that spread across her face was worth a million bucks. Who cared if she rolled gutter balls all afternoon? However, when she returned home, we would discuss the possibility that she was suffering from anorexia.

With a few hours to myself, I decided to track down Frank Novak. Hoping to reach him before he went to work, if today was even a workday, I drove to his house. He didn't answer when I knocked on the door. The burgundy Cavalier that had stood in his driveway the night before was nowhere in sight.

Rather than approach him cold at the library, I took the opportunity to get a feel for who he was. The drapes for the picture window were hanging open, so I stole to the window and peeked inside. The living room was sparse, decorated with an easy chair, a pole lamp, and a bookcase filled with antique books. One thing seemed out of place in the serene setting—a shotgun hanging over the stone fireplace.

Suddenly, a white Pekinese leaped onto a stool by the window and began to bark shrilly. I recoiled, not from the size of the dog but from the exposed teeth.

From the neighbor's yard, an elderly woman carrying a snow shovel said, "Did Moby Dick scare you, dear?"

"Moby Dick? Big name for a little dog."

"Frank loves that book. Melville's his favorite writer. What are you doing, poking around?"

"I'm looking for him. Do you know where he is?"

"At the library, I imagine. He's often there, even if it's closed." She leaned forward and lowered her voice. "I think he enjoys the smell of books." The woman chuckled and returned to her project. Over her shoulder she said, "You can catch him tonight at the library. It'll be open."

Nosy neighbors. My favorite people. Max had told me more than once to embrace them as sources of information.

Before heading to the library, I decided to take Vikki's earrings back to her house. I parked in front of the A-frame and, before heading inside, opened Vikki's file and added my case notes about her family and Rocky. When I'd written all I could, I glanced at the sheet. Max would have been proud of me. My college term papers hadn't been as comprehensive.

As I made my way up the path, Vikki's neighbor, Garrett, lurched at me. Where had he come from? I sidestepped him, hands ready to defend myself.

"Vikki's gone." He drew to a halt.

"Yes, I know."

"She was such a good person." His hair was mussed, his shirttail tucked half in and half out of his jeans.

"Yes, she was. How is sobriety going for you, if you don't mind me asking?"

He licked his lips. "Okay, today, but her death has thrown me for a loop."

"Detective Sergeant Shaper said you were with AA buddies playing poker the night she died."

"Yeah."

"When I saw you at the crime scene, you smelled of beer."

"I fell off the wagon."

"Why?"

"Stress with my job. I almost got canned."

"What do you do?"

"I'm a tech guy. I tweak apps. Work from my house." He hitched his thumb. "I missed a huge deadline that day. See, my car broke down and I didn't have Internet access, and my boss was super angry. That night I met up with my buddies, and one thing led to another."

"They let you drink?"

"They sort of have to. An alcoholic can't get better if he doesn't see the signs and help himself." He ran his fingers through his gnarled hair. "I started day one of sobriety right after the police told me about Vikki. I've had a lot of day ones." He brandished a hand. "What are you doing here?"

"Returning something."

"Gotcha." Without saying goodbye, he trudged to his house next door.

I shook off the jittery feelings about Garrett—he had to be innocent if more than one buddy vouched for him—and strode up the path.

The sheriff's department tape was gone. I used my key and slipped inside. Vikki's bedroom, which the officers had returned to order, smelled of cinnamon. I switched on the overhead light and crossed the woven carpet to the dresser. A potpourri of dried flowers in a silver bowl sat atop a lace runner. Little framed pictures of flowers and trees cluttered the bureau. Three swan figurines nestled on a mirror. At the far right lay a shiny black jewelry case, and next to it, two brass trees: one with slots to hold earrings, the other to hold necklaces.

I pulled the earrings from my purse, looped them through slots, and eyed the necklace tree. One space on the tree was empty. Was a necklace missing? I recognized the strand of pearls. I couldn't remember having seen the antique locket before. I examined it and my breath snagged. The initials *GVB* were inscribed on the front—the same initials as in her Bible. I popped the locket open. Inside was a photograph of a baby with chestnut-red hair. The *V* had to stand for Victoria. What did the *G* and *B* denote?

The front door slammed.

Seconds later, Detective Sergeant Shaper strode into the room. "Well, well, well, look who's here."

Like a child with her hand in a cookie jar, heat rushed up my cheeks. I stepped toward him to plead my case. "I have a key. The tape was down. I brought back Vikki's earrings." I pointed to the jewelry trees. "She would want things in order."

Shaper didn't say anything, but he was staring at me with a glint in his eyes.

"Why are you here?" I asked. "Are you following me?"

"Don't get paranoid. I live just up the way." He hooked his thumb over his shoulder. "I was driving by and saw a light on and movement, and since the good doctor who owns this place is still in San Francisco, I decided to check it out thinking a prowler might have seized an opportunity. As it turned out, an enthusiastic investigator was messing with the crime scene." He winked.

It was a friendly wink. Cool. He wasn't upset with my being here.

"I'm through. I'll leave."

"Hold on." He blocked my exit. "I spoke to Detective Brandon. She said you left her a message that Miss Carmichael's family wants nothing to do with her."

"Adoptive family."

"Tell me about them."

"They were rustic. I didn't get the feeling they had any part in her death."

"Did you give Brandon their address?"

"Of course. Is there anything new you've learned that you'd care to share with me?"

He regarded me with those piercing eyes. "Nope."

"Okay, then." I headed for the front door and stopped, my hand on the knob. A sob caught in my throat. On the floor to the right stood Vikki's black knee-high after-ski boots, the ones with fur-lined cuffs. She'd spent an entire week's paycheck on them.

"Are you okay?" Shaper asked.

I pivoted. "Did Detective Brandon tell you about Rocky Yeats?"

"Deputy Kim is following up. She's dealing with all aspects of the casino."

I grunted.

He tilted his head. "What's wrong? Why don't you like her?"

"Karen said she's not seasoned as a homicide detective."

"Trust me, Kim comes with a long list of creds from SFPD." Shaper stepped toward me. "Listen up. Karen Brandon is going through a case of badge envy at the moment. Take what she says with a grain of salt."

"She wants you to respect her."

"I will if she does her job."

We stood for a moment, at an impasse.

He broke the silence. "How's your niece doing?"

"She's out with friends."

"Which means she's feeling better. Glad to hear it."

I glanced at my watch, eager to meet Frank Novak. "Are we good?"

"Good with what?"

"My having been here." I dangled my key to prove I hadn't broken in.

"Yes, Miss Adams. The owner hasn't requested your friend's personal belongings be vacated yet, and you've got a key, so we're fine. By the way"—he took another step toward me; his cologne smelled like warm almonds—"I agree with Detective Brandon about what went down at the springs."

"Thanks. I'll sleep better tonight." I strode out of the house.

Shaper followed. "Where're you off to since your niece is out?"

I swung around. He was standing with his hands shoved into his jeans pockets. "None of your business."

His laughter continued until I drove off.

Chapter 26

The library was located at Boatworks Shopping Center next to the rustic two-story warehouse. On the lower floor of the warehouse was a terrific restaurant with a view of the lake and marina. On the upper floor were jewelry and art shops.

A sign in the library's foyer promised that any book could be obtained within twenty-four hours because, though limited in size and therefore selection, the library had an interlibrary agreement with the much larger Auburn Library.

Tables in the main body of the facility were packed with teens and adults poring over periodicals and books. To the right was a bestsellers area. Straight ahead was a section devoted to inspirational works. In the children's room to my left, kids and adults sat on the floor or at child-friendly tables. Due to the warm temperature inside the building, visitors had shed jackets and sweaters.

"Miss Adams." A man in a baseball cap waved. He was nestled in a beanbag chair with a boy and girl sitting on either side of him.

I peered hard trying to place him and then it dawned on me. Mr. Lazar, my latest process-serving coup. He scrambled out of the squishy chair and shuffled toward me. His cheeks were ruddy; his eyes looked clear and focused.

"I just wanted to say thank you," he said.

"For?"

"I've attended two AA meetings since I saw you. My wife promised every time I go, I can spend an hour with my kids. If not for you—"

"You did it. You took the first step, sir."

"Daddy," his daughter called out.

Lazar smiled, a couple of days sober and eons more confident. "Gotta go."

I headed toward the checkout desk, where four people stood in line waiting for an elderly clerk to issue them books. Had Karen not warned me about Frank Novak's appearance, I would have been looking for a younger man—a potential boyfriend of Vikki's. As he examined each book he stamped, he reminded me of a ferret foraging for food. Pale arms with liver spots jutted from his blue plaid shirt. A pair of glasses dangled from a chain around his neck.

In minutes, it was my turn to talk with him. He looked up, his rheumy gaze meeting mine.

"Frank Novak?" I asked.

He slipped on his black-rimmed glasses and grinned. A few of his teeth were missing, and he smelled of chicken noodle soup. "That's me."

"I'm Aspen Adams, a friend of Vikki Carmichael's."

"Vikki, Vikki, Vikki. So sad." Frank bobbed his head. "Murdered."

"May I call you Frank?" When I spoke, he moved his mouth in rhythm with mine, pronouncing the words along with me.

"Everybody else does." His gaze moved to a spot over my shoulder.

I turned, expecting to see an impatient patron at my heels, but found no one. I refocused. "I'd like to ask you some questions."

"That deputy already grilled me." When he said *grilled me*, he drew imaginary quotation marks in the air.

"Who? Detective Brandon?"

"No. An Asian woman. Kim."

I was glad to hear she was on top of things, but that didn't stop me from wanting a few answers myself. "Do you know Billy Tennyson, Vikki's boyfriend?"

"Never met him."

"He said you and Vikki spent a lot of time together." The movement of his mouth as I spoke was disconcerting. I wriggled my shoulders to shake off the tension.

"I wasn't her boyfriend." Frank twirled the numbers on an old rubber date stamp with his index finger.

"I didn't say you were."

"I wasn't."

"Gotcha."

Frank pushed his glasses higher on his nose. The move left a streak of blue ink along the ridge. "I'm gay." He was nothing if not blunt. In fact, he was such an odd duck that I couldn't fathom what he and Vikki had talked about.

I took another tack. "Vikki visited the library a lot, I heard."

"She was thirsty for knowledge."

"Did she ever meet anybody here, other than you?"

"Nope. This isn't that kind of place. The library is for people interested in learning."

"And Vikki was hungry for that?"

"Yep."

"Do you know if she had any other boyfriends?" A more specific question might bring straighter answers.

"Just Billy." He cleared his throat. "He was her ex-boyfriend." This time he mimed quotations around the *ex*.

"Did Vikki talk to you about other men in her life?"

Frank pursed his lips. "She never told me their names, but one time she confessed she chewed them up and spit them out." He chortled.

An odd sense of humor was better than none, I supposed.

"I think it had to do with her being abandoned as a child," he added.

Aha. He was an amateur psychologist. How many books had he read on the subject? I'd bet there were quite a few of them in the library, judging by how crammed the shelves were.

"She was always reading books about adoption and abandonment."

"Which books?"

"You'll find them in the religion and psychology section."

"You put religion and psychology together?"

He *tsked*. "Of course not. But the one hundred and two hundred aisles are back to back."

"Excuse me," a woman behind me said. "Can you hurry up? I need to check out."

Frank's cheek twitched. He signaled to me. "I'm sorry. You need to move."

For an hour, I searched the books on the psychology shelves looking for some sign of Vikki's having read one, perhaps a credit card receipt or movie ticket stub used as a bookmark, the kinds of things I would have used. Not until I opened the book *The Beauty of Tao* did I find evidence. A ski lift ticket drifted to the floor. When I picked it up, I recognized Vikki's trademark smiley face on it, but this time she'd drawn an X through it and black droplets dribbling from the eyes.

I perused the pages. The contents didn't seem to have anything to do with adoption. Dog-eared pages marked sections about the inner soul, the essence of energy, and the ease of fertility. But nothing screamed *This is why I was murdered.*

Disheartened and knowing I had to pick up Candace, I left. At the same time Mr. Lazar and his children were in the parking lot, climbing into his Chevy.

He saw me and cocked his head to one side. "You don't look very happy, Miss Adams."

"I'm not." I pulled my keys out of my jacket pocket. "I was researching a project, looking for books a friend of mine might have read, but I only found one."

"Did you try the computer's database? If she was a regular, she'd have an account." He held up his library card. "We all have one. Whenever we check out a book, there's a record of it in the computer. Frank can check for you."

"Mr. Lazar, you're a genius. Thank you."

I dashed into the library. Frank was hovering over a cart of returned books. "Mr. Novak?"

He turned, his face pinched, his glasses teetering at the tip of his nose. "Yes?"

I told him what I was after.

"Vikki never checked out books."

"Not even one?" She'd come to the library and had never taken a book home?

"Nope. She read the books, and that was that."

"In the psychology section," I said.

"Yes, as well as the religion section."

"Earlier you said she read books about adoption and abandonment."

"She read about religion, too. Perhaps she wanted to find peace about being abandoned."

"Is that why she turned to the Source of Serenity?"

"What's that?" he asked.

"A church."

"I don't like church. Never been." Frank hunched down and beckoned me to draw near. I did. He whispered, "The religion section is the quietest section in the library. She liked to write there."

"What was she writing?"

"Don't know. She always closed the book when I came around. I think it held her deepest secrets or something." He grabbed a few books and shuffled toward the back of the room.

I paused. Frank had said *the* book, like Vikki had always read the same one. I hurried to the religion section and pulled out a handful of books. I flipped through pages. Nothing leaped out at me. I returned them to the shelves and scanned a few more. Zilch. I took a step back and stared at the myriad volumes, so many that the titles began to blur together. Tomorrow, I'd uncover whatever Vikki might have read in those books. Right now, I had to pick up Candace.

Halfway to the bowling alley, my cell phone rang. I recognized Candace's new number.

"Aunt Aspen? It's me. A bunch of us want to go out for pizza." Her voice bubbled with enthusiasm. "Is that okay?"

"Who, exactly?"

"Well, Zephyr is the adult in charge, and Waverly and Justin and a few more. Please say I can go."

"As long as Zephyr is there, I'm okay with it. Did I give you enough money?"

"Yes. Zephyr said she'll bring me home. I've got my key." The delight in her voice was infectious. "Thank you."

The moment I ended the call, the phone rang again. I answered, "What now, sweetie?" thinking Candace had forgotten to tell me something.

"I rank as *sweetie*?" Karen Brandon chuckled.

"I thought you were my niece. She just called asking if she could go out with friends."

"Since she's busy, how about dinner seeing as I bailed on you last night? I make a mean spaghetti."

Karen's loneliness was palpable. What kind of friend would I be if I said no? Returning to the library would have to wait.

Chapter 27

"Vikki's folks don't want to have a funeral for her?" Karen called from her kitchen.

The savory aroma of sautéed onions made my mouth water as I roamed the living room. Karen had ordered me to stay out while she made her masterpiece. The task of setting the table soothed me. "Her father said she wouldn't want it, but her mother asked me, as I was leaving, to give her a good one."

Televisions in both the living room and kitchen were blasting twenty-four-hour news. Karen once told me she hated silence. The noise was obliterating the babble of the brook outside her dining room window.

"Nothing like having secrets," Karen yelled over the din. "When the coroner releases her body, you can be in charge."

"If I can't find her sister."

"Sister?"

"Yes. She has an adoptive sister, Lynanne, who might be living here. Has anyone with that name contacted your office yet?"

"Not that I'm aware of."

"She must know Vikki died. It's been on every news channel. On the other hand, their mother said they weren't close. She's ten years older than Vikki and left home at sixteen."

Karen rounded the corner, handed me a glass of red wine, and returned to her post. "Have a seat on the couch. I'll be out in a minute."

The combination living room and dining room had been decked out with rust-colored chairs and lamps. The Berber carpet matched. A royal blue sofa and armchair faced the fireplace. The walls were impersonal and barren of art or mementos, which saddened me as much as it had when I'd visited the Carmichaels.

I said, "I tried to find out who the birth parents were."

The strident sound of jars slamming on the kitchen counter startled me. What sauce was Karen making?

"I contacted the wife of the lawyer who handled the adoption. He had died and his records were a mass of confusion. There was no way I'd find the information unless I had weeks to review his files."

"Ridiculous," Karen shouted.

Sensing she wasn't commenting on what I'd shared, I poked my head into the kitchen. Had a tornado passed through? Empty olive jars filled the sink. A spaghetti bag lay on the floor. The neatnik in me wanted to clean up, but I stayed put.

Karen pointed at the television. "Did you hear that? The idiotic city council." She took a long sip of wine. "Can't they do anything right? The jerks might be dropping the moratorium on new construction in Lake Tahoe again, and they're considering allowing more piers to be built. Make you a bet the bill gets passed." She whipped a five-dollar bill out of her jeans pocket and slapped it on the cutting board. "C'mon. Five bucks."

"I don't bet."

Karen shoved the bill back into her pocket and gulped down the rest of her wine. "If I could be on the council, I'd make things right. If I ruled the world . . ."

Leaving her to her rant, I left the kitchen to explore her home. I had visited once before to pick her up for a book club meeting because her car had broken down.

"Come back," Karen yelled before I reached the bathroom on the right. "Tell me about Vikki's parents."

Thwarted, I returned and leaned against the doorframe.

"They're different," I said. "Her father wanted the children to be nature-loving kids. The girls didn't go for it. Vikki told me her mother was a fabulous cook, but the cookbooks in the house were untouched."

"Some cooks wing it."

"Mr. Carmichael said when Vikki went off to college—"

"Speaking of which, did I tell you that I'm thinking of taking a few more courses over in Reno so I can get a full-fledged degree instead of the two-bit junior college thing I have from Sacramento? The rough-and-tumble academy training doesn't seem to be impressing my colleagues." Karen cut a hard look at the television. "Dang it. We get a dolt for mayor and everything goes haywire."

"Why don't you turn the TV off?"

"Can't. Got to keep current."

Loneliness could create all sorts of quirks, I mused.

When Karen shouted at the TV again, I left her. I paused in the foyer to inspect a gun case made out of walnut. It held four antique rifles and a half dozen nineteenth-century and contemporary pistols. Beneath each weapon was a brass plaque denoting the maker and year.

Karen sidled up to me, glass of wine in hand. "You win." She crossed to the television in the living room and switched the sound to mute. She returned and eyed the display case. "Those are my dad's. He had a penchant for collecting." She sipped her wine. "My preference is the .45 Colt revolver with the four-inch-long barrel and tooled silver handle."

"It's nice." I didn't like guns, but I could appreciate craftsmanship.

"My dad loved to hunt. He always dragged me along."

"Did you enjoy the outings?"

"Not that much, but having a brother made me battle for my father's attention. My brother? He hated to hunt." She plucked at her messy hair. "Dad was mine for those few minutes." Her fingers drifted down her neck to the class ring that dangled from a thin gold necklace. A charm peeked from beneath the ring.

"Is that your father's?" I asked.

"Berkeley, class of fifty-two. He was a lawyer, did I tell you?"

She had. A number of times.

Karen dropped the ring. "Man, I miss him."

"Has anything been resolved with your brother and the will?"

After book club a few weeks ago, she had confided how much she hated the yelling matches with her brother. She was challenging the validity of the document, claiming their father had Alzheimer's at the time he'd written it, making it invalid. I didn't know what it contained. Maybe her father had bequeathed more to her brother. Conflict with family was never easy.

"I've got my attorney dealing with the issue. Pain in the butt." Karen gulped down half of her wine. Was the dispute with her brother the impetus for her drinking? "These guns." She patted the cabinet. "They're mementos of a simpler time when I didn't have to prove myself." Without further explanation, she strode into the kitchen and topped off her wine. "Did I ever tell you that I was attacked in Sacramento? One night after work. I keep the guns on display as a reminder that I will never be a victim again." She picked up the television controller. "I'll bet you there are no women's sports on tonight." She slapped a five-dollar bill on the counter and started clicking through the channels.

I didn't have cable. What was the point? I hated watching television. Reading filled my idle hours.

"Ha! Told you. Nada. Nothing. Pay up." She opened her palm but quickly fisted it. "Oh, that's right. You don't bet." She scooped up her five-dollar bill.

I was beginning to wonder whether Karen had a gambling problem as well as a drinking problem. Had Shaper been hinting about both issues earlier?

Switching conversations as fast as she changed channels, Karen said, "Yeah, the attack came from behind. There's nothing like that feeling of vulnerability. I've carried a gun with me ever since. Even when I'm not on duty. Jerks that mess with a woman don't deserve to live."

Her edginess was worming its way into my system. Why was I at her place? Because she'd invited me and I was a supportive friend. Was it worth the angst churning in my stomach?

I said, "Do you have any antacids?"

"In my bathroom under the sink."

Karen continued talking as I made my way down the hall. "The Sacramento police never accepted my account. My own buddies on the force disavowed any knowledge. It's one of the reasons I left the area."

I missed the rest of her account as I turned into a room that was simple, at best. No color. No artwork. Against the far wall stood a bed made with a crisp white sheet and brown blanket, tucked so tightly that the surface looked firm enough to bounce a quarter on. The dresser was maple and barren of personal items. A bookcase was stocked with police procedurals. No fiction. An ancient Panasonic television sat on a rolling cart. An oak desk stood against the window. An HP combination printer/fax sat on the desk, as well as a pile of bills. The topmost bill was marked *Two months overdue*. I wondered whether Karen's gambling had crippled her financially.

I chastised myself for prying and stepped into the tiny bathroom. Like everything else, the counters were devoid of personal items, not even a perfume bottle or a jewelry box. As much as Karen had loved her father, I was surprised that she hadn't displayed a photograph of him. Anywhere.

In the medicine cabinet, I found a single bottle of generic ibuprofen. No antacids. She said they were here, so I continued to search. Under the sink, I found a bottle of peroxide, a hair dryer, and a curling iron. Way in the back, I caught sight of a box of Tums. I'd been hoping for Zantac, but anything would do at this point. My stomach was rumbling. I downed two, turned out the light, and returned to the dining room. If I could have left before dinner, I would have, but I didn't think Karen would appreciate the rejection.

I returned to the living room and suggested we switch off all the televisions, even the one in the kitchen, and put on some music. Grudgingly, Karen obliged. During the meal, she downed two more glasses of wine and shared stories about her best days on the ski slopes. Around ten, after helping her wash the dishes, I thanked her for the meal and split.

Before I slotted the key in the Jeep's ignition, the televisions were blaring again.

Just as I arrived home, Candace was climbing out of Zephyr's car. For fifteen minutes, she bubbled with enthusiasm about her day. After brushing her teeth and climbing into bed, she fell fast asleep.

Minutes later, I snuggled into bed and opened an Agatha Christie mystery. I read for an hour, but my eyes wouldn't stay open.

Seconds after turning off the lamp on the nightstand, however, I was awakened by a gagging sound coming from down the hall. I tiptoed toward Candace's bathroom and put my ear to the door. My heart snagged. She was vomiting again. I raced in and found her hunched over the toilet bowl, her nightgown clinging to her with sweat.

"Candace? Sweetie." I drenched a towel with cold water and braced it against her neck. "Are you sick?"

Candace craned her neck to look at me. Her eyes were watery. "Please, Aunt Aspen, I'm f-fine."

"No, you're not. In the morning, we're going to the doctor."

"No," Candace cried. She wrenched herself from her hunched position and covered her mouth. Through splayed fingers she said, "I . . . I ate too much. That's all." In her eyes was a panic I couldn't comprehend.

Biting my lip so I wouldn't blurt out anything that might rile her, I cleaned her up, ushered her to bed, and stroked her hair. When I was certain she'd fallen asleep—again—I searched her purse, duffle bag, and dresser drawers. I didn't find any evidence of drugs. I checked the pockets of her jeans and my ski jacket. Empty. What was going on? This was not anorexic behavior.

A horrible thought cut through me. Could Candace be bulimic and inducing herself to vomit? A number of patients I'd treated at BARC had struggled with the disease. Most often it started with peculiar eating habits. A patient might choose specific eating rituals, like chopping her food in the same size bites, alphabetically, geometrically, as Candace had done that first night. Other patients might feel riddled with guilt for having eaten something, like Candace had after downing a Big Mac.

I moaned. *Bulimia*. I hoped I was wrong.

Chapter 28

The landline telephone rang the moment I returned from my morning run. I answered, still out of breath. I tucked the receiver between my chin and ear and leaned against the kitchen counter to stretch my calves.

"Hey, little sis, did Candy tell you I called last night?" Rosie sounded hoarse, as if she'd been up all night partying.

"No." I stood erect. Tense. The hairs on the back of my neck prickled. Was she the reason why Candace had vomited?

"I didn't think so. I knew you'd call me back if she had. You're Miss Responsibility."

I kept mum. I wasn't up for a fight.

"Listen, I'll cut right to the chase," she went on. "I could use a loan. A hundred bucks would do it."

"No."

"You've got my kid."

"And I'm feeding her. Get a job, Rosie."

"Why don't you get a frigging life!" She hurled a few nasty zingers before ending the call.

I'm rubber and you're glue, I thought childishly.

After setting the receiver in the cradle, I stared down the hall. The first episode for Candace had happened after she'd heard her mother's voice on the answering machine. Who knew what tongue-lashing Rosie might have given her last night?

The door to Candace's room squeaked open. I ducked into the kitchen and started making breakfast. She appeared at the kitchen door, her face glowing and moist with sunscreen. She had dressed for skiing in my baby blue sweater and powder pants. "Aunt Aspen, I feel fine this morning. Please don't make me go to the doctor."

I glanced from her to the telephone and back.

"Justin's going to be in ski school today. It's his last day. He's going home tomorrow. I've got to see him again." Her eyes sparkled with anticipation. "Please?"

"Sweetheart, you'll see him in Auburn."

"No, I won't." Tears burst from her sweet eyes. "He's moving in two weeks. His dad got a job in Columbus, Ohio." She flung herself into my arms.

I rubbed her back and cooed, "Okay, you can go skiing, but I'm warning you, if you have another"—I hesitated—"incident, we're off to the doctor. Repeated vomiting can ruin your intestines."

"How?" She wrinkled her nose.

"It makes you less resistant to infection."

Candace pushed apart from me and picked at the pilled lint on the sweater. "I'll be good. I swear it was the pizza."

"Ready for breakfast?"

"I'm not hungry. I'll eat a power bar in a little while." She scooted out, avoiding my glance.

A short while later, after eating an omelet with cheddar and stowing the last of my breakfast dishes in the dishwasher, the telephone rang. I braced for another onslaught from my dearly beloved sister.

"It's me. Did I wake you?" Dan sounded chipper.

My shoulders relaxed. "No. I've been up for hours." The hour prior to my run had been dedicated to paying bills.

"Want to go on a bike ride?"

A ride might clear my head and help me see things about Vikki's murder, motherhood, and life in general in a new way. "Yes, but I have to drop Candace at ski school and pick up some documents at the courthouse for Max first." My job description of process server wasn't accurate. I was often called upon to be a go-fer. "Why don't I meet you in the parking lot by Tahoe Books in three hours?"

"Perfect."

• • •

I was still mulling over the case as I pulled into the lot by the bookstore. Dan was arched forward over his mountain bike and decked out in yellow Neoprene biking pants, a turtleneck, and a black and yellow jacket. With his day's growth of beard, he reminded me of an ornery hornet ready to attack. His smile dispelled the notion.

"Hello, gorgeous." He bussed me on the cheek.

It took a minute to get my mountain bike off the rack, but after I'd mounted it and ridden a mile, the cobwebs in my mind melted away.

"You look pretty in pink," Dan said.

A sweater, leggings, gloves, and the requisite helmet were all I needed to keep warm as I rode. I'd chosen the crimson shirt because I didn't want to wear makeup and knew that the hue highlighted the natural color in my cheeks.

Riding past Crystal Bay Cove was inspiring. A handful of homes or condominiums did nothing to hamper the view. Buoys bobbed on the water. An outboard motorboat roaring across the water glistened in the sun.

Because the ride from Tahoe City north around the lake was nearly flat, we weren't out of breath when we stopped for a cup of coffee at View by the Lake, a café that, in addition to coffee, sold homemade candy by the pound and freshly made pastries.

"My treat." Dan took off his ski hat, beat it against his leg to remove icy particles that had formed from the morning moisture, and ordered a black coffee and what had become my drink of choice, latte with extra steamed milk and a dash of chocolate. He set the drinks on a wooden table in the corner closest to the windows and sat down.

After grabbing a couple packets of sugar, I joined him, dumped both sugars into my coffee, and stirred.

"So what's going on with Vikki's murder investigation?" Dan leaned back in his chair, his long legs stretched out in front of him, a man comfortable in his own skin.

I regarded him for a long moment and wondered why I wasn't in love with him. He was a catch, just not my catch.

He asked how the police were proceeding with Vikki's murder investigation. I had no idea. Shaper seemed proficient and Karen was busting a gut trying to win his approval.

I brought him up to date about what I'd learned: finding Vikki's family and my list of possible suspects: Rocky Yeats, Billy Tennyson, and Reverend Brock, though I couldn't figure out his motive. I simply didn't like him; he was slick.

"You're becoming a real investigator." His eyes sparkled with humor. "A regular Columbo."

"Max is a good teacher. She makes me write everything down. I've got a file for Vikki that's stuffed to the gills with my notes."

"The key to every article I write are the research notes I take."

"Notes." I snapped my fingers. "The librarian—his name is Frank Novak—he told me Vikki was always making notes. He thought she might be writing some kind of article."

"You know, she wanted to give me a piece for the magazine, but it never materialized," Dan said. "All she gave me were the photos." He drank the rest of his coffee. "I think she planned to do a pictorial overview of avalanches."

"She was an excellent photographer." I regaled him with stories of a few of my photographic outings with Vikki. She'd taken pictures; I'd hiked.

In the middle of one of my accounts, Dan started twirling the bicycle lock key he'd placed on the table. At the same time, he worked his tongue along the inside of his mouth.

"What's wrong?" I asked.

"I'm leaving in a couple of days for a lengthy assignment."

"Where to?"

"The Himalayas."

"Wow," I said, then chuckled. I was beginning to sound like my niece.

Dan gazed at me, his eyes full of sadness. "You don't care that we won't see each other for a long time, do you?"

"Dan, we had this conversation."

He nodded. "We did, but—"

I reached out. "And you said you were okay with my decision."

He yanked his hand away. "I guess I'm not. I love you, Aspen. I can't get past it." Color rushed to his cheeks. "Man, I'm blowing this. I—" He fiddled with the key.

I grew still. Why couldn't I give him what he wanted? He was a terrific guy. The best. So why was Nick Shaper's face popping into my mind?

"I don't want to lose our friendship," I said.

"You won't. You never could." His smile eased the tension, but the disappointment in his voice was palpable. "I'd hoped, given time, that you'd . . ." He rose to his feet. "I'll be outside." He tossed his empty cup in the garbage and strode out the door.

A good man is walking out of your life. Why aren't you running after him?

I took my time leaving the café. When I arrived at my bike, Dan had climbed onto his and was ready to roll.

"Race you back to town," he said.

An hour later, I kissed him goodbye in the bookstore parking lot, wondering if I'd ever see him again. An ache gripped my heart, but I didn't give it voice.

After I turned left at the Y and headed south on Highway 89, the sight of the Homewood ski area, a modest resort with slopes visible from the highway, comforted me. Its parking lot was packed. The line for the chairlift was short. Skiers whisked down the hill beneath the lift.

Nearing the Homewood Market, I thought of my parents. Whenever we would visit Lake Tahoe in the summer, they would take us to the decades-old market and let us skip through the store barefoot, enjoying the fragrance of spicy roasted chicken and fresh-baked donuts. Each time, we were allowed to choose an ice cream treat from the huge blue chest that stood inside the entrance to the right. I'd learned from my father that on any given day ice cream was the ideal food. A bite or two, he said, could solve the world's problems.

No question about it, I could use a few problems solved. I'd possibly lost Dan as a friend, I couldn't help Karen with her drinking issue, my errant sister was the bane of my existence, my niece might be battling a troubling disease, and I hadn't figured out who had killed Vikki. Yet.

Upon entering the store, the huge blue chest beckoned me. I selected a plastic cup of vanilla/orange sherbet and ate it while I shopped. Five minutes later, I left the store with a roasted chicken, the makings for a salad, and a loaf of crusty French bread.

A few feet from my loaner Jeep, I spied a black Ford truck idling. Sitting in the driver's seat was Billy Tennyson, smoking a cigarette. Anxiety swept through me. The way he was leering at me unnerved me.

Deflect and diffuse, I told myself. It was a phrase I'd often used as a therapist. We were in a public place. There were lots of people around.

I marched toward him. "Hey, Billy."

"Hey, yourself."

"You're a long way from home."

"I've got to pick up a few costumes at Wyatt's."

Wyatt's was an eclectic costume shop south of Homewood owned by a colorful cross-dresser. When Wyatt wasn't at the shop, he was lounging on the beach or skiing on the slopes.

"The girls are adding a new number," he went on.

"Another Marilyn Monroe song?"

"Nah. They're branching out. This one's by Madonna. 'Material Girl.' Lots of spangles." He took a deep drag on his cigarette. "I stopped here to get a soda first. Got a problem with that?"

"No, of course not." I forced a smile.

Billy shut off the engine. "Could you move? I can't get out of the truck if you're standing there."

"Oh, sure." I backed up a couple of steps.

"You look good, by the way." He climbed out. "A sunburn suits you." Was he coming on to me? He tossed his cigarette on the ground by my feet and crushed it with the heel of his boot—a stained Timberland Trekker. He grinned. "See you."

As he strolled into the market, I hurried to my car. When I'd first met him, trusting my gut instinct, I'd marked him off my suspect list. For that same reason, he was going back on the list, his undying love for Vikki notwithstanding.

My cell phone rang as I was pulling into my driveway. I answered.

"Aunt Aspen. It's me."

Candace sounded hyper. My upper lip broke out in a sweat. Was she sick again?

"Justin is so cool," she gushed. "We had lunch together. And skied together. And he's so smart."

"Smart is important."

"This day is going down in my diary. Do you know what he said? He said he's going to write me from Ohio. I gave him my friend's email address since I don't have one."

"That's great."

"Oh, and Waverly asked if I could go to the barbecue place with them for dinner."

I breathed a sigh of relief. How great was it that she wasn't sick? How cool was it that she was living on cloud nine?

"Her mother's going," she added, giving me the woman's name and cell phone number. "She said you could call if you wanted to talk to her. Later, if it's okay, can I go to a movie? It's a stupid Seth Rogan movie, but everyone's going."

A pang of sadness swept over me. Vikki had loved Seth Rogan. To her, there was no one funnier.

"Well? Can I?" Candace asked.

"Yes, you may." I gave her a midnight curfew and hung up.

Seconds later, Candace's words replayed in my head. She was going to write about her day in her diary. I had written in a diary until I turned twenty-nine, and then I tossed it out, no longer in need of those memories. Frank said Vikki was always writing. Did she have a diary?

I called Shaper; he answered after the first ring. I asked if he'd found Vikki's diary. He said no one on his team had and asked why. Having nothing to go on, I said it was a hunch and ended the call. I knew what I had to do.

Chapter 29

Inside the A-frame house it was cold. I kept my jacket on while searching Vikki's bedroom. Under the bed. In the closet. I rummaged through the dresser. Nothing. I looked for fake drawer bottoms and such. No diary. I scoured her bathroom. The kitchen. The living room. I checked for phony books on her bookshelves. Zilch.

An hour later, I rang Gwen on her cell phone. I needed help.

"Hi, there," she answered, her voice loud to rise above the boisterous lunch crowd. "What's up?"

"Where would you hide a diary?"

"In a panty drawer."

"I checked there."

"In a shoebox."

"Nope."

"Why are you asking?"

"Frank Novak, a librarian, said Vikki was always writing. I'm wondering if she kept a diary."

Gwen slammed something on the bar counter. The sound jarred me.

"Are you okay?" I asked.

"I dropped a tray. I'm flying solo. Chef called in sick, and my backup bartender got the cold of the century, but that's not important right now. A diary, huh?" As glasses clattered and corks popped, she recited a number of places she would have hidden a diary: inside a pillowcase, between the mattresses, at the bottom of the laundry hamper, inside a recipe box.

I thanked her for rekindling my imagination, wished her luck with customers, and restarted my search, methodically checking every nook and cranny of the house.

When I returned to the bedroom and searched the bed, I laughed out loud. As Gwen had suggested, I found a handcrafted book bag, imperceptible during my initial search because the material matched the linens, wedged between the bed and nightstand. A pink-and-burgundy-striped book was in one slot. A gold pen was in the other.

I perched on the bed and turned to the first page, which was easier to read than Vikki's datebook. Yes, there were doodles down the margins, but the handwriting was neat and legible. Her memoir began on the day she'd moved to Lake Tahoe. Dominating the pages was her amazement with the beauty and aroma of the area. Subsequent pages told of her various encounters with new people: a woman at the cash-only line at Safeway, a hunk who had helped her pump gas, a doctor at a bookstore, a ski lift operator who'd smiled. Everyone seemed to rate in her diary, even a gambler at the casino had rated.

Had an argument with a gambler today. I hate fighting.

In the margins were aimless doodles, similar to the drawings in her datebook, as if she were trying to come up with what else to write.

The next few entries were short, about two or three sentences each. She mentioned Billy early on.

Billy's a jerk. Never returns calls. Voice mail stinks. I want to break up. What a louse.

Frank seemed to be the person who understood Vikki's quest for knowledge.

Dear Frank. How he loves those books. Wish I could find him a boyfriend. He's so shy, it's going to be hard.

Not once did Vikki write that she was afraid of either man, making me think my reaction to Billy at Homewood Market was over the top. She didn't mention Rocky at all.

When I reached a section about Vikki's adoptive sister who was living in Tahoe, I held my breath.

Lynanne came for dinner. She hates when I call her Lee-Lee. Heh-heh. And, man, she's a picky eater. She's fit, so I guess that's why. Boring.

Could Lynanne, aka Lee-Lee, be the *LL* that Vikki had scribbled in her datebook? Why hadn't Vikki introduced us? Maybe Lynanne had moved out of the area. The entry was from two months ago.

One about Vikki's parents caught my eye.

Poor Mom and Pop. Hope they'll forgive me for leaving. I wish they would read my letters. They always send them back.

Vikki wrote about her birth mother, as well.

Wish my mother hadn't been so freaking weak. If she'd kept me . . .

An hour in, even though my eyes were tired, I continued to read.

An account of her search for religion cropped up. She mentioned Ed Brock.

Eddie's so funny. That toupee. What is up with that? Like the whole world doesn't know? Vanity thy name is Reverend. LOL

Her writings about the Source of Serenity, which she'd abbreviated using the initials *SOS*, waffled between loving spirituality yet hating dogma. After one reference, she'd drawn a cartoonish stick figure with a dialogue bubble. She'd written the word *Help* inside.

I laughed at her play on words: SOS meaning *help*.

Reading further, one entry caught me up short.

I feel the new life growing inside me, yet still I wonder. The life gives me hope.

Was Vikki talking about her spiritual life, or had she been pregnant? If the latter, why hadn't she told me? Was this the secret she'd wanted to tell me? I made a mental note to ask Karen if the coroner knew the answer or whether someone from the sheriff's office had asked Vikki's doctors for her records. If she had been pregnant, whose was it? Billy's? Had they fought about it? Did he kill Vikki because she wanted to keep it and he didn't? I pictured her face the last time I'd seen her. Her skin had been glowing.

I scanned the remaining entries. On the last page of the journal, she wrote:

I know the fate of the life inside me is mine to determine. No one else's. With this life, I understand faith and yet I see the lack of faith, and I am moved to tears.

I choked back a sob and closed the diary. How I wished Vikki had confided in me. Knowing I had to hand the diary over to the sheriff's department—it could be key to the investigation—I pulled out my cell phone to call Karen. At the same time, my phone rang, shattering the quiet. I swiped to answer.

"Miss Adams? It's me. Tess Marks. From the Gemstone." Her voice was hushed, as if she were trying not to let anyone hear her. "I have some information that I think you'll want to know."

"One of the dancers told me you didn't think it was important."

"Now it is. I have a break in two hours." Tess ended the call. No details.

Chapter 30

"Karen, open up." I pressed her doorbell and knocked on the door of her cabin a third time. The receptionist at the sheriff's department said she had gone home sick. I could hear her moving inside.

When she answered, she growled, "What do you want?" In her left hand she clutched a tumbler filled with amber liquid.

I held up the burgundy book. "I found Vikki's diary."

"Bully for you." She pronounced each word carefully. Too carefully. "You know, if you show up with all the answers, you're going to get me fired." She tramped into the living room, leaving the door ajar.

I followed and closed the door.

Karen whirled around. "They already think I'm incompetent."

"What happened?" I slipped the diary into my jacket pocket.

"You wouldn't understand."

"Try me."

Karen downed the liquid in her glass. "Today . . ."

"What was today?"

"The anniversary of my abortion."

My heart wrenched. What a memory to have to bear.

"Daddy made me. I hated him." Her movements were jerky. "He said I'd ruin my future and I'd suck at being a mother."

I reached for her.

Karen careened toward the couch. She fell onto the chenille cushion and sank down, her knees touching her chest. The liquid sloshed over the rim of the glass. She tried to clean it up with her thumb.

"Karen," I said, "let me help you into bed."

"No," she snapped.

I recoiled.

"I'm sorry," she said. "So many things wrong with me."

"No, there aren't."

"They'll find out." Karen rubbed her nose with the back of her sleeve. "I'm a failure. Everything I've ever done . . ." Her head flopped to the right. She jerked it back to center. "They'll fire me."

"They can't fire you because you had an abortion."

"That guy."

"Which one?"

"Joey Blain. The snowboarder. He did it. He killed Vikki."

The jump in conversation jolted me. "How do you know?"

"I went to Alpine earlier. I cornered him. He gave me attitude. I could see it in his eyes." She smacked her leg. "In seconds, he lawyered up and slapped a restraining order on me."

Oh, no. Had she been drunk at the time?

Karen looked at me dully. "I'm so tired of having to prove myself. I could never please him."

"Your father?"

"My brother."

I felt like I was on a merry-go-round whirling at top speed.

"He's an idiot." She slogged into the kitchen, where she poured herself another drink.

I trailed her. "Karen, don't. You need to sleep."

She glanced at the glass and back at me. The clock on the wall ticked loudly. After a long moment, she set the glass on the counter and allowed me to usher her to the bedroom. It took a few minutes to help her undress. When she slumped onto the bed, she whispered, "Don't tell Nick. Please."

"You need some professional help."

She clutched my hand. "You help me."

"I can't."

"You're a professional. Oh, wait. No, you're not." She cackled. "You bagged on that, didn't you?" Her eyes closed and reopened. She licked her lips. "That was mean, wasn't it?"

"Yes."

"I'm vile."

"You're drunk. Sleep it off, and I'll call you later."

"Don't tell Nick."

Against my better judgment, I said, "If you promise to get help."

She couldn't. She'd passed out.

• • •

A half hour later, I strode into the investigation agency, Vikki's file in hand. The temperature was hotter than hot, which meant Max wasn't alone in the office.

Sitting at the work desk was Darcy Doherty, a strong-featured woman in her forties whose specialty was locating hidden money. She could follow fund transfers better than the Treasury Department. She looked up and acknowledged me with a wiggle of her fingers.

"Hello, sugar." Max lumbered toward me, a stack of files in her arms. "Been busy? You look disappointed."

"A friend is struggling."

Max led me to the table, set the files down, and said, "I'm all ears. Sit."

I perched on a chair. "I think Detective Karen Brandon is an alcoholic."

"The best thing you can do is point it out to her when she's sober."

"I know." My shoulders slumped. I wanted to help Karen through her pain, but I knew I couldn't make her stop.

Max patted my shoulder. "Did you get a call from a woman named Tess?"

"Aha. So you're how she tracked me down." I checked my watch. "I'm headed to see her after I do a bit of work here."

I filled Max in about everything: the Carmichaels, Vikki's adoptive siblings, Richard, aka Rocky. I mentioned my encounter with Billy Tennyson and added that Shaper had alerted me to the fact that the killer wore a size ten Trekker.

"Billy looks like he wears a size ten," I said.

Max, who was notorious for pointing out holes in an investigation, said, "Any adult could walk in size tens without stumbling."

I told her about the appointment Vikki had set with *MM* the night she died, and I recounted how Vikki had referred to her sister Lynanne as *Lee-Lee*. "The initials *LL* in her datebook might stand for her."

When I got to the part about Joey Blain, Max said, "Do you think he's guilty?"

"Detective Brandon thinks he is. She's been riding him hard, due to his attitude."

"You didn't answer my question."

"I don't know what his motive would be. Rejection?" I told Max about discovering Vikki's diary and learning about the pregnancy.

"*Alleged* pregnancy." Max clasped my wrists, grounding me. "What else is bothering you?"

I chewed on my lip. "I'm haunted by the design Vikki drew in the snow. She was a doodler. In her datebook. In her diary. I think whatever she drew was significant. That detective discounted my theory."

"Stick to your guns." Max tapped her fingertip on the tabletop. "This young man, Billy Tennyson. Did you interview his brother to corroborate his alibi?"

"I intend to." Deputy Kim probably had by now.

"How about checking out Rocky Yeats now that you know his connection?"

"I will."

Max cuffed me on the shoulder. "Coffee's hot."

The last thing I wanted was coffee. The acid churning inside me was making my insides raw.

Darcy ceded her spot at the computer to me. I typed in *USSearch.com*. A message emerged: *Site not accessible*. I pressed *Refresh*. Nothing. I pounded the desk and swore.

"Been there, done that," Darcy said. "Wouldn't be human, otherwise."

Five minutes later, after uttering the word *abracadabra* more times than I cared to admit, USSearch.com opened its portal. I typed in Billy Tennyson's name and all varieties of it, William, Bill, Bilford—I'd gone to school with a Bilford. After a long while, the choice of William A. Tennyson in Reno, Nevada, appeared on the screen. I clicked on the link.

The choice of *Cursory Search* or *Exhaustive Super Search* appeared. It never ceased to amaze me how much personal data could be found on the Internet, gathered from data bits that led a trail to a person's front door.

I clicked *Exhaustive* and waited as a history of Billy's family materialized. He had been born in Reno. He lived by himself. Nothing odd about that. No second names were on any of his rental agreements. The request for financial information showed that he had applied for bankruptcy when he was twenty-three.

Max leaned over my shoulder. "A pretty typical age to find out that credit cards are difficult to manage. That doesn't say anything about his character."

Billy's criminal background arose next. I reviewed his high school record—pretty good grades. He dropped out of high school in his junior year to go to a trade school. I continued reading and learned that someone had sealed Billy's criminal record at the age of sixteen. "How can I view sealed records?" I asked Max.

"You can't," she said. "Don't read too much into it. He could've done something as minor as stealing hubcaps. Now, if he committed a crime after the age of eighteen and spent time in prison, you could take a look at those records." Max picked up my file on Vikki and flipped through it.

I paused on an Internet page to read Billy's high school sports activities. He had participated on the cross-country team and had also been a member of the rifle and archery association. Seeing the latter made my skin prickle. Maybe the hunter who'd admitted to shooting at me at the springs had been mistaken about his location. What if Billy was the one who'd fired?

After printing the information, I instigated a search on Richard "Rocky" Yeats. His information came up more quickly. He had a criminal record that included three standout incidents. With a crowbar, he'd beaten the truck of a guy who had run him off the road. Paying damages had gotten him out of that fix. Using a baseball bat, he'd assaulted a guy who had broken into his house to steal his collection of baseball cards. The court had punished him with community service. For the third incident, he'd attacked his ex-wife with his fists. She had waived the charges. Three get-out-of-jail-free cards. How lucky could a guy get?

A reminder chimed on my cell phone. I was supposed to meet Tess in less than forty-five minutes. I asked Max to print out the remainder of my findings and hit the road.

Chapter 31

When I arrived at the Gemstone, the cabaret was empty of customers. The next show didn't start until eight. A single light illuminated a path to the stage. Tess, standing center stage, was shaking icy particles from her hair. She had dressed in tight jeans tucked into a pair of fur-cuffed boots. Even in the cold weather, she dared to wear a cropped sweater that revealed her midriff. She beckoned me to a corner booth. Before sitting, she glanced around.

"I don't see Rocky if you're wondering whether he's watching us," I said.

"I'm not. He's still ice fishing. Due back later today. I'm on the alert for Billy." She slouched at the table, her legs slung into the aisle. "He's why I called you. After you stopped by, Deputy Kim came around asking questions. Billy seemed spooked, so I followed him. To his brother's house."

I waited for more.

"I listened through the door. I heard him say that he would kill his brother if he didn't lie about being with him the night Vikki was murdered."

"Did he admit he killed Vikki?"

"No."

I sighed. "You could've told me all of this on the phone. Why did you really reach out?"

She crossed her legs and toyed with the candle on the table. "Deputy Kim gave me the go-around, too. She asked where was I the night Vikki was murdered."

I hadn't considered Tess a suspect, though she appeared strong enough to have overpowered Vikki. I glanced at her boots. Her feet were a lot bigger than mine, maybe not a man's size ten, but like Max said, an adult could walk in large Trekkers without stumbling.

"What did the detective claim your motive was?"

"Jealousy. I used to have a thing with Billy. Him and me . . . it's been over a long time." Tess pushed the candle aside. "You know, that detective wasn't very thorough."

Aha. Her dirt on Billy was an appetizer. The big news was yet to come.

"Don't you think Kim should have searched the Gemstone for places Vikki might have stored personal things? She never asked to see Vikki's locker."

"Vikki was no longer an employee," I countered. "She hadn't worked here in quite a while."

"But she still had one. I told Deputy Kim. She said she'd tell her boss. Nothing came of it." Tess leaned in. "Rocky never cleaned it out. He's lax that way."

"Why tell me?"

Tess toyed with the hair at the nape of her neck. "You seem to be on the ball, and Rocky thinks you're cool."

Swell. Just who I needed giving me a seal of approval.

"What's in the locker?"

"Who knows? I keep mementos in mine. I got a necktie this guy and me used when we had a fling a month ago." She hopped to her feet. "Want to see Vikki's stash? I know the combo."

Was Tess lying? Did she know what was inside? Was there something more on Billy that she wanted me to discover in the locker? I couldn't figure out her angle, but I couldn't walk away from fresh information, either.

"Okay, show me."

She led me to the poorly lit locker room fitted with a dozen drab green lockers, many riddled with dent marks.

"This one was Vikki's." Tess twisted the lock once to the left, twice to the right, and three times to the left. "Ta-da." The door swung open.

On the door of the locker, Vikki had taped a photo of Billy having a smoke. Most costumes hung on hangers or hooks, but one, made of lime green feathers and not much else, sat in a lump at the base of the locker. I removed it and discovered a pair of black stiletto heels beneath it, as well as a book of matches from the casino and some wadded-up Kleenex.

On the upper shelf sat a shoebox. I grabbed one of the tissues, wrapped it around my fingers to avoid getting fingerprints on the cardboard, and lifted the shoebox out. I set the box on a bench and rummaged through it: laundry receipts, used casino bingo cards, and photos of the other dancers acting silly. At the bottom of the box lay more than a dozen postcards from various places around Tahoe, including Emerald Bay, Mount Rose, and Northstar Ski Resort.

With the tissue still protecting my fingertips, I withdrew three of the cards. They were addressed to Vikki with no postage stamp. On the left were handwritten notes. As I read, my stomach tightened. All the notes were confessions of love. All had been signed by Richard.

I dropped them in the box as if they were hot coals and said, "The sheriff's department needs to see this."

"What did you find?" Tess asked.

"Postcards. From Rocky."

"What do they say?"

"Nothing."

"You can't think he had anything to do with her death. He's a pussycat."

I shot her a hard look. "You don't know that, and you can't mention this to him. Do you promise?"

"Yes." Tess sighed. "Rocky killed Vikki? Man."

"No. This is not proof of that. I'm calling the police. Don't touch these."

Tess saluted.

Using my camera, I took a picture of the opened shoebox before replacing it where I'd found it. Why had Vikki kept the postcards? What had her relationship been with Rocky? The missing components of her life plagued me.

• • •

On the drive home, I called Karen. She didn't answer. She was probably still sleeping. I left a voice-mail message that I'd found something at the Gemstone. I went into sketchy detail and asked her to call me. I debated whether I should loop in Nick Shaper but decided against it. Karen needed my support. I'd give her until morning to respond.

When I got home, I heated up the roasted chicken I'd bought in Homewood in the microwave and set a breast and wing on a plate. Then I threw some chopped romaine lettuce onto the plate and plopped two tablespoons of homemade Caesar dressing on top. I didn't need gourmet, just fuel. I poured a glass of sauvignon blanc and turned on the news.

Gloria Morning's perky face smiled back at me. "The sheriff's office is no closer to solving the murder—"

I switched off the television, not eager to watch her enjoy another moment of her newly found fame. Instead, I selected an iTunes playlist of jazz and nibbled at my food. The effort to solve Vikki's murder and the emotional grit required to care for Candace had depleted me of energy. Even Dan's confession of love had drained me. Why had he chosen this week of all weeks to confront me? Hadn't he sensed how frazzled I was?

An image of Nick Shaper inspecting the books in my living room flitted through my mind, followed by another of him grilling me at Vikki's. His smirk. That wink. A sudden impulse to call him hit me. Not to discuss the case. To talk. I convinced myself that would be a bad idea and sipped more wine.

Was I certain that Rocky had written the postcards? I didn't know what his handwriting looked like. What if Tess had planted the cards? What if she'd killed Vikki? What if telling me that she'd overheard Billy and his brother was a lie? Was I wrong to have left evidence in the locker? No. The photograph I'd taken would prove its existence.

Scratch-pick-tick.

I froze. Something or somebody was trying to get in through a window. I turned the music down. The scraping sound repeated. From my bedroom.

Grabbing the corked wine bottle, I tiptoed down the hall and peeked around the bedroom door. The drapes were closed. I didn't feel a breeze. I stole to the window, raised the bottle of wine, and pushed the curtain aside. A broken tree limb was brushing the glass.

"Get a grip, Aspen." I lowered the wine bottle. Feeling a chill, I shrugged on my green down vest, returned to the living room, lit a fire, and called the number Candace had given me.

"Hi," I said when Waverly's mother answered. "I'm Aspen Adams, Candace's aunt."

"Of course. What a sweet girl she is. The kids are having a great time. Do you want to speak to her?"

"No." I didn't want to worry Candace. Knowing she was fine was good enough. "I wanted to thank you for inviting her."

After I ended the call, loneliness flooded me. I cleared my plate and wineglass from the table, hoping the humdrum job of washing dishes would soothe me. As I spritzed the plate with dish soap, I heard footsteps clomping up the stairs to the front porch.

On edge, I grabbed the wine bottle again. The notion that I should rely on my self-defense training flitted through my mind. I shoved it aside and hurried to the door. I peeked through the sidelights. My breath caught in my chest.

Chapter 32

Nick Shaper stared back at me with a look of moderate concern. He was wearing a pair of jeans and navy sweater over a white turtleneck and holding a silver gift bag stuffed with matching tissue paper.

I opened the door. "What're you—"

"I came to give this to your niece."

"That's nice but she's not here. She's out with friends again."

He dangled the gift on one finger. "It's a stuffed animal called Ski Bunny. Does she like stuffed animals?"

"I'm sure she does."

His face flushed, which made him appear almost vulnerable. "Here." He handed me the gift and eyed the wine bottle in my hand. "Is that an invitation or a warning?"

My cheeks warmed. "I heard a noise. Earlier. Your footsteps startled me so—" I hoisted the bottle. "Want a glass? Are you off the clock?"

"I'll take a beer, if you have any." He strolled into the foyer while I closed the door. "It's chilly out."

"You should have worn a coat, Detective."

"Call me Nick, and yes, I should have."

We smiled like idiots for a moment. Shaper slipped his hands into his pockets. I strolled into the kitchen, set the gift on the counter, and peeked into the refrigerator.

"How's a Heineken sound?" I asked.

"Terrific."

Happy with a chore to do, I popped open a bottle of beer. Shaper sauntered into the dining area. I could see him through the pass-through. He crossed to the window with the distant view of the lake and looked out. There was an aura of calm about him.

"I heard you found Vikki's diary," he said. "Where?"

I tensed. Was this the real reason he'd dropped by? To reprimand me for entering Vikki's place a second time? "Between the mattress and the nightstand," I said.

"Anything in it I should know?"

I sighed with relief. He wasn't going to execute me. Not tonight, anyway. "Vikki had an adoptive sister in Tahoe. Her name is Lynanne, nickname Lee-Lee." I grabbed my glass of wine and the beer and joined him in the dining area. I hadn't noticed when he'd come in that he was wearing cologne. The tangy scent stirred me. Flustered, I handed him the beer, opened the door to the balcony, and strolled outside.

Shaper followed.

"Karen said she hasn't contacted your office, which surprises me. Vikki's face has been in all the papers and on the news."

"Maybe she doesn't live here anymore. People come and go."

The lapping of the waves on the shore echoed from below.

Shaper gazed at me with a depth I couldn't fathom. I twirled my wine, liking his attention yet uncomfortable with it.

"I think Vikki might have been pregnant." I told him about the *life within me* comment in the diary.

"Deputy Kim didn't mention a pregnancy. She reviewed the coroner's notes."

"Is it possible the coroner missed it?"

"An exam for rape as well as for pregnancy is standard in an autopsy. The examiner goes through the brain, the organs, everything."

The image made me cringe.

"The prosecutor needs that kind of comprehensive evidence," Shaper went on, "so when he goes to trial, he can prove the injuries were inflicted by the defendant." He took a sip of beer, his gaze still fixed on me. "Anything else you've unearthed? Don't keep me hanging."

I filled him in about my discoveries on the Internet—Billy's history and Rocky's dubious past, including the assaults. I told him about my visit with Tess and her story that Billy lied about his alibi. I concluded by telling him about Vikki's locker and the box of postcards.

"Why didn't you lead with this tidbit?"

"I—"

"You didn't touch them, did you?"

"I used a tissue. Right after I found them, I called Karen and left her a message, and I took a photograph in case Tess—"

"We'll retrieve them. I'll have the lab review them."

"Unless Tess alerted Rocky and he destroyed them. Also, what if they're fake? What if Tess wrote them to set up Rocky? What if she lied about overhearing Billy? She's a suspect, right? Deputy Kim questioned her because she and Billy were involved once."

"More than involved. She was in love with him."

"There must be a twenty-year age difference."

"Love can be blind. One of her coworkers heard her shouting at Billy a week ago in the parking lot that she'd kill him if he went back to Vikki."

"Kill him, not Vikki."

"Maybe things got out of hand." Shaper pulled his cell phone from his pocket, sent a text message, and stowed the phone.

"What did you text?"

"Tess has blond hair, just like the evidence we found at the site."

"Karen told me the hair could have come from your people or other visitors to the beach."

"Why are you defending Tess?" Shaper tilted his head.

"I'm not. Does she have an alibi?"

"She says she was gambling. I've got Kim interviewing the dealers at the casino." Shaper wiped moisture off his beer bottle with his thumb.

"Would you like to see Vikki's diary?" I turned to go inside.

"No. Later." Shaper rested his hand on my arm. "Let's not talk about the case for a while, okay? I'm beat."

I took in his tired face and nodded. After brushing ice crystals off one of the chairs of the patio set, I sat. Shaper leaned against the railing. Together, we let the serenity of the evening envelop us. Squirrels raced through the trees near the porch. A soft breeze caressed my face.

After a few minutes, Shaper said, "You know, that night at the council meeting when I first saw you, I wanted to introduce myself."

"Why didn't you? You don't strike me as a shy guy."

"Gun shy."

"Because you're still married?"

"Separated. And Detective Brandon has a big mouth."

"No, Gwen does."

Shaper laughed. "That's the last time I belly up to the bar."

I shivered, realizing the conversation was taking a personal turn for which I was unprepared. "How about something to eat?"

"I could do with a snack."

I went to the door and yanked on it. It didn't budge. "Shoot. Locked out."

"Happen a lot?"

"More than I care to admit." I shrugged. "Close your eyes so you don't see where I keep my breaking and entering screwdriver." When he refused, I gave in and reached into my pocket. I withdrew my Swiss Army knife, explaining why I carried it as I jimmied the latch on the door.

"Was your father a Boy Scout?"

"Eagle Scout." I opened the door, returned the Swiss Army knife to my pocket, and stepped inside.

Shaper followed, which surprised me, seeing as I thought he would've preferred to have a moment to himself.

I placed a brick of cheddar cheese on a cutting board. "If you're determined to crowd me, then grab some English muffins from inside the fridge."

Shaper opened the door and withdrew the packet.

He sliced two muffins and said, "Now what?"

I loaded the muffins with cheese, slid them into the toaster oven, and set a timer.

"Tell me about your niece," Shaper said. "I feel like there's a lot of backstory."

"Her mother, my sister, is a drug addict." I put two napkins on a tray. "Rosie has no idea how to hold down a job, let alone put food on the table. She hops from friend to friend because she can't make the rent." I leaned against the counter, exhaustion catching up to me. "Candace is a terrific kid, and Rosie is blowing it."

"It stinks when people disappoint you, doesn't it?" Shaper put a hand on my shoulder.

The nearness of him jolted me. My heart rate kicked up a notch. Every fiber in me screamed to keep my distance. He was investigating my friend's case. I pulled away. "Another beer?"

"Sure."

I fetched one and handed it to him. "Here." My hands were clammy and trembling. Shaper didn't notice, or if he did, he didn't comment.

The timer dinged. Shaper removed the muffins from the toaster, placed them on the napkins, and picked up the tray of snacks. "You know"—he led the way to the porch—"the first time I saw you, you were in a heated discussion with some guys about pollution in the lake. Five of them, to be exact."

"Ah, the fearsome tourism bloc."

Shaper held the door for me as I passed through.

"What a gentleman. Where'd you learn your manners?"

"Good old Mom."

I sat down in the chair I'd occupied earlier, leaned back, and studied the man in front of me. He was candid and confident, and against my better judgment, I was beginning to like him. A lot.

Shaper cleaned off a second chair and sat. He bit into one of the muffins and swallowed. "You don't put up with any bull, do you?"

"Nope. Gwen tells me it's a trait men hate."

"Gwen's wrong." Shaper clinked his beer bottle against my wineglass and polished off his snack.

After a while, he asked me questions about my past. I didn't want to load him down with details of my failed marriage, so I told him about the family cabin, the many summers I'd spent at Tahoe, and even a bit about my Indian heritage. Precious memories, he said, were gems that needed to be taken out and polished. Dan hadn't ever been curious about my history. To him, the past was gone. There was no need to dwell.

At around eleven, the temperature dropped to fifteen degrees. We moved inside by the fireplace, and over the course of the next hour, I became the listener.

"I wanted to play center field for the Giants," Shaper said, "but that dream was dashed by a torn ACL in my right knee."

"Ouch."

Stories about college ensued. "Worst memory ever? An SAE pledge trashed the engine of my sixty-six Mustang with eggs. That car was my prized possession." Shaper's laugh was throaty, appealing. "The poor heap never ran the same, chewing instead of chugging."

As he started to talk about his years with the San Jose Police Department, his face tightened. One incident in particular affected him. "I was a patrol cop. On a high-speed chase. A drunk driver was swerving everywhere and wouldn't respond to the siren." His eyes clouded over. "It ended with the car slamming into a tree. The driver and the two passengers died. My partner and I were brought before the review board for that one." The line across his forehead deepened. "We were exonerated, but I still have nightmares wondering what we could have done differently."

I asked about his sister. He was surprised I knew about her, but he didn't hold back. And then, without prompting, he told me about his marriage. No details, just that it had failed.

Around midnight, he stood. "It's late. I should go."

"I'm waiting up for Candace if you'd like to stay a while longer."

"Another time." He strolled to the foyer.

I followed close behind and caught myself staring at a pulled stitch near the hem of his sweater.

Shaper turned. "How about that diary?"

"Oh, sure. Right away." My cheeks burned with embarrassment. Had he seen me staring at his backside? I hurried into the kitchen and returned with the diary. I handed it to him, but he didn't take a peek.

"Good night, Aspen. Tonight was . . . enlightening."

Without another word, he opened the door and tramped down the steps into the darkness. A cool wind and a few pine needles blew into the cabin. I closed the door, but for a long time afterward, I pictured Shaper's face. In particular, his mouth.

Chapter 33

When the lights of Waverly's mother's SUV flared through the sidelights, I hurried to the foyer and whipped open the front door.

Candace leaped out and waved goodbye. "Thank you." She hurried to me, her cheeks flushed with energy. "We had so much fun." She chatted all the way down the hall about how silly boys were because they laughed at stupid jokes and how cute Justin was and how much she would miss him.

When she was dressed for bed, she hurried into my room and plopped on my bed. "Can we have a slumber party? I've never had one."

"You want to invite some girls over?"

"No, I mean tonight. You and me. Please?"

I looked at her fresh face and my heart whelmed with love for her. "Of course. I'll get cookies and milk."

"No, that's okay, I'm not hungry."

"You're not going to get fat eating cookies and milk," I chided, "and you can't have a slumber party without them. Plus, I'll give you a hint, if you eat them off my plate, they're free calories." At the door, I turned back. "Get your pillow."

Candace bounded off the bed and skipped down the hall.

We ate and talked until one—big slumber party—when her eyes wouldn't stay open any longer. A day on the slopes and that much enthusiasm was bound to wear out anybody.

For a while afterward, I lay on my back, staring at the dark blue shadows on the ceiling, thinking about Vikki and the diary and Tess. Had she found out about Vikki's pregnancy? Had that sent her over the edge?

I glanced at the clock. It was a little after two. Maybe I could reach her at the cabaret. She would have finished her set. I tiptoed to the kitchen and dialed the number. Billy answered. I asked for Tess.

"She split. Who's this? I'll give her—"

I ended the call and returned to bed. I had just drifted off when my landline telephone rang. I answered.

"It's me," Gwen said, her voice raspy. "Man, this place was crazy tonight. Did I wake you?"

"No."

"Why are you whispering?" Gwen asked. "Did you get lucky?"

"My niece wanted to have a slumber party with me."

"How sweet."

Pressing the cordless receiver to my chest, I slipped out of the bedroom and closed the door. "What's up?"

Gwen sighed. "I met a nice guy tonight. I think we might go on a date."

"Great." I swallowed a yawn. "I had an interesting night, too. You'll never guess who stopped by. Nick Shaper."

"Ha! So what happened?" she asked leadingly.

"He came to give Candace a gift."

"Why?"

I realized I hadn't told her about the incident with Candace the other night and filled her in.

"I hear it in your voice," she said. "You're interested in Nick."

"No." I was glad she couldn't see me. I'd started toying with my hair, a clear indication I was lying. "Let's talk about something else."

"Have you discovered anything new on Vikki's case?"

I told her about the diary and Vikki's adoptive sister and the postcards from Rocky. Gwen asked if Vikki had mentioned her in the diary.

When I told her no, she said, "Good thing. I revealed a lot of personal details about my love life to her. Wouldn't want that getting around."

"Things you haven't told me?"

"Yeah, I've got secrets up the wazoo." Gwen chuckled. "So what's up with your niece? Are you going to keep her?"

"She's not a puppy."

"Your sister treats her worse than a dog."

"Don't start," I rasped.

"The kid needs a mother," Gwen went on. "A *good* mother. You could do it."

I wasn't so sure.

"Social services wouldn't give you a fight, I bet." She continued to feed me advice. I agreed with some but not all of her suggestions. Considering her relationship with the daughter I'd never met, she wasn't going to win motherhood medals.

After we ended the call, sleep came quickly. However, a series of nightmares plagued me: Rosie hitting Candace; a stranger lighting the cabin on fire; bullets shredding the pillows on my bed.

Close to four, I sank into an even heavier sleep and dreamed of my father and me as a young girl playing on the sand by the lake. He drew a line in the sand with his toe and dared me to cross it. I did and he tackled me. My mother, fitted with angel's wings, came soaring toward us. She landed on top of me and twisted my face toward the sand. The lines we had drawn turned into childish stick figures. "Here's Mommy and Daddy," she cooed. "But where's Aspen?" I couldn't breathe. I was choking. "Let me go," I cried. From behind, Shaper pulled my mother off of me and raised me to my feet. In my hand was Vikki's diary. I screamed, "The life within me!"

And awoke gasping for air.

I glanced at Candace, who was sound asleep on the other side of the bed, her hair feathered out on the pillow. The vision reminded me of Vikki, which made me flash on the drawing beside her body and the doodles in her diary and datebook. None of them were the stick figures of my nightmare, but they were important. I knew it at my core.

Chapter 34

At two minutes past seven, my cell phone jangled, tearing me from a murky haze. I reached to silence the phone, but Candace had already answered. She stood by the nightstand, her hand cupping her mouth.

"Yeah, Mom. Uh-huh."

Rosie. What the heck did she want?

Candace sounded dull. Uninterested. With cell phone in hand, she tiptoed out of the room.

A half hour later, another sound woke me. A horrible retching. From the bathroom. Followed by a thud and silence.

I raced down the hall and threw open the door. Candace lay on the floor, her hair and face a mess from the incident, the cell phone by her knees. I checked her pulse. Sluggish. Her eyes were dilated, her breathing ragged. I grabbed my phone, scooped her into my arms—she was light; too light—and hurried to the kitchen for my keys.

Careful not to drop her, I lugged her to the Jeep. Holding her with one arm, I whipped open the door. I settled her in the passenger seat, connected the seat belt, draped her with the blanket I stowed in my gear for emergencies, and switched on the car so the heater could warm up the interior.

After brushing the half inch of fresh snow off the windshield, I said, "I'll be right back." I returned to the cabin for my purse, boots, and winter coat.

On the way to the hospital, I heard a *pop*. The Jeep heaved. My stomach lurched. Had I blown a tire? Forward or rear? I didn't feel any drag. We weren't slowing down. I tapped the brakes. The car skidded on the new snow and fishtailed. I tried to straighten the car out, but I must have overturned the wheel. The Jeep swerved.

An oncoming car blared its horn. Then another.

If I hit the brakes and skidded again, the car might veer off the road and flip. Instead, I aimed for the dirty snowdrift up ahead. Using the driver's side, I skated along it. Shards of brittle snow shot into the air. As the Jeep slowed, I cranked the wheel left and pitched the front end into the drift. My head snapped forward and struck the steering wheel. Our airbags inflated and quickly deflated.

At a standstill, I switched off the engine and checked on Candace. She was fine, although still groggy. Her seat belt had held her in place. I hopped out of the car and looked at the tire. Shredded. Accidental or intentional? I couldn't focus on the probabilities. I dialed 911 on my cell phone. Within minutes, a fire engine and EMTs arrived.

The emergency room at Truckee Hospital wasn't busy when we arrived. Once the team had wheeled Candace into a sterile room, a doctor tended to me. She sewed twelve dissolvable stitches in my forehead and covered them with a bandage. She said I'd heal with steady doses of antibiotic ointment and rest.

An hour later, Candace's attending doctor, a pleasant-looking older man with blue eyes and a reassuring smile, shambled into the waiting room carrying a manila folder. "Miss Adams, I don't mince words. Why is Candace on Prozac?"

"Prozac?" My mouth fell open.

"You didn't know?"

"No. I'm her aunt. She's here for a visit. I—" I swallowed hard. I'd searched Candace's bags. Where had she hidden the pills? Why had she taken them? "Are you certain?"

He nodded. "Prozac can stay in your system quite a while."

"So it's possible she didn't take the medicine recently?"

"It's possible." The doctor tapped his leg with the file. "This morning, I believe she induced herself trying to eliminate the drugs from her system. She confided to a nurse that her mother gave her the pills. To help her diet."

I groaned. "I'm going to kill my sister."

"I've discussed the dangers with Candace; however, you may want to give her this literature on bulimia, as well."

I sagged, my suspicions confirmed.

The doctor withdrew a brochure from the manila folder. "I'm not positive Candace's mother understood what she was doing."

"My sister is the world's expert on drugs, Doctor. She knew what she was doing."

"The binge-purge cycle is hard to break," he said.

"I haven't seen Candace binge."

"What is binge eating to her might not be binge eating to you." The doctor pointed to the pamphlets. "There are some physicians in the immediate area who can help with treatment, and there are organizations online that can provide support." He turned to leave. "She'll need to stay with us for a day or two."

Anger raged through me. I recalled my chat with Gwen. Could I get custody of Candace? How would I be as a single parent? I'd hate to become her guardian and make things worse.

As I waited for the moment when I would be allowed to see my niece, I stewed. For being blind. For being stupid. For being rash. When I realized how much negative energy I was churning, I turned my focus to Vikki's murder. I called Tess on her cell phone. She answered on the third ring.

After I identified myself, she said, "What's up?" I'd awakened her.

"I was talking with Detective Sergeant Shaper, and he told me your alibi. He said you were gambling on the night Vikki died."

"At the Nugget. You know the place?"

I did. It was a casino in South Lake Tahoe not far from the Gemstone Cabaret.

"Nobody seems to remember me being there, though," she admitted. "I've asked."

I couldn't imagine anyone not remembering her. She was a knockout. Maybe dealers were taught not to stare? "There should be video."

"Uh-uh. I mean, yeah, there are cameras, but even those seemed to have missed me. I've asked. I think it's because I moved from table to table. I kept getting crappy hands. At one of the tables, I was sitting with a detective, if you can believe it, except she might not recall because she was blasted."

"What did she look like?"

"Blond-in-a-bottle, cheeks chiseled enough to carve ice. Karen something."

"Brandon?"

"Yeah, that's it." The sound of a match and the intake of a deep breath suggested Tess had lit a cigarette. "I've seen her a ton of times.

She gambles a lot. I do, too. I saw her another time, a few months ago, at the Emerald when Vikki picked a fight with her."

"Vikki knew Detective Brandon? Are you sure?" Karen said she'd never met her. On the other hand, maybe she had been so drunk that she'd blanked out the memory.

"Yeah, the broad—sorry, the *detective*—was giving the dealer a hard time. Out of nowhere, Vikki stormed up to her and told her she hated drunks. Rocky showed up and got in the middle before Vikki could punch her."

"Rocky?"

Tess sighed. "He was always protecting Vikki. Like a shadow. That's why I can't accept him being the guy who offed her." She clicked her tongue. "But then you don't think he's the killer either, do you, seeing as you're asking me about my alibi?"

"I'm trying to gather all the information I can."

"Do I need a lawyer?" She coughed. "Never mind. I know the answer." She ended the call.

A nurse drew near and whispered, "Ma'am. You can go in now."

I slipped into Candace's room and was shocked by how pale she was. She was asleep, her hands resting on her stomach. An IV was inserted in her left arm. In the bleak privacy, I berated myself for not having acted sooner. Why had it taken another incident to make me seek help?

Sitting in the chair beside her bed, I studied the room. White walls, white sheets, and white blinds.

Candace stirred. "Hi," she whispered.

I jumped to my feet and kissed her cheek. "When you're up to it, we need to talk. It doesn't have to be now."

She sucked on her lower lip. "The doctor told you about—"

I nodded.

"I didn't want to take it." Tears leaked out of her. I handed her a tissue. "This morning I told Mom I'd had an episode. She said she couldn't handle my ups and downs and got mad and said she was going to make me take more medicine. I . . . I . . ."

I petted her shoulder. If only I'd answered the dang phone. "She knew you were sick?"

Candace nodded and wiped tears away with the tissue.

"And that you were making yourself vomit on purpose?"

She nodded.

"Why do you do it, sweetie?"

"Mom said it's my fault that she's fat. She said I needed to stay skinny so people would know—" Candace coughed hard. "Would know she was skinny once, too."

I grabbed the cup of water that was sitting on the bedside table and turned the straw toward my niece. "Drink."

She sipped. "Why doesn't she love me? Why am I an embarrassment?"

The question caught me off guard. "You're not. You're exactly who you should be." Rosie was the embarrassment.

Candace drank more water and continued. "There's this dress my mom got from a friend. A hand-me-down. It's green and cute. Size two. I think if I could fit into it, maybe she'd love me."

Her naiveté frightened me. Would she starve herself to gain her mother's love? Murderous thoughts coursed through my brain.

I squeezed her hand. "We'll talk about all of this later. For now, you're going to stay here. The doctors will take care of you for a day or so. They'll give you something to eat."

"No," she wailed. "I'm not hungry."

"You won't get fat. I promise." I kissed her on the forehead. "You need nourishment. Protein." My stomach knotted at the fear in her eyes. "Trust me." I stroked her hair and the ridge of her chin until her eyes closed.

When she was asleep, I tiptoed from the room and called Gwen. She didn't answer. I phoned Max. She didn't pick up, either. I needed to talk to somebody. Anybody. I dialed Karen. She answered after one ring. I explained what had happened to Candace and asked her for the name of a good custody lawyer.

"Are you sure you want to do that?" she asked.

"Positive."

"Single parenthood is the most challenging task you'll ever undertake."

I was in no mood to argue.

She gave me the name of her lawyer, the one handling her father's estate. "Josephine Quill's the best. She does it all. Divorce, custody, wills. I'll touch base with her and tell her you'll be calling."

When I climbed into yet another loaner that my mechanic had delivered—a clunky Dodge Colt with a busted window that wouldn't roll up the whole way—I realized I hadn't asked Karen about the altercation with Vikki or whether she'd seen Tess at the Nugget the night Vikki was killed. I called back but reached her voice mail.

Chapter 35

Icy rain hit the windshield as I drove to Quill Law Offices. I cranked the handle for the driver's window but the darned thing wouldn't roll up. The forecast called for heavy rain and sleet later. Swell.

"Tea?" Ms. Quill's receptionist offered as I entered.

I nodded. I was chilled to the bone.

Josephine Quill was a luminous woman with gold hair and peach-toned skin, but I didn't let her appearance fool me. She was all business, her manner crisp. Her office was comfortable, fitted with a modest-sized desk, two ladder-back chairs, and a white chenille love seat. A hint of cinnamon from the lit candle on her desk hung in the air. Black-and-white photos of the lake lined the walls.

After talking for a half hour spewing out all the anger I harbored for my sister, I leaned back in my chair, spent.

Quill perched forward at her desk, her hands folded around a mug of coffee. "I understand what you're going through." She offered me a box of tissues; I declined. "I sense your pain. My brother was a drug addict, too." She paused. "He didn't die from an overdose. He died from emaciation. His body couldn't take the punishment anymore." She adjusted the scarf around her neck, a green one decorated with black skiers jumping moguls. "So let's get this process started, shall we?"

"I want to make sure Candace is okay with it."

Quill nudged her mug aside and folded her hands. "Nothing is set in stone, of course, but there's a lot of paperwork to get the ball rolling. The courts will put up a fuss because you're single, but seeing as you're a relative and the father is nowhere in the picture—he'll need to be served, of course—and if your sister cedes custody . . ." She splayed her hands.

I couldn't see Rosie ceding anything.

"Are you prepared to handle the cost of raising a child?" Quill asked. "The doctors' visits, clothing, braces, education?"

"Is anybody ever ready?"

"Some parents save for years before having their first child. Others"—she tipped her head—"wing it."

"I'm not a wing-it kind of woman."

"Do you have savings? A steady job?"

"Yes and yes."

"Do you know college can cost upward of two hundred thousand dollars, depending on the institution and the kind of education your niece will seek?" Quill leaned forward, forcing me to think hard. "Is she a good student?"

"I don't know. I haven't asked. She's smart."

"Does she have braces?"

"Not yet."

"Ten thousand dollars, minimum."

The financial strain was going to be profound, but I thought of Candace's sweet, vulnerable face and ached to help her. No matter the cost.

"I'm ready," I whispered. "Whatever happens."

• • •

When I climbed into the Colt, I refocused on the investigation. Rocky Yeats's name came to mind. Had someone from the sheriff's office asked him about the postcards yet? Had they pinned down his alibi for the night Vikki was killed? How I wanted to ask him a few pointed questions even though Deputy Kim had already interrogated him.

I called the Emerald Casino. Rocky wasn't in; he'd called in sick. Using a ploy I'd heard Darcy use, I asked for the payroll office and convinced an accountant that I was an IRS agent seeking answers about inconsistencies in Richard Yeats's tax returns. I needed to speak to him in person. If she would please supply his current address . . .

The woman was sympathetic. From her tone, I suspected Rocky might have made inappropriate advances to her in the past.

Forty-five minutes later, I arrived at Rocky's house in Tahoe City. The white paint on the ranch-style home was so thick the grain in the wood had disappeared. A single scrawny pine looked lonely on the dormant grass. A blue double-cabin truck stood in the driveway.

Just as I climbed out of the Colt, the skies let loose. To avoid getting soaked, I raced to the front door. I knocked on the screen door's metal rim. As I did, a notion struck me. Had Rocky caused the tire blowout on the Jeep? Had he figured out that I'd informed the police about the postcards and slashed my tire as payback? Concerned about entering his house alone, I spotted a neighbor across the street and waved. The neighbor responded in kind. I knocked again.

"Yeah, yeah, hold your horses," Rocky barked. When he opened the door, his thickset body blocked most of the frame. His hair was messy and his shirt hung open, exposing a hairy, soft belly. Not his best look. He registered who I was and buttoned his shirt.

"Hope you don't mind me stopping by. You weren't at work. I wanted to ask you a few questions about Billy without him around."

"How'd you find out where I live?"

"The Internet." I offered my brightest smile, unwilling to get the accountant in trouble. "May I come in?"

"Be my guest." Rocky kicked the screen door open with his foot.

Before entering, I waved again to the neighbor, making sure Rocky registered the exchange.

The living room was messy. Shirts, socks, and shoes on the floor and sofa. CDs in a pile on the finger-smudged coffee table. Empty bottles of beer on a side table. Ashtrays overflowing with crushed butts. The single newish-looking item in the room was the entertainment center fitted with a flat-screen television.

"Cool system," I said.

"Yeah, I treated myself. I expect to come into some money soon."

I glanced around for a place to sit but was afraid I'd need a penicillin shot afterward.

Rocky indicated the sofa, making no effort to remove his dirty laundry. "You want some bottled water?"

"Yes, please," I said, surprised that he'd have that in stock.

As he tramped into the kitchen, I cleared a spot on the sofa and took a moment to collect my thoughts. The half dozen black velvet paintings of scantily clad women on his walls made it difficult to concentrate. How was one man blessed with this much taste?

Rocky returned and tossed me a plastic bottle. "Go ahead, ask."

I pulled a pad and pencil from my purse. "When did Vikki and Billy break up?"

"A couple of months ago. Man, he was ticked."

"Vikki must have broken it off," I said, knowing she had.

"She sure did." He slid his tongue along his teeth and ended with a *click*. "She was fed up with him playing the field."

"With Tess?"

"With a couple of broads." He grinned. "Excuse me. *Women.*"

How Tess and Mrs. Carmichael could think Rocky was a sweetheart baffled me.

"When did you begin working at the Gemstone?" I asked.

"Six years ago."

"Enjoy your job?"

"Yeah, it's okay. The pay's good."

"Are you from New York?"

"Originally. My folks moved here when I was young. I lost the accent."

Not really.

Rocky tilted his head. "You said you wanted to ask questions about Billy."

"I do." I readied my pencil. "He started at the Gemstone after you, is that correct?"

"A year after."

"He has a brother."

"Yeah. The guy's a bartender."

"Billy claims his brother is his alibi for the night Vikki was killed."

"If he says so."

I wanted to take a peek at the rest of Rocky's house. According to Max, seeing where someone lived could give an investigator real insight. Setting my bottle of water on the side table, I accidentally—on purpose—knocked it over. "Oh, geez. I'm sorry."

Liquid threatened to soak the CDs. I leaped to my feet and hurried to the kitchen. The sink was filled with dirty dishes. I grabbed two strips of paper towels and accidentally—on purpose—dumped the remainder of the roll into the sink.

"I'm such a klutz," I said to Rocky as I returned to the living room. "I knocked the rest of the roll in the sink. Do you have more?"

Rocky grabbed them from me. "I'll do it."

"Mind if I use the restroom?"

"Go ahead."

I moved down the hall and slipped into the bathroom, which was painted dark blue and smelled of heavy cologne. I closed the door and turned on the water faucet. Seconds later I peeked out. Rocky had disappeared into the kitchen. I heard him muttering and slamming cabinet doors. Apparently, he needed to search for more paper towels.

Taking pains not to make a sound, I left the water running and tiptoed to the sole bedroom in the house. To say I was shocked by what I saw was an understatement. Standing next to the unmade bed was a mannequin with long chestnut-red hair. The doll's eyes were blue. Her lips were bright pink. She was dressed in clothes that I recognized—a tight burgundy sweater, torn jeans, and a necklace of multicolored crystal beads. Vikki's. She'd thought she'd lost them. Had Rocky filched them from her locker or her home?

On the scratched nightstand stood an eight-by-ten picture of Vikki in a blond wig and cabaret costume. Beside the silver frame, an incense burner and a box of matches. More than twenty used matches filled a chipped ashtray.

Over to the right, a state-of-the-art computer hummed on an old maple desk. I touched the mouse; the monitor came alive. Screensaver photos of Vikki in a variety of cabaret outfits floated across the screen.

Rocky's obsession skyrocketed him to the top of my suspect list. I needed to tell Shaper. I scurried to the bathroom, flushed the toilet and switched off the faucet, then closed the bathroom door with a *clack*.

I sauntered into the living room as Rocky was coming out of the kitchen with a full roll of paper towels in one hand, his cell phone in the other.

"I've got to be going," I said.

"That's all you wanted to ask?" He raised an eyebrow.

"I wanted to verify what others said."

"How'd you get my address? It's not on the Internet. I checked." Rocky blocked my exit.

My breath caught in my chest. I slipped my hand into my purse, clasped the can of pepper spray, and forced a grin. "You caught me. I contacted the DMV. On occasion, they help out investigators."

"They shouldn't."

"But they do. Now, if you'll let me pass." I met his gaze. "Thanks for your time, Mr. Yeats."

He stepped aside. "Call me Rocky."

"Rocky." I gestured toward the CDs. "And, again, sorry about the water mishap."

"No problem. We all have our slob days."

Chapter 36

Driving north on Highway 89 toward Truckee, I called the North Lake Tahoe Station and left a voice mail for Nick Shaper. When I arrived at the hospital, I learned the staff had moved Candace to a private room. I sat in the chair at the side of her bed, cooling her forehead with a wet towel. Asleep, she looked so vulnerable. Slender arms on top of the sheet. Hands flat. Nails chewed to the nubs. At least her breathing was steady.

An hour later, the door opened and Shaper stepped inside with a foam cup in hand. "Got your message," he whispered. His parka was wet from rain. His hair was moist, too. "Came as soon as I could."

"I'm glad you did."

"Nasty little bump on your head." He reached out to inspect it. "Need driving lessons?"

"Very funny."

"Coffee?" He held out the cup. "One cream, one sugar. How'd I do?"

"Good guess." I took a sip of coffee.

"I checked with the lab. Rocky Yeats didn't write those postcards."

"You're sure?"

"We've compared the handwriting on his paperwork at the casino."

"He could've used his left hand as a ruse."

"To what end?"

"I don't know." I fought a yawn. And lost.

Shaper pulled up a chair. "For your information, I sent my deputies to take a look at Rocky Yeats's place, like you suggested. They reported back. He had it bad for Vikki Carmichael, but they believe his alibi is valid."

"What's his alibi?"

"Working at the Gemstone. He did go on an errand but not long enough to drive to Vikki's and back."

"Do you think Tess set him up to sow confusion?"

"That's the likeliest guess, but anyone with access to those lockers is suspect."

If not Tess, then who? I pictured Billy at Homewood Market and flashed on him squishing the cigarette with the heel of his boot. "Billy Tennyson wears Timberland Trekkers. They were stained with something the color of wine."

"I'll check it out." He gestured to Candace. "Is she doing okay?"

"She'll survive."

Candace stirred but didn't wake. I stood and brushed hair off her face. As I did, a memory of Vikki lying on the beach came to me. I jerked my hand away.

Shaper shot to his feet. "What's wrong?"

I stared at my niece. What was unsettling me? If only I could put my finger on it. "Nothing. Tired."

"Go home. Get some sleep. Your niece has plenty of caretakers." Shaper's gaze was full of compassion.

"You're right." I kissed Candace on the forehead, tucked the sheet under her chin, wrote a quick note saying I'd be back first thing in the morning, and walked out of the room with Shaper.

When his arm brushed mine, a jolt of passion shot through me. I stumbled.

Shaper righted me. "You aren't okay. You're trembling. I'm going to follow you. To make sure you get home safely."

"It's out of your way."

"No, it isn't. I told you I live nearby."

I kept my gaze forward, afraid Shaper would see what I was feeling.

"No argument," he added.

• • •

The rain had subsided. For now. Twenty minutes later, I pulled into the driveway. Shaper drove in behind me. I didn't see Rosie's dented Toyota until it was too late.

She lumbered out of her car and stomped toward me. "Get Candy. I'm taking her home."

More than twelve hours had passed since Candace and her mother had spoken on the phone. What had prompted this visit?

Shaper leaped from his Wrangler and blocked Rosie's access to me.

Feeling braver, I said, "Your daughter is in the hospital, thanks to you."

"What are you talking about?" Rosie tried to skirt around Shaper, but he continued to obstruct her path.

"She's sick," I said. "She's been throwing up."

"So what?" Rosie squared her massive shoulders. "You don't go to the hospital unless you need a blood transfusion. Doctors will—"

"Stop," I yelled. "She's in the hospital because of the Prozac you gave her." I stepped around Shaper, my fists balled.

"I did no such—"

"She's got a disease, Rosie. She's bulimic."

"Bull. She eats."

"She doesn't have anorexia, you idiot." No way would I admit that I had thought the same at first. "She's bulimic." I fought the urge to spell it out. "She vomits on purpose."

"Okay, fine. If she needs a shrink, she needs a shrink," Rosie said. "She's always been as edgy as a . . . a . . ."

"An addict needing a fix?"

My sister curled her lip. "I know what's best for my girl."

"She's not *your girl*," I said. "She's your daughter, but you're not going to see her again if I have anything to do with it. I'm filing for custody."

Rosie's gaze drifted to the right for a split second. Shaper had edged beside me.

"If you want her, get a job and get clean if you can." I glowered at her. "Fat chance of that."

"Why, you little—" Rosie lunged.

Shaper knocked her shoulder. Not hard. Just enough. Rosie stumbled before regaining her balance. Shaper unzipped his parka and exposed the gun in his holster.

Rosie shimmied tension from her shoulders. "Sure, let a man fight your battles, Aspen. You always were a wuss." She marched to her car and slammed the door. Before driving off, she said, "You'll regret this."

The roar of her engine and screech of the tires did nothing to dampen my resolve. I was going to remove Candace from Rosie's miserable clutches, no matter what.

When the putrid smoke from the car cleared, I turned to Shaper. "Thanks for standing up to her."

"You were doing that pretty well all by yourself."

"It helped having a guy with a gun by my side." I frowned. "I told the hospital to bar her from seeing Candace. Think she'll make trouble?"

"She never asked where Candace was."

"Good point." I walked up the stairs and slipped my key into the lock. "Want to come in?"

He grinned. It didn't take a rocket scientist to see the answer was yes. I opened the door and switched on the lights. He stepped in behind me and closed the door.

I turned to ask if he wanted a beer but halted. He was staring at me. In a good way. As if committing every inch of my face to memory. My landline phone rang, startling me.

Shaper gestured for me to answer it. "It could be the hospital."

I stepped into the kitchen and lifted the receiver. "Hello?"

"Hi." It was Dan. He sounded agitated. "I'm sorry about . . . you know."

"I'm sort of busy right now."

Shaper moved into the archway, head tilted.

Dan cleared his throat. "I left you a couple of messages. You didn't respond."

Had he? I glanced at the answering machine. It was blinking. With all the hoopla, I hadn't noticed. "Sorry."

"I want to see you again before I leave town. Can I come over?"

"No," I blurted. "Candace. She's in the hospital. She's got . . . an upset stomach." The lie sounded feeble. "I'm stressed out. I'll call you in the morning." I didn't wait for his response. I replaced the receiver in the base and turned to Shaper. "How about that beer?"

He shook his head. "How stupid of me not to think you had other men in your life, not to mention, I've been inappropriate. I need to conclude the investigation before we . . ." He let the sentence hang. "Good night, Aspen." He walked to the door.

Before I could find my voice, he left.

Chapter 37

The next morning I stood on the back porch in my robe and drank in the fresh air. The morning sun was doing its best to peek through the dark clouds. The projected sleet storm hadn't hit . . . yet. Even so, a chill cut through me. I couldn't believe a week had gone by since Vikki was murdered.

To boost my mood, I returned inside and dressed in my favorite sweater, jeans, and Uggs. Then I headed to the hospital. About a mile away, I stopped at a flower store, bought a vase with a depiction of Emerald Bay's castle, and filled it with yellow pansies. Ever since I was a little girl, I'd loved the dainty flowers.

When I stepped into the hospital room, Candace was sitting up in bed eating a meal of scrambled eggs and toast. Her color had returned; her eyes looked focused.

"Hi." I kissed her cheek.

She wiped her mouth with a napkin and smiled. "I'm sorry for the trouble I've caused."

"I'm just glad you're all right." I handed her the flowers.

"Ooh, those are so pretty. Thank you."

I sat on the chair beside the bed.

"Cool sweater," she said.

I grinned. "Yes, you can borrow it." I'd worn the red one with white snowflakes.

After a long pause, Candace asked how her mother was going to pay for the hospital bills. I told her she wasn't, I was, and then I broached the subject of her living with me full-time.

Candace shivered. Her eyelids fluttered.

"If you don't want to, it's okay."

"No, I want to. It's—" She plucked at the edge of the sheet.

"What?" I stood and rested my hand on hers.

"Mom will hurt you."

"No, she won't."

"Yes, she will."

The fear I'd felt the other day returned. "Sweetie, has she hit you?"

Tears welled in her eyes. I wrapped my arms around her and pulled her close. Man, what a nightmare her life must have been. Why hadn't I done anything about her situation before? Because I was so involved with my own pitiful life that I couldn't see day for night.

"Shh." I settled her on the pillows and played with strands of her hair. "We'll talk about this later. First, we're going to get you healthy again."

Before coming to the hospital, I had read the pamphlet the doctor had provided. Though I believed I had a full understanding of bulimia, the written material opened my eyes further. The disease was rarely life threatening—unlike anorexia—but the problem of purging had to be conquered. A tuned-in adult could help Candace find a better self-image, but I couldn't imagine Rosie being lucid enough to try.

Concern flooded through me. "You rest."

"Okay. I love you."

"Love you, too."

Candace's eyes fluttered closed. Seconds later she was asleep.

As I was leaving the room, I glanced back and again flashed on an image of Vikki lying in the snow. Her hair, like Candace's on the pillow, had been flared out, as if positioned. Had the killer lovingly placed it that way to make her look radiant?

My cell phone hummed. I'd set it on mute. "Hello?"

"It's me." Karen was out of breath. "Shaper and I are going to meet with Billy Tennyson. He wants you to come along and give us your take." She sounded peeved. Was she upset because Shaper asked to include me? Or had he confronted her about her drinking problem, and she thought I'd revealed her secret?

"Sure. Of course. Glad to oblige."

"We're leaving in an hour. Meet us at the office." She clicked off.

• • •

Taking Highway 80, Nick Shaper, Karen Brandon, and I made our way to Reno. Shaper drove. Karen rode shotgun. I sat in the backseat of the Wrangler behind Shaper. A fire had devastated the region last year. I was pleased to see new growth in the forest that lined the route. Newly planted pines looked strong and healthy, too.

"Good work on picking up on the pregnancy angle, by the way." Karen had donned a blazer and crisp white shirt over pleated slacks, and her hair looked washed and styled. She'd even applied eye makeup. "Somehow that tidbit had eluded Deputy Kim." She seemed pleased about her cohort's blunder. Was she glad she wasn't the sole screwup?

Shaper added, "The coroner said Vikki was eight to ten weeks along."

How could Vikki not have told me? I pushed the thought aside. *Secrets. Everyone had secrets.*

"Is Billy Tennyson expecting us?" I asked.

"Yes," Karen said. "It's his day off. Hence, the trip to Reno. You're along for the ride because Nick says you have a good rapport with him."

I wasn't so sure after the encounter at the market, but I kept mum.

"The DA is getting antsy to make an arrest," Karen said. "His office has been calling around the clock saying Lake Tahoe doesn't need this kind of bad publicity. It affects tourism. By the way, the coroner has set the body for cremation if it isn't claimed within a week. The Auburn storage facility is overbooked as it is."

I gasped. "I thought you said the autopsy wasn't complete."

"It is now."

"I'll claim it"—a lump the size of a snowball formed in my throat—"seeing as her adoptive parents have declined to handle the funeral arrangements and her sister hasn't come forward. Is that okay?"

"Nick?" Karen asked.

"Make it happen."

Karen nodded to me. "Oh, side note. Joey Blain is innocent. He was giving a half-pipe seminar."

"That late at night?" I asked.

"Seems those things go into the wee hours. Kids nowadays. They have stamina. I'm sure pot was involved."

"Why did he lawyer up?" I asked.

"Because I'd crowded him." She laughed and knuckled Shaper on the arm. "Can you imagine me crowding anyone?"

He grinned. "You? Never."

A short while later, Reno appeared on the horizon. Neon lights gleamed twenty-four hours a day, seven days a week. Reno did its best to draw elite crowds, but the place played second fiddle to Las Vegas.

At the first stoplight, Shaper made a sweeping right and pulled in front of a sixteen-unit building painted a faded pink. We climbed out of the SUV and headed inside. The railings were rusted from moisture, the rubber matting on the stairs chewed with wear. In other words, it was a dump.

Using the intercom by the security gate, Shaper rang Billy.

"Yeah?" a voice crackled through the speaker.

"Detective Sergeant Shaper, Mr. Tennyson."

"Come on up." A buzzer blared.

No elevator. We climbed the stairwell.

Shadows hovered along the second-floor walkway. Near a unit at the far end, Billy reclined against the doorjamb, his thumbs hooked through the loops of his tattered jeans.

"Good morning," he said, his voice raspy. "Sorry about the appearance. I overslept."

The detectives strode into the apartment. Billy eyed me while tucking in his shirt. "After you."

I stepped inside, a riot of emotions rushing through me. He did it; he didn't do it. Vikki had loved him; she'd broken it off with him. Someone had arranged her hair lovingly. Billy? Was he the one who'd set Rocky up by planting the postcards in the locker?

Though Billy was disheveled, his apartment was neat and tidy without a hint of dust. A stereo sat on a gold table with casters. At least a hundred classic records in sleeves devoid of frayed corners were stored beneath. Against the wall stood a plush leather sofa with a glass-topped coffee table in front of it. A pair of black chairs with slatted backs stood on either side of an archway. Myriad Grateful Dead posters puzzled me. He'd used them as wallpaper. Either he was a true fan or this was his way of debasing the group.

A glimpse into the kitchen proved that the living room had not been spruced up for the police. It, too, was spotless, with white and black tile counters and decorative canisters nesting on top. Candles were everywhere. Three live plants were thriving.

The bankruptcy data that had appeared on USSearch.com came to mind. Maybe Billy's credit had failed because of his buying sprees.

"Nice place." Shaper sat in one of the slatted chairs.

"Thanks."

"Lousy neighborhood." Karen sat on the sofa.

"No kidding."

Why was I here? When I'd interviewed Billy, I'd had control. Now I was a fifth wheel. I propped myself on the arm of the sofa. Shaper looked at me, his gaze questioning. I shrugged.

"Get you some water? Or a smoke?" Billy pulled a package of Marlboros from his shirt pocket and held them out. "You have to smoke outside, though. This dump has rules."

Karen reached for one, yanked her hand back, and chuckled. "Bad habit. I quit."

Billy slid the second slatted chair up and straddled it.

From behind a door that I assumed led to the bedroom came a long howl followed by a series of yips.

"Sorry. It's my dog." Billy turned and yelled, "Shut up, Eddie."

Karen continued. "Mr. Tennyson, let's get straight to the point. We happened to come upon some information, and the coroner confirmed it."

"Yeah, what's that?"

"Miss Carmichael was pregnant at the time of her death. What do you know about that?"

The devastation on Billy's face was instantaneous. His eyes welled with tears. Either he was a terrific actor or he hadn't a clue. "Whose was it?"

"Yours," Karen said.

Chapter 38

"No, it can't be." Billy stood and paced the living room while wringing his hands. "A baby. She never said. But you're wrong. It's not mine."

"Mr. Tennyson, sit down," Karen ordered.

Billy did, but his hands continued to wrestle with one another.

"How do you know for sure that the baby wasn't yours?" she asked.

Billy sat taller. "Because I'm sterile."

Karen glanced at Shaper. Aha. She'd been riffing. She didn't have DNA proof.

"Look, I know what you're thinking." Billy waved his hands. "That I killed Vikki because I wanted her to have an abortion and she wouldn't, but you're barking up the wrong tree."

"Why's that?" Shaper asked.

"Because I would've loved that baby." He rubbed his neck hard. "Oh, man, how I would've loved that baby. I told Vikki I wanted kids and that I was, like, willing to let her go to a sperm bank so we could have kids."

Had Vikki's secret been that she'd visited an insemination clinic?

"Man, I loved her so much, I'd have done anything to get her pregnant." Billy's eyes glistened with pride. "All she talked about was wanting kids."

"What if she got pregnant by somebody else?" Karen asked. "How would that make you feel?" She paused to let the idea sink in.

"Look, we broke up." Billy flipped his chair around and sat the normal way. "You split, you can have sex with other people."

"Did you?"

"Sure. I'm human. That doesn't mean I wouldn't have taken her back like that." Billy snapped his fingers. "Even pregnant."

"Are you having an affair with Tess Marks?" Karen pressed.

Billy rolled knots out of his neck. "No."

"She says you are."

"She's full of it. She's got a thing for me, but I don't have a thing for her. She's, like, old." The skin on Billy's neck turned splotchy.

"Supposedly, she overheard you warn your brother to lie about your whereabouts the night Vikki died or else."

"She's only saying that because I told her to take a hike." His gaze narrowed. The other side of him, the darker side I'd witnessed outside Homewood Market, was emerging.

Shaper leaned forward, elbows on his knees. "Rocky Yeats was an old friend of Vikki's, wasn't he?"

Billy glowered. "From high school, yeah." He pulled the pack of Marlboros from his shirt pocket and tapped one out.

"Could he be the father?" Shaper asked.

Billy tossed the packet on the coffee table. "No way. Tess wanted nothing to do with him."

"You meant Vikki, didn't you? *Vikki* wanted nothing to do with him." Shaper slid his chair closer.

"Vikki, Tess. None of them wanted to date Rocky. Something's off about him."

Karen said, "But you weren't sure when Vikki rejected you if Rocky was the reason, were you?"

"She'd never go for him." Billy smoothed his dirty blond hair with the hand holding the unlit cigarette. Strands fell on his jeans; he plucked them off one by one. "He wrote her love letters, but—"

"How do you know that?" Karen cut in.

"Vikki showed me. She had a stash of them. All on blue stationery. In flowery envelopes. I made her burn every one of them."

"She kept his postcards," Karen said.

"Uh-uh. He didn't send her postcards."

"Are you sure?"

Billy's gaze wavered. "Look, Rocky is as big a suspect as I am, isn't he? What's his alibi?"

"He was working at the club," Shaper said.

"He takes breaks. Long breaks." Billy tossed the cigarette on the coffee table. "I loved her, don't you get it? No strings. I told her we could adopt, but she didn't want to hear about that. She said adoption was no magic wand."

I'd heard Vikki use that phrase in another context. Unable to restrain myself, I said, "What do you think she meant by that?"

Billy looked at me for the first time since I'd entered the apartment. "I'd bet it had something to do with her being adopted."

Karen said, "Mr. Tennyson—"

Shaper put his hand on Karen's arm to stop.

Out of the corner of my eye, I saw Karen bridle. Shaper nodded at me, so I continued. "You and Vikki discussed adoption at length, didn't you?"

Billy stared at the tips of his shoes and chewed the right side of his lower lip. He was hiding something. "She said adopted kids had baggage. The birth parents always show up sometime down the road, bringing a whole lot of guilt." He slumped. "She said some DNA carries bad genes, and bad genes make mistakes."

"Vikki never met her birth parents," I said.

"Yeah, but she felt worthless because they didn't want her. She said people who give up their babies have bad genes."

Karen said, "Her birth parents are dead. Aspen"—she looked at me—"didn't you tell me that?"

"No, I said I couldn't locate them."

"They might be dead," Billy conceded. "Then again, they might not. Vikki talked about them as if they were alive. Sometimes she, like, talked in riddles. She enjoyed puzzles. You know, those rebus things and those cross sticks?"

"Acrostics," I corrected.

"Yeah, them. I called her my little decoder." Billy studied the ceiling as some happy thought flitted through his memory. He lowered his chin and his gaze came to rest on a framed picture of a beagle.

"Is that Eddie?" I asked, trying to put Billy at ease, a stratagem I'd often used at the rehab center. If I could get a patient to talk about the thing he loved, when I returned later to address his problem, he trusted me.

"Yeah."

"He's cute."

"Yeah, real cute. But when I'm at work or when I have guests, he stays in the bathroom."

"Why?"

"So he doesn't piddle everywhere." Billy snickered. "Eddie. Stupid name for a dog, but that's what Vikki named him."

"You got the dog from Vikki?"

"When we broke up." He sighed. "She thought a dog could replace her."

"Why'd she name it Eddie?" I asked, already knowing the answer.

"Because of the reverend at SOS."

"Source of Serenity," I said, explaining for my colleagues.

"Yeah. The reverend had a deep effect on her." Billy kicked the leg of his chair. "Vikki knew how I hated that place, but she was a kidder. 'Eddie will be your daily reminder of devotion,' she said. The dog is cool, though. He licks me a lot."

"He looks a little like Reverend Brock," I joked.

Billy chortled. "Yeah, he does. Without the toupee."

"Brock?" Karen blurted. "Aspen, you never mentioned meeting any Reverend Brock."

"Yes, I did. The night I gave you the ride home. From the casino."

Her jaw started ticking. Had she forgotten? Was her memory a blank? I'd suggested she send people to interview him. Hadn't she followed through?

I cut a quick look at Shaper. Anxiety shot through me. I couldn't tell him the truth about why Karen was upset. Even though I planned to end our friendship, ratting her out would be low. I had to give her time to join AA and put her life in order.

Choosing my words carefully, I said, "We talked about a lot of things that night, like your breakup with your boyfriend."

"Brock," she nodded. "Of course. I remember now." She mustered a smile, but I could see she was still searching her memory.

I turned to Shaper. "I started to tell you about him a couple of nights ago when I saw you at the Tavern, but you were—" I waved a hand. "Anyway, I asked my boss to check him out."

"And?" Karen challenged me with a stare.

"Before moving to Lake Tahoe, Brock was a dentist. In the Gilroy area. Squeaky clean, no arrests. He was going through divorce and moved here a few years ago. He started this church—"

"That's enough, thanks. We'll look into him." Karen's lip curled up in a snarl.

Man, she could be nasty. Drunk or sober.

"My two cents," Billy went on, "Vikki may not have liked the church, but she trusted the rev."

When I'd first met Billy, he said Vikki had good instincts.

"Are you done with me?" Billy asked. "I've got an interview for a gaffer job in an hour and want to shower up. Universal Studio's doing a film in Reno in a month. I'm meeting with the assistant director."

"Have you tried to get other jobs like that?" Shaper leaned forward, casual, conversational.

"Yeah. I always come up short. My résumé is a little brief. I'm hoping this one pays off."

"Good luck to you. Thank you for your time, Mr. Tennyson." Shaper rose and headed for the door.

Karen and I followed.

"By the way, Mr. Tennyson"—Shaper turned back—"do you own a pair of Timberland boots?"

"Yeah. Pretty sure everybody does." He flashed a winning smile.

"Could I see them?"

"Uh, sure." Billy went to his bedroom and returned with the boots. "Here."

They were as tarnished as I'd remembered.

"Size ten?" Shaper asked.

"Nine. I've got small feet, but it's not true about, you know . . ."

"Tell me about these stains," Shaper said.

"I had a burger about a week ago. The catsup bottle splatted. The crud oozed all over me. Had to toss the shirt. Forgot to clean these up."

It sounded like a pat explanation. Had he rehearsed it?

"You don't mind if my lab tests these, do you?" Shaper asked.

"No, sir."

"I'd also like you to test for sterility. To corroborate your account."

Billy balked. "My doctor has records."

"We'd prefer if our own doctor verifies it."

Billy scratched the back of his neck. "Seems pretty personal."

"Murder is personal."

Chapter 39

On the way to the car, Shaper said, "Size nine's too small for the cast we have."

"We should run them through anyway," Karen said. "Icy snow isn't the ideal casting medium."

Despite his edginess, Billy's account had rung true to me. At the moment, I didn't think Karen would care to hear my opinion.

During the remainder of the ride, I sat in back and listened to Shaper and Karen exchange opinions. When we reached the parking lot at the Placer County Sheriff's Office, a quaint building that had been erected in the sixties when the Winter Olympics took place at Squaw Valley, Karen bolted from the car, claiming she had to enter data from the interview on the computer.

Over her shoulder, she yelled, "Aspen, write up everything you have on Ed Brock and the Source of Serenity and email it to me."

"Sure thing." I started toward my loaner.

"Hold up." Shaper caught up to me and clasped my forearm. "Off to a fire?"

"What's her problem?"

"You have a knack."

"For what, ticking her off?"

"For getting to the heart of the matter. She's spent years trying to rise in her career, and she'll never have the ability you have. You're a natural."

A *natural.* My cheeks warmed from the compliment. I glanced at his hand on my arm. He released it.

"Tell me about this Ed Brock guy." Shaper leaned against my driver's door, blocking my getaway.

"He's a self-proclaimed guru of a new order of spirituality."

"Like a cult?"

"No."

"Have you interviewed other members?"

"His assistant. No members. I think Brock subscribes to what he professes though. I had some pamphlets, but—" I closed my mouth.

"But you gave them to Karen that night, and she doesn't remember. Had she been drinking?"

I chewed the inside of my lip.

"I'll take your silence as a yes. It's okay. We all go on a binge every once in a while. Her dad's death has messed her up. It shows in her work." Shaper gazed at me. "Don't worry. I'll cut her some slack."

I nodded, realizing he understood, given his sister's situation. We stood staring at each other for a long moment. He was so close I could hardly breathe.

"About last night," he said.

"Let's not talk about it. This . . . *us* . . . can't go anywhere. Not until . . ."

"The case is closed."

"Right. Plus, you're married."

"Get a room, Shaper," a guy in a gray SUV yelled as he swerved into the lot. He parked fast, hopped out of the truck, and headed into the station.

Shaper stepped away from me, his cheeks flushed, his embarrassment endearing. "Come with me to meet Reverend Brock." He bounced his keys in his palm.

"I can't. I've got to see Candace."

"I'll bet she's sleeping, and there are attendants standing by."

"Karen will be ticked off."

"She'll survive."

After I climbed into the Wrangler and buckled the seat belt, Shaper took off. The temperature outside was rising, promising snow-destroying rain, not sleet, would arrive sooner rather than later. Despite the foul weather, the lake looked peaceful and calm. Shaper navigated the twists and turns north with ease.

I said, "I don't like Brock, but I don't think he's the killer."

"What makes you say that?"

"Billy said Vikki didn't like the church, but she trusted the man."

"Could Brock be the father of her baby?"

"He's in his fifties."

Shaper glanced at me. "So?"

"Okay, sure. Young women date men in their fifties, but I don't see it. Not Vikki." I faltered. With all that I'd discovered about her in the past week, I wasn't sure. I'd been blind about my husband's appetites. It pained me to think I was still wearing blinders when it came to my close friends.

When we walked into the Source of Serenity, the scent of oranges was prevalent. Somewhere down the hall, people were chanting to achromatic music. I signaled for Shaper to follow me. We stopped outside the room and peeked in.

A mirror spanning the length of the far wall reflected at least fifty people on their knees, heads bowed. Ed Brock, in what I suspected was his stock uniform—silver-studded cowboy shirt, jeans, and brown boots—caught sight of me. He signaled to his watch and held up one hand, spread-fingered, meaning five minutes.

Shaper and I returned to the foyer. He kept himself busy by reading pamphlets and opening drawers at the admissions desk.

When the chanting group disbanded, Reverend Brock ushered them out, shaking hands with each and muttering words of encouragement.

After the crowd left the building, Shaper introduced himself to Brock and flashed his badge. Brock beckoned us to follow him into the room that was decorated with newspapers. The moment I stepped inside, fingers of dread clawed my intestines. I hated the place.

"Interesting wallpaper, sir," Shaper said, on the same wavelength as me. He recited a few headlines. "SDS Survivors, 200 Commit Suicide."

"As I told Miss Adams, we keep these notices up to remind our devoted of the treachery that exists in the world," Brock said. "We are not a cult. We do not wish for our believers to destroy themselves or to seek heaven in an unspecified location. We want them to be wary of false promises. *'For all who do evil hate the light and do not come to the light.'"*'

"Many autocrats think they're doing right by their people," Shaper said. "The sway that one man can hold over the minds of many is powerful."

"I do not intend to sway but to inspire."

"Do you hold services all day every day, Reverend?"

"We provide the faithful with opportunity." Brock circled the pine desk and took a seat in a high-backed leather chair. He indicated Shaper should sit in the chair opposite him. I remained standing.

Brock threw me a disparaging look. "You can't think I was involved in Vikki's murder. It was a heinous act."

"I'm sorry, sir," Shaper said, "but until we know more, everyone who knew her is under suspicion."

"You've made no arrests, so you're widening the net."

"We're taking pains to question everyone who might have been associated with the deceased. Ours is a small staff."

"As is mine."

Shaper leaned back in his chair, but he looked far from relaxed.

"I told Miss Adams that I have an indisputable alibi." Brock folded his hands across his stomach.

"Which is . . ."

"On the night Vikki was murdered, I was here with my flock."

"All night?"

"At the time in question."

"And what time would that be, sir?" Shaper rested his elbows on the arms of the chair.

"If I recollect, she was murdered sometime between ten Wednesday night and two the next morning. Correct?"

"Give or take."

"Well, I was here until one a.m. Thursday morning."

"You told me eleven on Wednesday night," I said.

Brock hesitated. "I must've said eleven because that's when the prayer meeting ended. We had a fellowship meeting afterward to induct new members into the church."

"Induct?" I said. "What it this, a club or an army?"

Brock frowned. "*Induct* in every sense of the word means to draw into unity. To initiate. To welcome. It is simply a choice of words."

"Words are your stock in trade," I said.

"Indeed. We followed the induction with a small affair. We served tea and cakes. At least ten of the devoted attended."

Shaper said, "Sir, did Miss Carmichael confide in you as her spiritual leader?"

"All my believers do."

"*Your* believers?" I cut in.

"*Our* believers." Brock fingered the medallion that hung on a gold chain around his neck. To regroup after the faux pas? "We are a big family, each relying on the other as we travel down the path of righteousness. I am here as an instrument to guide the flock."

"In any of your discussions with Miss Carmichael, did she happen to mention she was pregnant?" Shaper asked.

The color drained from Brock's face. "I had no idea. Poor child."

"The infant or Vikki?" I asked.

"Both. What a painful thing to go through without a husband."

"She never mentioned it, sir?" Shaper asked.

"Never."

"Not even to your assistant?" I asked.

"Lily keeps her distance. She doesn't care to overstep her bounds."

"Does stroking the medallion calm you, sir?" I asked.

Brock stopped caressing the necklace. A sadness filled his face. "Vikki gave this to me."

"Does the symbol mean something?"

"I don't have the faintest idea." Brock wiped a bit of sweat off of his upper lip. "Vikki said it would bring me inner peace. I wore it because I didn't want to let her down."

"Do all of the faithful give you gifts?" I persisted. Vikki had given Billy a dog and the reverend a medallion. Out of the blue, she had given me a frame with an etching of Tahoe on it. She'd said I should think of her whenever I looked at it. Were gifts her way of establishing bonds with friends?

"Some do, not all," Brock said. "Vikki was—how can I put it?—such a needy young woman. In search of her soul. She wanted people to appreciate her." He pursed his lips as if holding something back.

"May I?" I drew near and eyed the medallion. It featured a curvy design, like a tree with blazing branches emanating from it. I gasped when I realized it was the necklace Vikki had been wearing in the photograph Dan had given me.

"What?" Shaper eyed me.

"Vikki started wearing this necklace about three months ago. She called it her *magic wand*. I think she believed that if she wore the necklace, everything would get better. I asked her what needed to *get better*, but she didn't elaborate." I sighed. "Why would she give it to you?"

"It was a thank-you for being the one who had brought her into the world. *Spiritually*," he added hastily and reddened. "A rebirth if you will. Do you mind?" He nudged me out of his space. "As I said before, Vikki claimed this would give me inner peace, as I gave her inner peace." Perspiration formed on his upper lip again.

Secrets sure could make a man sweat, I mused.

Lily rapped on the door and entered without invitation. "Ed?" She seemed startled to find anyone else in the room. "I'm sorry. I'll come back." She flipped her braid over her shoulder and retreated.

"No, dear, please come in." Brock beckoned her to his desk. "What is it?"

Lily leaned close to him and whispered something in his ear. What was their story?

"It seems I have an important phone call," Brock said. "Anything more, Detective?"

Shaper shook his head and rose to leave. "I'll take a list of the faithful who were with you last Wednesday, if you don't mind."

"Lily will provide that."

Shaper headed to the door and paused. "One more thing." He winked at me out of view of Brock. "Were you having an affair with Vikki Carmichael?"

Brock bolted to his feet and gripped the edge of the desk so hard his knuckles turned white. "No. I would never."

Out of the corner of my eye, I caught sight of Lily. Anger flickered in her gaze. Was she mad at Shaper for accusing Brock? Or jealous of Vikki? Maybe she was in love with Brock and had killed Vikki in a jealous rage.

"Thank you, sir," Shaper said. "We'll wait in the foyer." He took me by the elbow and led me out. "You're not fond of him, are you?"

"No, but I can't put my finger on why."

"Sleazy comes to mind."

"Or insincere. I need the restroom." I pivoted and strode down the hall, opening doors and inspecting as I had before. I slipped into the file cabinet office where I'd first seen Lily. She'd been a biathlete. Did I hope to see a rifle lying around like the one used to shoot at me in the wilderness? No, a biathlete would have been able to take me out with one shot. Unless, of course, she'd intentionally missed because she'd wanted to scare me.

A door opened farther down the hallway. Heart racing, I hurried back to the foyer and joined Shaper. Seconds later, Lily appeared with a list of names in hand. She offered it to Shaper.

"Thank you, Miss—"

"Smith."

He stared at her. "How well did you know Vikki?"

"We were quite friendly."

"Do you think she was having an affair with Reverend Brock?" Shaper asked, showing no mercy. He must have picked up on her discomfort, too.

Lily's jaw ticked with tension. After a long moment, she said, "Let me assure you, Reverend Brock does not dally with the flock. Relationships with the devout can create unwanted turbulence in a world of serenity."

"Are you part of the flock?" I asked.

"No, I mean, yes, I'm a believer, but I work here. I'm not a—"

"Flock member?"

She lifted her chin. "What are you intimating?"

"Nothing."

Shaper grabbed my elbow and ushered me toward the door.

The chilly air outside was refreshing, the scent of pines welcome. Still no rain. But soon.

"If she's not involved with the reverend," I said, "she wants to be." I climbed into the Wrangler and buckled my seat belt.

"C'mon, Aspen, she didn't kill Vikki. She's too small."

I shared the possibility that she'd shot at me Sunday. "She was a biathlete, which means she's strong beneath that slim exterior."

Shaper sighed. "Does our hunter's confession mean nothing?"

I shrugged.

"She certainly doesn't wear a Trekker size ten," he said.

I didn't counter that lots of people could stuff a foot into a larger shoe.

"Don't you trust me?" He sounded testy. "Do you want me to do a background check on everyone who belongs to the church?"

Tears pressed at the corners of my eyes. "I want you—" I drew in a sharp breath. "I want you to find my friend's murderer."

"We're doing all we can."

"It's not enough," I snapped.

Shaper yanked the car into reverse and screeched out of the lot. He didn't say a word on the drive to Tahoe City. I tried to apologize for overstepping. He didn't acknowledge the attempt. When he dropped me at my car, he didn't say goodbye.

Frustration churning in my gut, I switched on the ignition of the Colt and sped to the hospital to check on Candace. The whole way, I muttered negative, nasty things about Nick Shaper. I didn't mean one word.

Chapter 40

Candace had to stay in the hospital one more night, so I spent the rest of the afternoon and early evening playing cards with her. The doctor wanted to make sure she ate well and drank plenty of fluids before releasing her. Who was I to disagree?

Once she fell asleep, I drove to the library. My stomach grumbled, and I knew I should eat, but something was niggling at me about the medallion around Brock's neck.

Having arrived half an hour before closing, I raced to the religion section and grabbed some of the same books I had already perused. Nothing clicked. I set them aside and chose a few more. I laid them out on the long table and opened the top one.

What was I looking for? Symbols that matched the medallion. Something that would explain why Vikki had considered the necklace her *magic wand.*

A pile of books accumulated on the table: *Religious Truth*, *Fertile Mind and Fertile Soul*, *The Seeds of Doubt.* Zilch.

I gathered a few books relating to Eastern religions, as well as some about Indians of the Tahoe region. Vikki had loved exploring caves, so the first one I opened was *Cave Dwellers of the Ancient Americas.* A catalogue of pictographs appeared: house, horse, weapon, and family. Nothing matched the medallion's artwork. The Eastern religions books were useless, as well.

From behind me, a man cleared his throat. Frank Novak was hovering at the opposite end of a bookcase, his glasses hanging around his neck. How long had he been watching me? He drummed the edge of the middle shelf. "I see you found more books that Vikki liked."

Hadn't he told me he didn't know which books she'd read? Had he been afraid to admit he'd been observing her?

I said, "Which ones?"

"She loved nature." Frank bracketed the word *nature* with imaginary quotation marks and shuffled toward me, his feet never leaving the ground. He picked up a well-thumbed paperback with a green binding and handed it to me. "This book was her favorite."

Nature's Way.

I flipped through and saw photographs of women birthing babies in lakes and swimming pools. Perhaps Vikki was searching for the natural way to have her baby.

"Why this one, Frank?"

"She said she was going to give it to her birth parents." He clasped his liver-spotted hands in front of him. "She seemed to think it would help her talk to them." He gestured to the picture of a newborn submerged in water while emerging from a woman. "They live here," he added. "Her parents."

My pulse quickened. "Are you sure?"

He checked his watch. "It's closing time." He turned on his heel and left.

Unwilling to leave, I flipped through the pages of *Nature's Way* looking for something, anything, that Vikki had thought was important. The first few doodles didn't catch my attention. They blended in with the book's artwork. But when I realized pages were filled with them, I turned back to review them.

Indeed, they were Vikki's drawings, just like the ones she'd added to her diary and datebook.

In the chapter called "Parenting Is Natural," images similar to the ones on Vikki's medallion appeared. Up and down the margins. Sometimes in pairs.

On one page, the arcs faced the text. Vikki had scribbled the word *mother* beside them. On another, the arcs faced the edges of the book, and she had written the word *father*. Mirror images of the same picture.

I retrieved *Cave Dwellers of the Ancient Americas* and turned to the catalogue of pictographs. On the fourth page, near the bottom, the symbol for father caught my eye. It looked just like Vikki's drawing.

Realization hit me like a thunderbolt.

Ed Brock wasn't her lover. He was her father. Her *birth* father.

• • •

I dialed the North Lake Tahoe Station, only to learn Shaper was out. I told the officer on duty that I needed either Detective Shaper or

Brandon to call me ASAP. Next, I called Max to share the news, but she didn't answer.

Needing to talk to someone, I sped south on Highway 89 toward home. Overhead, a lightning bolt streaked the sky. Before the count of ten, a rumble of thunder shook the car. Seconds later, sheets of icy rain began streaming through the Colt's busted window. I cursed and leaned to the right to avoid getting too wet, but to no avail.

Up ahead the neon light for the Homewood Tavern gleamed. A glass of wine would take the chill off. A piece of plastic wrap and some tape might keep the rain out of the car. I pulled into the parking lot and drove toward the kitchen entrance for supplies.

As I rounded the corner, I spotted Gwen under the eaves, her red hair highlighted by the overhead lamp. She was standing very close to a semi-bald man wearing a bulky parka.

I struggled out of the car, kicked the door closed, and bounded toward her. She touched her companion's arm and pointed toward me. The man turned and his jacket fell open. The oyster pearl and silver studs on his shirt gleamed.

Ed Brock sans toupee.

Before I could make my way to them, Brock ducked out of sight and Gwen went inside. I attempted to follow her but the door was locked.

I dashed through the rain to the front of the restaurant and hurried inside. Gwen was at the bar, wiping down the counter. A few people sat on stools. A number of tables were filled, but not as many as usual. The storm had kept them away.

Gwen looked up.

"What gives?" I drew near and hitched my thumb. "You saw me a second ago. I know you did."

"Water?" Gwen poured me a glass and slid it down the counter.

I caught it with one hand. All the patrons had been served. Gwen occupied herself by inserting corks into wine bottles, avoiding me. I moved to a stool nearer to her.

"The guy you were hanging with. Is he the new date material you mentioned?" I asked. Indirect questions were best on a fishing expedition.

Gwen turned her back. Silence ensued. I wracked my brain trying to come up with a reason why she wasn't being forthcoming with me.

She knew Ed Brock. Big deal. Was she embarrassed because I'd bad-mouthed him before?

Then it dawned on me. Was she Vikki's mother? No way. She would've admitted the truth; she and Vikki had been pals. On the other hand, Vikki's mother had put her up for adoption. Maybe it had been too difficult to face reality.

What had Gwen said her daughter's name was? Gabriella. Was that the *G* in the initials written in Vikki's Bible as well as on her locket?

"Have you heard from your daughter?" I asked. "I'd still love to see a photo of her. Does she have a social media presence? Maybe I could check out her Facebook page."

"She doesn't have one." Gwen headed toward the sink.

I rose and moved with her. "Does she have your curly red hair?"

"Last time I checked, she was blond, but years have past."

"You know, you and Vikki sure looked alike. You could have been her—"

"Sister?"

"I was going to say mother."

"A mother who would kill her daughter? Is that what you're intimating?" Gwen whirled on me. A few of the patrons looked in our direction. She lowered her voice. "Darlin', you are way out of line. When I said you should investigate Vikki's murder, I had no idea you'd be suspecting every Tom, Dick, and Mary."

"Hold it."

"Ed told me how you grilled him. Pointing fingers with no foundation. You're so danged impulsive that you'd even consider me, your good friend, a suspect. Do you think I killed her to keep my secret? Ridiculous."

Anger boiled within me. To divert suspicion from himself, Brock had convinced her that I was nuts.

"You want to know why I spent so much time with Vikki?" Gwen continued. "Because my daughter abandoned me. It felt good to be looked up to." She slapped a wet towel on the metal drain table and rubbed with vigor. "No, I am not Vikki's mother, but I'd sure as heck have told you if I was."

I slumped onto a stool. "Vikki had a locket and a Bible with the initials *GVB* on them. I thought maybe the initials stood for—"

"Gabriella Barrows?"

"I was thinking Brock." I stared at Gwen.

She shook her head. "Look, Aspen, you want somebody to be responsible for Vikki's murder. I get that, but I'm not your gal. I got knocked up once. After that big mistake, I had my tubes tied. Gabby's twenty-eight. I'm forty-three. I did not have twins. You do the math. And FYI, her middle name is Anna. For my grandmother."

"Vikki's adoptive parents were told the *V* stood for Victoria."

"That settles that." Gwen heaved the wet towel into the sink, lifted the hatch, and left the bar.

Dang it. I'd warned Max that I wasn't cut out for investigating. I had no right jumping to conclusions the way I had. I didn't want to tear my friendships to shreds to pursue a career as a PI.

On the other hand, I needed a few more answers. I hurried after Gwen into the kitchen. She was tending to French fries. She slipped paper sleeves into three cone-shaped baskets, shook a basket of fries free of oil, and dumped them into the cones.

"I'm sorry," I said, taking one of the fries. "What's with you and Ed Brock then?"

She gave me the stink eye. "You can't help yourself, can you? Fair warning: curiosity killed the cat." She planted a hand on one hip. "Ed came in with a bunch of friends a few weeks ago. We hit it off. We've dated twice. We haven't slept together, if you were wondering. Not that I don't want to. He's quite attractive and smart. But I'm not a believer. I think he hopes to convert me."

"Why did he run off when he saw me?"

"He said he'd had enough of you for one day." She set the baskets on a tray.

"I believe he's Vikki's birth father. A DNA test will prove it."

"If you say so," she said over her shoulder as she headed toward the restaurant. "I've known him for a nanosecond, so I can't confirm or deny. But you know what? I'd bet he'd make a pretty good father." Using her hip, she pushed through the swinging door.

I caught the door before it could slam me in the face. "Except he wasn't. He didn't own up to it. I think Vikki figured it out."

"Tell Shaper, Aspen." Frustration peppered her tone. "He and his team can handle this. It's time for you to hang up your sleuthing hat."

Dismissed and wounded, I marched to the Colt and opened the front door. Water gushed out. I climbed in and shoved the gear into reverse, almost ramming into Karen Brandon as she pulled up in her dark green Explorer.

She jammed on the brakes, hopped out, and jogged to my window. I rolled it down. A baseball cap diverted the flow of rain from her face. "I called the hospital, but they said you hadn't been by."

"I was there all afternoon."

"That niece of yours—"

"I'm taking her home in the morning." I held up a hand to stave off the flow of accusations Karen seemed ready to hurl every time we discussed Candace. "I have something to tell you about Ed Brock."

"What?"

I filled her in about the medallion and the images I'd found in the library. "I accused Gwen of being the mother." I explained why.

"You're an insensitive idiot."

"Thanks. That didn't sting too much."

Karen wiped rain off her chin. "You deserved it."

"When I found out that Vikki's birth mother lives here, I thought—"

"How do you know that?" Karen gripped my door.

"Frank Novak the librarian said so."

"Okay, I'll handle this. I left a message for Shaper that I was tracking you down. We're on it. Go home and get some sleep. You look a wreck."

"I'm stopping my side of the investigation," I said.

"Good idea. It's taken its toll on you. Not everyone is cut out to be an investigator. Maybe you should consider going back into therapy."

"Maybe." Grief swept over me as I pictured Vikki in the morgue, her body unclaimed, her murder unsolved.

"We'll get the creep who did it, Aspen. Promise." Karen squeezed my forearm. "I'll call you when we make an arrest."

"Thanks."

"By the way—" She faltered. "I'm going to AA. It meets every night at the high school. Thanks for giving me the nudge I needed."

She turned to go and spun around. "Please know that you can call me if you think of anything else. I value your opinion."

"There is one thing. The swirls Vikki made in the snow."

"What about them?"

I felt like I was reaching for something through thick fog. I could make out the shape but not the object.

"It'll come to you," she said, picking up on my frustration. "When it does, call me."

Later, I awoke with a start. I'd fallen asleep in the armchair in the living room. I stared at the fireplace. The fire had fizzled. Embers remained.

Think, Aspen. Something had awakened me.

The design in the snow.

Might Vikki have written the letters of someone's name except the letters swirled together? No, it wasn't a name.

I flashed on the doodles Vikki had drawn in *Nature's Way*, specifically the symbol for *father* and knew that was it. Vikki had been trying to convey that her father—Brock—had killed her.

Reneging on my plan to pull out of the investigation, I called Shaper at the station. He wasn't in. I left a message and tried Karen on her cell phone. She didn't answer.

Neither called me back.

Chapter 41

When I awoke the next morning, my skin looked tired, my hair was limp, and my appetite was nil. I didn't hear from Shaper, Karen, or my aunt before I headed to the hospital.

For three hours, I completed paperwork to check Candace out. Every *t* had to be crossed and *i* dotted. While waiting for the attending doctor to approve the exit report, I checked my cell phone for messages. None.

I'd brought warm clothes for Candace because the temperature had dropped to a chilly fifteen degrees again. Maybe I'd overdone the amount of clothing. She protested the second turtleneck. I conceded but demanded she wear the down vest.

When we reached the curb, the sky was once again packed with bloated clouds. Last night's storm was a precursor. Would the bigger storm hit today? Why couldn't the weather choose sunny and stick with it?

On the way home, I broached the subject of bulimia with Candace. I asked if she'd read the material the doctor had left for her.

Candace nodded and whispered, "I'll do better."

I clutched her hand. "I don't need you to do better, but I need you to see yourself in a better light. Do you know you're beautiful?"

"No, I'm not."

"Yes, you are. And smart and funny. I don't think you value yourself."

"Is it Mom's fault?"

Mother-bashing Rosie was not my aim. "No. Body image is an issue with lots of girls your age. Sometimes a therapist can help you gain a healthy perspective."

"I don't want to see a shrink."

I tabled the discussion and didn't raise the notion of gaining custody. She was too fragile, and, frankly, I needed to see what kind of battle Rosie might wage.

At noon I pulled into my driveway, exhausted. Temporary motherhood was proving to be a challenge. Patience and love, I kept reminding myself. Patience and love. Not until I was out of the car did

I spot Shaper sitting in the rocker on the porch, a pink teddy bear under his arm.

I stepped out of the car and frowned. "You don't call, you don't write. I don't have your cell phone number." I sounded waspish, but he deserved it.

"It's 555-1492," Shaper said. "The year Columbus discovered America." He strode to the car, handed Candace the toy and, ignoring her protests, lifted her out and carried her into the house.

On the way to the guest room—*her* room—he said, "We got some results today. Hamburger grease and catsup were found on Billy Tennyson's shoes, and he was telling the truth about being sterile."

I hitched my head. "Can we talk about this outside?"

"Sure." He laid Candace on her bed and ruffled her hair.

"Thanks for the bear, Detective."

"You can call me Nick."

"Okay." Candace grinned and color came into her cheeks.

"Sweetie, I'll be back in just a bit with some lunch. Here's the TV controller." I handed it to her and strode through the house to the back porch.

Shaper followed. He closed the sliding glass door and leaned up against the railing. "Also, we found a sperm bank where Vikki Carmichael was a recipient back in October."

He was all business. No swagger. No heat. Good. We needed to remain professional.

I sat in the chair I'd sat in the other night. "Have you spoken to Karen?"

"Yes. She and I agree with you. The symbol on Brock's necklace means *father*." Shaper sighed. "So the guy kept the information a secret and is a jerk for not coming forward on behalf of his daughter. It doesn't mean he killed Vikki."

"The image in the snow. I told you at the crime scene that Vikki had carved something with her pen. Remember? I think the drawing resembled the symbol on Brock's medallion."

"Aspen, come on, you were the only one to see the drawing. Is it possible you've imagined that the two match?"

"Don't reject my idea out of hand."

Shaper folded his arms over his chest.

I mirrored him. A standoff.

After a long silence, Shaper said, "We'll ask Brock to do a DNA test, okay? One other thing. Vikki's adoptive sister—"

"Lynanne."

"Is Lily Smith."

The news hit me like a loose ski careening down a steep incline. Vikki had referred to her as *Lee-Lee* in her diary. *Lily. LL.* That meant the initials *EB* in her diary had to stand for Ed Brock. "Why didn't you tell me before?"

"Walker and Kim just figured it out. They looped me in an hour ago." He held up a hand to stave the flow of my anger. "And you were busy at the hospital."

"Why hasn't Lily come forward?"

"Got me."

"Isn't that perfect?" I popped to my feet and paced the porch. "Vikki's father and adoptive sister get cozy in a church built for two. Somewhere there's got to be a motive."

"We don't believe Lily—Lynanne—had anything to do with Vikki's death. She, too, has a solid alibi. By the way, Rocky Yeats is MIA."

"He skipped town?"

"We've got an APB out—" Shaper's cell phone buzzed. He glanced at the number. "I've got to go."

"Is it about Rocky?"

"No." He moved to the door.

"Whatever it is, send Karen Brandon or Walker or Kim."

"It's personal."

"But I need to know more about Lily and—"

"I can't right now."

End of discussion. He strode through the house. I beat him to the front door and whipped it open. He gazed at me with sad eyes, but no words of explanation for his hasty exit came. The revving of his engine assaulted my ears.

Edginess made my skin itch. If Shaper or his deputies weren't interested in interviewing Reverend Brock further, I would confront him myself. If wrong, I'd be the first to admit my mistake. I called the

Source of Serenity and learned that Brock would be there for three more hours. However, I couldn't head to Incline until I found someone to watch Candace, even though she was fast asleep.

So I called my aunt and filled her in. Max promised she could be at my house within thirty minutes and told me to go. I checked all the doors and windows, wrote a note for Candace to advise her of the plan, and sped north.

Chapter 42

I found Lily in the file room stapling leaflets together. The sweet strains of Beethoven's *Eroica* serenaded her. Didn't she listen to anything else? I cleared my throat, but she didn't look up from her chore. I rapped on the door. "Lily?"

She whirled around, hand to her chest. "You startled me."

"I have a few questions for you and hoped you might help me out."

"I can't." Lily sputtered. "Ed said . . . I mean Reverend Brock said I don't have to answer to you. You're not with the sheriff's department." She whipped her braid over her shoulder and stared daggers at me.

"And you're not Lily Smith. You're Lynanne Carmichael."

She glanced right and left.

"Don't worry," I said. "Brock isn't here. I checked each room on my way to you."

She ushered me to the file room and closed the door.

I said, "Vikki called you Lee-Lee."

She bobbed her head. "Lynanne was too hard for her to pronounce. I was ten when our parents adopted her. I left home six years later." Lily toyed with her braid. "Our parents were, um, odd. I loved them, don't get me wrong, but they were reclusive and strict. No phones, no television. They didn't live in this century."

"So you ran away."

Her eyes pooled with tears. "I moved to Reno and changed my name. Thanks to my adoptive brothers, I was good at cards. I became a dealer at the casino to earn money and got my GED. Then I applied for scholarships and got into college. Two years later, I became a biathlete. But in my junior year, my scholarship was yanked. Sixteenth in trials didn't cut it. I couldn't keep up the payments." She shrugged. "I went back to being a dealer. I had to make a living."

"How did you reconnect with Vikki?"

"I was working at the Emerald when she came in three months ago."

"Tess told me Vikki assaulted a drunk customer who was harassing a dealer. Were you the dealer?"

"Yes." A tear slipped down her cheek. She brushed it away.

"Why was Vikki there? She'd quit dancing by then."

"She'd stopped by to see friends. When she saw the fracas"—Lily chopped the air with her hand—"she came over. She recognized me from family photos and said it was fate that we reconnected. We had coffee. Caught up." Another tear. Another swipe.

"Vikki got you the job here."

"That's right."

"What about you and Reverend Brock? Are you in love with him?"

She gasped. "You can tell?"

"It's pretty obvious."

"I fell in love at first sight." Her cheeks turned crimson. "He doesn't love me. He's worried what others might think. Because of the age difference."

"Did you know he was Vikki's father?"

"I didn't. Not right away." Lily wove her hands together and squeezed so hard that the blood drained from them. "I remember when Vikki was little, she was desperate to know who her birth parents were. She said our parents told her they were dead, but she didn't believe them. I said even if they were alive, locating them might not be worth the trouble. I'd met mine, and they were real jerks."

"But she was insistent."

Lily nodded. "After a while, though, she stopped talking about it. And then I left . . ."

I perched on the edge of the desk, waiting for more.

"When I ran into her at the casino, Vikki divulged that she'd moved to Lake Tahoe because she'd discovered her birth mother and birth father were living here. I'd asked her how she found out. She said she'd talked to an adoption lawyer and gone through tons of his files."

I pictured the boxes in the attorney's attic, surprised that his wife hadn't mentioned Vikki's visit to me. Maybe she hadn't known. Her husband would have still been alive.

"When she revealed Ed was her birth father, I was in awe of her resolve. That's why she'd become involved with the Source of Serenity. She was a natural investigator. I think that's why she liked you so much. She respected you."

"She talked to you about me?"

Lily nodded and rubbed the bridge of her nose. "When I asked whether her birth mother was a good person, she dodged the question."

"I'm confused. It wasn't Brock's wife?"

"No." Lily toyed with her braid again. "Vikki was adamant about that."

Both of her parents in Lake Tahoe. Not married. Coincidence or fate?

After a long pause, Lily's lower lip started quivering. "Ed and Vikki had the same mannerisms. Their laugh was the same and their eyes crinkled when they smiled. I think that's why Vikki had wanted me to meet him. She wanted to know if I saw what she saw." She sighed as a memory flitted through her mind. "They were so orderly."

"You obviously loved her."

"I did."

"Why haven't you come forward then?" I rasped. "She's in cold storage at the morgue, lying in a drawer waiting for someone to claim her. Your adoptive parents don't want to. How about you?"

The door opened and Lily jumped.

"Miss Adams, what a surprise." Ed Brock strode inside, his cowboy shirt cleaned and pressed, his toupee in place.

"You know what galls me?" I stepped toward him.

He stiffened.

"You knew Vikki was your daughter, and yet you didn't claim her as your own flesh and blood." I pointed at his medallion. "That necklace. She gave it to you."

His fingers moved toward it.

"She was murdered," I went on, "and yet you didn't come forward to demand justice. Did you kill her?"

"What? Heavens no. I would never harm—" His face collapsed. He slumped into a rattan chair against the wall. "You're right. I knew she was mine the moment I met her. Quite by accident. On the mountain. On a Sunday. Something inside me leaped for joy but at the same time filled me with dread."

"Because you had an affair. Your secret would be exposed. Your pristine reputation tainted."

He rubbed his jaw with his knuckles. "I was married when Vikki was conceived. Unhappily. But married. The woman, Vikki's mother—"

"Why keep the secret now?" I opened my palm. "You're divorced. Your children are grown."

"Because I promised her mother that I would. If she'd made her pregnancy public then, she would have destroyed my career. She didn't." Brock looked up, his eyes flush with tears. "I won't wreck hers now."

"Is that when you became religious?" I asked.

The reverend bowed his head. "Vikki gave me this necklace in honor of—"

"Fatherhood."

He clutched the medallion with fierce passion. "My heart broke when she died."

Bile rose inside me. "How old was her mother when the two of you—"

"Seventeen."

So she was young but not too young. Was it Tess? Did Rocky—Vikki's protector—find out and threaten to ruin her career? Had Tess been disgusted that her own daughter wanted to have a baby with Billy, the man she adored?

"Come on, Reverend. We're talking murder. Tell me her name."

"I can't. I'm a man of my word."

"Right, a man of your word. A married man who played the field and never had to pay the price until now."

"Now hold it—"

"Vikki. Your own flesh and blood was crying out to you, and you ignored her. Do you want to know what I think?" I clenched my fists. Lily mewled. My gaze didn't leave Brock's pathetic face. "Vikki threatened to expose you. She wanted to take down your mini-empire. Your cash cow. She gave you that medallion to wear because it was her version of a scarlet letter."

"No."

"FYI, she drew something in the snow to convict you. I saw it. I told the police."

"She couldn't have. Wouldn't have. She knew I loved her. I'd embraced her. I had made a promise to reveal everything to my family before Christmas. I—"

I held up a hand to silence him as an image flickered in my mind. Vikki. The strands of her chestnut-red hair flared out. The drawing. I gagged, the response so convulsive that I clutched my chest. "I'm wrong."

"I told you that."

"Yours wasn't the necklace Vikki was wearing in the photograph."

"What photo—"

I sliced the air to silence him as a realization flashed in my mind. The necklace in the picture Dan had given me was smaller. Daintier. And the arcs on the charm were curved to the left, a mirror image of the arcs on Brock's medallion. The word *father* wasn't what Vikki had been trying to illustrate; it was *mother*. Karen Brandon wore that necklace. A college ring partially concealed the symbol.

Karen was a woman with a reputation—a *career*—to lose.

My cell phone buzzed. My aunt was trying to reach me. Probably to tell me she'd arrived at the house. I sent it to voice mail, intent on processing the rest of my theory. When Vikki pulled the drunk customer—*Karen*—off Lily at the casino, had someone called out Karen's surname? Was that how Vikki had connected the dots? I imagined her reaching out to Karen afterward. Becoming friends. Giving Karen the necklace. Did the appointment I'd seen in Vikki's datebook with *MM* on the night she was killed stand for *Mama*?

No, no, no. My reasoning was off. Karen had an alibi. Tess had seen her gambling at the casino the night Vikki was murdered. Except no one could remember seeing Tess there. Had Deputy Kim found surveillance footage yet? Maybe Tess, knowing how often Karen frequented the place, had used Karen to cover her own flimsy alibi.

The reverend was staring at me, his face flushed with concern.

I said, "Is Karen Brandon her mother?"

Brock's defeated expression confirmed it.

As I raced from the building, I heard Brock arguing with Lily that he had to contact Karen.

The moment I was in the loaner I dialed Shaper's cell phone number. I received an instantaneous message that he was unavailable. I started to tell him my discovery when the call ended. I saw the word *Roaming* and tossed my cell phone into the cup holder.

I didn't need Shaper. I knew what I had to do.

Chapter 43

Ominous clouds filled the sky. We wouldn't escape the storm's wrath today.

I drove along North Lake Boulevard, the impending cruel weather matching my angst. Why would Karen kill Vikki? Would bearing a child out of wedlock twenty-plus years ago ruin her career today?

No, I was missing something.

My cell phone buzzed. My aunt had left me a message. It would be risky to listen to it at the brisk rate I was driving. I figured she was reassuring me that she and Candace were having a grand old time and to take as long as I needed.

Nearing Tahoe City, I considered stopping at the sheriff's office and bringing Shaper up to speed in person but decided not to. He had already rejected the notion that the carving in the snow was significant. He would scoff if I told him I'd figured out it was the symbol hanging around Karen Brandon's neck. If I mentioned that Karen's footprints and hair would be found at the crime scene, he'd say that of course they would; she was first on the scene after me. I'd counter that when Karen killed Vikki, Vikki's blood must have splattered on Karen's clothing. He would argue that she was smart enough to ditch it all. No evidence, no conviction.

I glanced at the station's parking lot as I passed. Shaper's Wrangler wasn't in the lot. I slammed my palm against the steering wheel. What personal business could be taking the whole day? Who had called him and made him stand at attention?

Stop, Aspen. He's busy. Move on.

As always, traffic drew to a snail's pace near Tahoe City. Stuck in the mire, I tried to recall everything about the morning I'd found Vikki. Karen said she'd been on her way to the grocery store. Was that a lie? She'd raced down the snowy slope to join me, adding her own footprints to the mess. Had she straddled Vikki on purpose in an effort to obliterate the drawing in the snow? I flashed on Vikki's hair. Someone had arranged it lovingly after death. Her birth mother?

Determined to find any possible evidence, I turned onto the street leading to Karen's cabin. Her Explorer wasn't parked under the carport. Even so, I stashed the Colt out of sight, slid my purse over my shoulder—in the event I needed to pretend to be paying a social visit—and stole through the woods along the stream.

Even though a soothing pre-storm breeze whistled through the needles of the pines, calm was not in my vocabulary. I climbed the stairs to the back porch and stopped. A man was talking inside the kitchen. I ducked down until I realized the noise was coming from the television. I peeked in a window. A male anchor was delivering the afternoon news. I tried the kitchen door. Locked. I shivered even though I was warmly dressed. Breaking and entering wasn't my forte.

A pile of wood stood in the corner of the deck. I considered grabbing a piece and smashing a window. Would a forced entry appear to be an attempted robbery so Karen wouldn't suspect me? She hadn't installed an alarm in the cabin; most people in Tahoe didn't. I lifted a log from the woodpile, hauled back . . . and stopped. The window to the right of the kitchen door was open a crack. If I could remove the screen . . .

Using my Swiss Army knife, I got to work. Six screws later, I removed the screen and shoved the window open. I shinnied up and pitched through the opening.

Head and hands first. I landed in a sink filled with soapy water and a couple of plates. As I scrambled to the floor, I noticed three empty bottles of scotch on the counter.

After using a dishtowel to dry off and to wipe my fingerprints off the counter and windowsill as well as to blot the water I'd tracked on the floor, I tiptoed to the foyer. The hooks by the front door were empty of snow gear. No jackets. No mittens. I sneaked down the hall into the bedroom. The small Panasonic television was turned on to the same channel as the TV set in the kitchen.

I set my purse on the dresser and began opening drawers. Karen's underwear, socks, long underwear, and shirts were neatly folded. No bloodstains. I didn't find any gloves. Perhaps she'd stowed those in her car.

Her closets looked ready for a marine sergeant's inspection. Each pair of shoes was turned the same direction, toes toward the room.

Browns beside browns. Blacks next to blacks. She had four pairs of Timberlands. One pair were Trekkers. And on the Trekkers were dark stains that looked like dried Chianti.

My stomach lurched at the gravity of what I'd found.

More. You need more.

In the bathroom, I noted the name of her hair color: *Ash blond by Clairol.* Could hair fibers at the crime scene be matched by the chemical makeup of the dye?

Not enough. You need to prove motive.

I returned to the bedroom, and my gaze landed on the overdue bills I'd seen on Karen's desk the other night. Would her gambling debts be a motive? How could killing Vikki have solved the problem? According to Shaper, Vikki didn't have a will.

I lifted a set of envelopes bound together with a rubber band. I sorted through them and discovered more overdue bills. About a third of the way in, however, I found a handwritten letter from Karen's father as well as a copy of his will.

The letter was dated the day before he died.

> *My dear daughter, I am so sorry for the pain and sorrow I caused you in your younger years. Putting your child up for adoption should not have been my decision. I have done much since then to try to right the wrong. I have asked your brother to search for your child. He has come up empty-handed, but his passion to find the girl is strong. If I die before I complete this task, I hope he will be able to fulfill your dream of motherhood. I ask your forgiveness. With all my heart, I did what I did out of love and the belief that I was giving you a better future.*
>
> *Lovingly, your father*

My stomach wrenched. Her father had put Vikki up for adoption, and her brother had known about it. How had that impacted Karen? She was contesting her father's will, claiming he'd had Alzheimer's and hadn't been fit to write it.

I opened the document and scanned the provisions. As I'd guessed, the father had planned to shortchange Karen, but not to benefit her brother. Her father stipulated that should his granddaughter be found, Karen's portion would be reduced by half, with the other half distributed to her daughter. No wonder Karen was fighting the will. She had soaring debts. Vikki had been an obstacle to Karen inheriting what she believed to be rightfully hers.

Using the HP printer, I copied the letter and will.

Rumbles of thunder shook the house.

A blare resonated from the television. I turned, expecting to see a warning for severe weather, but instead saw a bulletin on the screen: *News Update.* The male anchor said, "Another homicide has shaken the pristine area of Lake Tahoe. Richard "Rocky" Yeats, the manager of a South Lake Tahoe dance club, has been found shot to death." The man continued speaking as a picture of Rocky appeared in the upper corner followed by live action shots of deputies Kim and Walker at a local pitch and putt golf course. They were supervising the removal of the corpse from the trunk of a car. Gloria Morning, the on-site reporter, materialized like a stealth bomber. She shoved her microphone toward Kim and asked if the deputy was sure the deceased was Rocky Yeats.

It was. I recognized his slick hair and fighter's nose.

I returned the letter and will to the set of envelopes and dashed to the gun cabinet in the foyer. All of the guns were polished and set in the proper slots. All except one. The .45 with the tooled silver handle was missing.

Had Rocky figured out Karen killed Vikki? When I visited his house, he told me he was coming into some money. Had he blackmailed Karen? Had she lured him from the casino and shot him with the .45?

My cell phone hummed in my pocket. My aunt was calling again. Why was she being so insistent? I answered.

"Aspen, it's me. Candace isn't here. I've searched everywhere. I thought she might have gone for a walk, but I can't find her."

My stomach snagged. "She wouldn't have left without—"

My phone buzzed again. Karen was on the line. Had she sensed I was in her house?

"Aunt Max, hold on." I pressed a button to switch callers. "Hi, Karen, what's up?"

"Guess who I just spoke to? Ed Brock. You and I need to talk."

"Sure thing. I'll meet you at—"

"Come to Alpine Meadows, Aspen. Alone. Top of Summit Chair. I've got Candace. FYI"—Karen cackled—"if you haven't heard, a big storm is coming. Drive carefully. Those brakes or tires could give out at any time."

I groaned. She was the one who had sabotaged my car. Twice. She must have been the one to shoot at us near Rubicon Springs, too. Why? Because I was close to realizing Vikki's drawings could implicate her.

I switched the call back to my aunt, told her where I was headed, and bolted out of the house. Max begged me to wait for someone from the sheriff's department to show up. I couldn't.

"Shoot, shoot, shoot!" I cried as I scrambled into the Colt. Why had I left Candace alone? Scolding myself wouldn't solve the problem. I shoved the key into the ignition and turned over the engine. It sounded normal. I made a U-turn and drove down the hill testing the brakes; they worked.

As I headed toward Alpine Meadows, rain mixed with sleet started slamming the car and pouring in through the busted window. Due to the weather, traffic was moving at a snail's pace. Although the road was narrow and slick, I dared passing car after car. Even with my dicey maneuvers, getting to the base of the ski resort would take at least fifteen minutes. Each second was precious.

What would Karen do in the meantime? She'd already killed her own flesh and blood.

I telephoned the sheriff's office. "Detective Sergeant Shaper," I said. The receptionist informed me he wasn't in. She had no idea where he was. I spat out my name and said, "Tell him he needs to look into Karen Brandon's financial issues and her father's will. Tell him Karen kidnapped—"

Lightning blistered the sky; the connection ended. I pressed Redial, but the message on my cell phone read *No service.*

Chapter 44

The last of the cars and trucks with skis attached to the tops were exiting the Alpine Meadows parking lot. I pulled into a spot close to the lodge and leaped from the car. Sleet stabbed my cheeks. I sheltered my head with my hands and tore to the breezeway. From beneath, I peered at the slopes. The lifts were shut down. All of the attendants had gone.

Beyond Summit Chair, I spotted something that made my stomach churn. My sweater. The red one with white snowflakes that Candace had admired. Past the sweater, wide tractor tracks from a grooming vehicle headed up the slope.

I spied a Skidoo with a toboggan attached to its rear near the ski patrol room and tore to it. When I found a key in the ignition, I blessed the ski patrol, always prepared for an emergency.

Even in the sloppy snow, the Skidoo was getting good traction as I drove up the hill, but that wouldn't last forever. Well known among the locals was how rain falling on snow could produce some spectacular avalanches. A profusion of water could create a channel down to another layer of snowpack, add weight, and destabilize it. I had to get to Candace before that happened.

Halfway up the mountain, the air grew frigid and the sleet turned into snow. I steered the Skidoo up the steep, barren Alpine Bowl and pulled to a stop at the crest next to Summit's upper terminal. I saw a Thiokol groomer parked beyond but no sign of Karen or Candace. I climbed off the Skidoo and peered over the backside of the mountain, a wilderness area with no avalanche control and no easy way down. A few signs designating *Area Closed* had been planted along the crest. I didn't spot any footprints or ski tracks.

I pivoted and scanned the area. Where were they?

A concrete building with a lower level for snow vehicles and an upper level to house the ski lift operators looked empty. I dashed up the ramp to the unloading platform and stopped short.

Karen, dressed in ski gear, appeared. Thin winter gloves made it easy to manipulate the revolver she was aiming at me. "A Skidoo. How clever of you. I would expect no less." She was working hard to pronounce words, although she was slurring her *s*'s. How much alcohol had she imbibed? The effect in high altitude could be double that at normal elevation. "You're starting to enjoy the detective game, aren't you?"

"Where's my niece? If you've hurt her—"

"She's safe and sound." Karen pointed behind me.

Teetering more than thirty feet above the ground on a chair facing away from us—the lift at a standstill—sat Candace, dressed only in a turtleneck, jeans, and tennis shoes. She was hunched forward, gripping the safety bar. If she jumped or fell, she would break a leg or worse. If that didn't get her, the cold would.

If only I'd spotted her when I'd ascended the mountain. I'd been too intent on following the groomer's tracks.

"Candace, are you okay?" I yelled.

She couldn't see me. I didn't know if she could hear me. If she did, she didn't acknowledge with a response or gesture.

"I told Candace to be quiet or else. She's such a good girl," Karen said. "How I would've loved to have a daughter like her."

"You did."

"Vikki was never mine. She was never going to be mine."

"I went to your house. I read your father's will. I saw the letter."

Karen scoffed. "He was a piece of work."

"I also saw your bills. You're in debt. You killed Vikki for her part of the inheritance."

She shrugged. No contrition.

"What are you going to do with Candace and me?" I asked.

"You'll have an unfortunate accident, and she'll freeze to death. Those stupid attendants missed one passenger. Such a shame. As for me, I'll ski to freedom."

In my haste, I'd left my purse with pepper spray in the Colt. I said, "I've called Shaper."

"He won't come. He's a teensy bit busy patching up his marriage to that bimbo. Doesn't that just irk you? I know you like him."

Refusing to take the bait, I looked to my right and spotted a snow shovel standing by the shack door. The lift's chairs were out of the way.

One hung beneath the circular turn; another dangled four feet behind me. "I left a message for Shaper about you. And about the will," I added, lying.

Karen smirked. "I'll have destroyed any evidence by the time he gets there. Your word against mine."

"Rocky was blackmailing you, wasn't he? You shot him."

"You have no proof."

"Ow." I gripped my calf, pretending it had cramped up, and hobbled to my right toward the shovel. "I figured out who you were because of your necklace."

Karen fingered the chain around her neck. The *mother* symbol, which had been partially obscured by her father's class ring before, was now evident.

"When did Vikki give that to you?" I asked.

"When she told me she knew I was her mother. She moved to Tahoe to find me. Isn't that sweet?"

"And you moved here to be closer to Ed Brock. Am I right?"

She didn't respond.

"Have you been keeping tabs on him all this time?"

Karen frowned. "Ed. Such a trusting soul. He called me the moment you left his place. He thought you were off base thinking I would murder my own flesh and blood. He advised me to get in touch with you to set things straight."

"At first I thought he'd killed her," I conceded.

"Get real." She snickered. "He buys into that crap he's professing."

"How did you meet?" I inched toward the shovel.

"I was a junior in high school. He was in charge of our high school church group."

"I heard he was a dentist."

"That, too."

"And he lived in Gilroy."

"He moved after he knocked me up." Karen waved her hand. "I was so in love with him. He said he'd leave his wife for me and I believed him. How lame, right? Where was his religion then?"

"Where was yours?"

"Touché."

Never trust a man who swears he's had a vasectomy, she'd said to me. I hadn't picked up on the clue.

Candace started coughing. Her chair started to swing.

My insides wrenched. "Karen, let her go. Shaper will figure it out about the will. He'll learn you're in debt. He'll realize you needed Vikki out of the way. You'll still go to jail, with or without my help."

"No." Karen thrust her hand forward, but she didn't pull the trigger. Was she deliberating?

"Why kill Vikki?" I asked. "She wouldn't have wanted your money. She just wanted your love."

"It was my father's fault. All of it."

"Fathers can wield so much control, can't they? Why, you even became a tomboy to win his approval."

"Shut up."

"My father didn't want me to study psychology, but I didn't listen. I did what I wanted. Why didn't you?"

"He was cruel. Powerful." Karen looked as tight as a tick, as Gwen would say. Her eyes clouded, a distant memory drawing near. "When I first met Vikki, I didn't feel that twinge I thought I'd feel if I ever ran into my daughter."

"When did you meet?"

"A year and a half ago. She was still working at the Emerald."

I balked. "You told me you didn't know her."

"I lied."

That meant Vikki had known Karen when she'd pulled her off Lily at the casino. Vikki had kept that secret from her sister. And me.

"I'd taken a break from the tables," Karen continued. "Vikki followed me to the coffee shop and introduced herself. Cute girl was my first impression." Karen's head bobbed. Her gun hand trembled. Was the alcohol taking effect? Maybe I could wait her out, and she'd sink into a stupor. "She didn't tell me I was her mother. We simply chatted. A friendship ensued." Karen's face softened. Her eyes grew misty. "A few months later, when she gave me the charm for my necklace, she revealed everything. How she'd cajoled the lawyer for my identity even though I'd paid a lot of money to bury those files. He gave her a head start and told her I'd moved to Tahoe. I had to hand it to Vikki. She was tenacious."

"If she ever texted you or called you, there will be phone records."

Karen snickered. "No, there won't. Shaper put me in charge of that detail."

"You deleted them."

"Yep."

I cursed under my breath. She'd had autonomy. No one had checked up on her progress. "What does the *G* in the inscription *GVB* stand for?"

"You saw her locket."

"The *V* is for Victoria"—I edged closer to the shovel; one foot to go—"and the *B* for Brandon."

"Grace. It's Grace. Isn't that poetic?" Karen barked out a laugh. "I named her Grace because it's what I fell from."

"You gave her a Bible with the same inscription."

"The very Bible I discarded after my youth leader knocked me up."

"What happened the night she died?"

"I had a little too much to drink. I showed up on her doorstep. I wanted to talk her out of having the baby."

"She told you she was pregnant?"

"I was her mother. We had no secrets." Karen smirked. "Surprise. Surprise. She didn't like hearing that. She ran out of the house, taunting me over her shoulder, saying she'd gotten inseminated on purpose. She added that she was going to marry that no-good boyfriend. I was not the boss of her. Real adult."

"So you ran after her and hit her with a rock."

"You don't understand."

"She defied you. That angered you. You wanted control over her. How dare she have a mind of her own."

Karen's gaze narrowed. "I'm done talking."

Me, too. I lunged for the snow shovel.

Chapter 45

Karen startled and pulled the trigger. The bullet ricocheted off the shovel's blade. I swung the tool and landed a blow to her wrist. The gun flew out of her hand and slammed into the cement wall.

She charged me and grabbed the wooden handle. We struggled. She was bigger, but I wasn't drunk. I thrust my weight into her. She resisted and took control of the shovel. She heaved me into the wall.

My head jerked backward and hit the wall. The impact jolted me but didn't knock me off my feet. I leaned sideways and thrust the heel of my boot into Karen's thigh. She lurched backward. With a labored kick, I knocked the shovel out of her hands.

Screaming at the top of her lungs, she drove me into the wall again. At the same time, I spotted the gun. At the edge of the loading ramp, teetering at the top of a steep incline. I lunged for it, took hold, and caught myself before I went headfirst down the mountain.

I scrambled to my feet and swung around, gun aimed at Karen.

"You won't shoot," she said.

Who would convict me? I'd claim self-defense. Or temporary insanity.

"You're weak, Aspen. Spineless. You sat on your butt while the police blew the investigation of your parents' deaths. You turned tail and ran when a patient ended his life. Face it, you're pathetic. You can't kill me, and if you did, you'd hate yourself forever."

"You're wrong." I extended my arm and pointed at her heart. "My niece's life hangs in the balance."

"Speaking of Candace . . ." Karen dove to the left and punched the Start button. The chairlift groaned into motion. Fast. Faster.

"Help!" Candace yelled, breaking her silence. Her voice was thin, frightened.

I glimpsed her chair heading down the mountain, toward the rocky spine called Peril Ridge. Treacherous terrain lurked beneath.

Taking advantage of the distraction, Karen rammed the shovel's handle into my chest. I stumbled, fell backward, and plummeted down the barren Alpine Bowl slope. Ten yards. Twenty yards. I did everything I could not to lose my grip on the gun. When I came to a shaky stop at a level spot, I clambered to my feet.

Karen sprinted after me, heels skidding like skates. When she reached me, she wrestled me for control of the weapon. "You should've shot me when you had the chance."

Fury mounted inside me. She was right. I couldn't have pulled the trigger. But I could fight. I wrenched free and slammed the butt of the gun into her head. She staggered. I kneed her in the stomach. She reeled and tried to regain her footing but couldn't. Her boot slipped on an icy patch. Arms flailing, she careened down the steepest part of the ski run.

A look of total betrayal crossed her face as she toppled head over heels. Gaining speed. Like an out-of-control snowball. Rooster tails of icy snow sprayed upward.

Moments later, she crashed with a thud into the lone tree that could stop her, a broad-based pine at the intersection near the Roundhouse offloading chute.

At the same time, thunder rumbled and the clouds unloaded. A sleety mess of snow pounded me, but I couldn't slow down. Candace's chair was barreling toward the lodge.

I pocketed the gun and, although my legs felt as heavy as bags of sand, I scrambled up the slope to the Skidoo. I mounted it and drove beneath Candace's chair.

"Candace," I yelled, not sure if she could hear me. "I'll meet you at the bottom. Promise."

A high-speed chair moved fast. With no operator to control the speed, when Candace reached the bottom, the velocity might hurl her from the lift and then an oncoming empty chair would smash into her. The image made me cringe.

I sped toward the base terminal, bypassing Karen's crumpled body, and crossed under the lift. The chairlift was still moving fast. I aimed straight, bouncing over the uneven terrain, gripping the Skidoo's handles firmly to maintain control.

With seconds to spare, I swerved to a stop at the unloading platform and raced inside—just in time to hit the Slow button.

• • •

As I was ushering Candace to the ski patrol room, a deputy and my aunt arrived. They maintained their distance as the on-duty ski patrolman led Candace to a cot and covered her with a blanket.

After filling the deputy in about Karen, I called Shaper. This time, he answered.

I replayed the incident and Karen's confession. "Two ski patrolmen and one of your deputies are going to get her. It was"—my voice caught—"an accident."

"I'm on my way," he said, adding, "Aspen, before I hang up, I want to tell you that a handwriting expert confirmed Rocky didn't write the postcards you found in Vikki's locker. Someone forged them."

"Karen."

"Most likely."

"I think Rocky was blackmailing her. I think she shot him."

"She did. A receptionist at the Emerald Casino contacted us. She said a woman called Rocky right before he left work. We played the voice-mail recording Karen uses at the office for the receptionist. She confirmed Karen was the one who called. Also, thanks to your message, I've spoken to Karen's attorney. She'll be providing me with a copy of her father's will before close of business. You've got good instincts, Aspen."

I settled into a chair and let the weight of his words sink in.

Chapter 46

At thirteen, Candace may have felt she was nearing adulthood, but the moment she awakened, she badly needed holding. I cuddled on the cot with her for a long while as Shaper and others from the sheriff's office reviewed the crime scene. Karen was dead. I was not being charged.

When we were released, I took Candace home, and we nestled on the sofa until darkness came. That evening, when the storm subsided, I stepped onto the patio and drew in a deep breath. The spicy fragrance of pine offered the promise of new beginnings. Vowing to do whatever it took to make Candace's life better, even if it meant making a huge change to my own, I called Josephine Quill. She agreed to send a letter to Rosie forthwith to alert her as to my intentions. It would be hand-delivered. With signature required. I warned her that Rosie might not be easy to find. She assured me her delivery person was experienced in locating contrary characters.

A few hours later at dinner, I broached the subject I'd been avoiding. "Candace, I've started proceedings to gain custody of you."

She stirred her pasta without eating. "What does that mean?"

"I want you to live with me all the time."

"Forever?"

"Until you go to college."

"Would Mom live here, too?"

"No." My lawyer had warned me to tread cautiously. "Your mom will continue to live in Auburn and come visit you."

"Did you ask her if it's okay?"

I recalled the last incident with my sister and shuddered. If not for Shaper, Rosie would have pummeled me. "I did. She wasn't happy, but she'll agree. I've sent her an official letter."

Candace's lower lip quivered. "If I say yes, what will she do to me?"

"Nothing to you. I won't let her. She'll fight me in court."

"She can't afford a lawyer."

"One will handle it pro bono."

"Where will I go to school?"

"Locally. With Waverly. Are you okay with the idea? I want to give you a stable environment. I want to make sure that the bulimia . . ." I wrapped an arm around her. "That you stop doing it. It's not good for you. I want you to be healthy. And happy."

Candace bounded from her chair and threw her arms around me. Tears streamed from her eyes. "Yes, oh, yes."

After a minute, she pulled away, her eyes glistening with joy. "Can we get a dog?"

"Uh, sure."

"And plant some flowers? You don't have any."

"It's winter," I laughed. "Nothing grows in winter."

"Could Waverly spend the night sometime?"

"Of course."

Someone pounded on the front door. Candace leaped to her feet.

"Sit," I ordered and bolted to the foyer. I peeked through the sidelights.

Rosie stood on the porch, dressed in black and looking like a cobra poised for the kill. The light from the porch gave her gaunt cheekbones a ghoulish look, although her skin looked better. Almost healthy.

I retreated to the kitchen, fetched the can of pepper spray from my purse, and returned to the foyer. I opened the door, but before I could say hello, my sister barged in.

"Did you send this?" She flailed a letter.

Josephine Quill's delivery guy was fast. "Yes."

"You have a lot of nerve." Her face smoldered with anger, but she didn't make a move at me. I kept my hand poised on the pepper spray button.

Candace mewled.

Rosie shifted feet, edgy, uncertain, her hands dipping in and out of her pockets. She took a deep breath as if ready to launch into a tirade, but then she deflated. "You have no idea how much I despise you."

"You always have." A fact I'd been reluctant to admit until now.

"How could you do this to me?"

"When I realized you gave Candace the pills, I had to act."

"They were supposed to make her better."

I arched an eyebrow. "They were supposed to make her docile."

"This letter"—she flicked it—"says you're going to require that I go through a program and be clean for a year in order to get her back."

"That's the stipulation. She needs to be safe."

"I can't do that. I've tried."

"Try again."

Tears pooled in her eyes.

"You're straight today," I said. As a therapist, I'd learned to read the signs.

"One day. We both know that won't last." She leaned against the door and sighed. Beaten.

I refused to let myself cry. I needed to be strong for Candace. "One day at a time."

Rosie arched her eyebrow. "You know, Mom threatened to do the same thing regarding Candy. I made a couple of stabs at cleaning up. That appeased her. She didn't have the guts to do what you did. You're tougher than you look, little sis." She eyed her daughter. "I'm sorry, baby. You got a rotten apple for a mother."

"Oh, Mommy." Candace raced across the room and dove into my sister's arms.

"You'll be better off here." Rosie hugged her.

A pang stabbed my heart. The love was there but not the will.

"You want to get her stuff, call first, Aspen. That way, you know . . ." Rosie let the implication hang, but I got it. That way Candace wouldn't catch her mother with a needle in her arm. After one more passionate hug, Rosie walked out the door without looking back.

Candace cried for hours until all her tears were spent. The doctor at the hospital had given me the names of clinics to deal with her bulimia. I hoped whomever we found was also trained in dealing with fractured families.

• • •

After waking every hour to check on Candace and battling tumultuous dreams every time I fell back to sleep, morning sunshine came as a welcome relief. I took a speedy two-mile run and then showered and dressed and drank a strong cup of coffee. Fortified, I called Dan. "I'm sorry for not getting back to you," I said.

"From what I hear on the news, you've been busy." He sounded cautious and braced for the worst. "How's Candace doing?"

"Fine." I told him about the upcoming custody case.

"Good for you. I'm proud of you for taking this on." Dan paused. He let out a long sigh. "I never should've pressed you, Aspen. About us. I'm sorry."

"You are a good man, Dan, and a good woman deserves you. I'm the one who should be sorry."

"Yeah, you should." He laughed. "Friends?"

"Always. Have fun in Timbuktu."

"The Himalayas."

"Same thing."

The moment I ended the call, it rang again. I picked it up, chuckling. "What did you forget, Dan?"

"It's Gloria Morning." The avid reporter with the perky voice. "Do you think we could talk?"

"Not today, but I'll meet you the day after tomorrow."

"Will you give me an exclusive?"

"Yes." So far I hadn't spoken to a reporter. Shaper had handled the heavy lifting.

"All right. I told you we Stanford grads stick together." Her laugh was charming. "Terry's Coffee Shop by Homewood Market at ten a.m."

The day passed simply enough. Candace and I went shopping and purchased a few essentials to suffice until we could make the trip to Auburn and pick up more clothes. Next, we bought school items. Before heading home, we stopped at the Cobblestone Shopping Center and purchased the most indispensable component of a well-balanced new life—chocolates from the fabulous Belgian Chocolatier.

Once we put Candace's things away in what we now referred to as *her room*, she asked if she could call Waverly.

"Sure."

Ten minutes later, I was driving her to Waverly's for a sleepover.

"What will you do alone?" Candace asked before darting from the car.

"Read a good book."

• • •

After lighting a fire, I plucked a book from the bookshelf and chose Sinatra classics from my iTunes playlist. When "My Way" rang out, I joined in, the poignancy of the words moving me.

Midway through the song, someone rapped on the front door. *Not Rosie. Please not Rosie.*

I peeked through the sidelights, and my heart skipped a beat. Shaper, his jacket slung over his arm, was standing on the porch smacking his hands together to keep them warm.

I opened the door. "You should wear that coat."

"Nah. It's over thirty degrees out here. I only put it on when it goes below twenty."

"Then why carry it? Are you afraid the weather report could be wrong?"

He pulled a grocery bag from beneath the coat. "I'm using it to keep this hidden."

"What's in it?"

"A secret. May I come in?"

"Sure." I backed up and allowed him to step into the foyer. "Don't keep me hanging. What's in the bag?"

"A couple of steaks and a bottle of wine. If you aren't doing anything, I thought we could have dinner. The case is concluded. No conflict of interest."

"What about your wife?"

A slight hesitation crossed his face. A look of apprehension. "She's the reason I left the other day."

"I know. Karen told me."

"I'd wager she didn't tell you the truth."

"Which is . . ."

"My wife and I signed the papers to finalize the divorce. I'm free. To date."

The tension band holding my breathing in check released. "Is this a date?"

"If you'd like it to be." He grinned and set the grocery bag on the counter and removed the contents. "All the rigmarole took a long time. I didn't say anything because I didn't want to jinx the outcome."

"Congratulations." I handed him a wine bottle opener and fetched two glasses.

Expertly, he removed the cork and poured the wine. "I heard you've got Vikki's funeral planned for tomorrow on the beach."

"I could have held the service at the Source of Serenity, but Vikki loved the beach, and even though—"

"Don't second-guess yourself." He put a finger to my lips. "You made the right choice."

The scent of him filled my senses. He grazed his fingertip along my jaw and then lifted my chin. He kissed me lightly on the lips. When I didn't resist, he stepped closer and kissed me firmly.

After a moment, he pulled back and offered that charming half-cocked smile. "You okay with this?"

"Oh, yeah."

Chapter 47

The snow sparkled beneath the sun's bright gleam. The day was cold, but the storm had passed. Waves lapped the exposed stones that lined the shore. Vikki's friends and coworkers stood on the beach, exchanging stories.

I wove my way among them, thanking each for attending. Billy Tennyson gave me a hug, for closure I would suspect. Frank stood next to him. He smelled of soup.

Both Gwen and Tess were wearing hot pink in honor of Vikki. Ostensibly, Gwen had forgiven my blunder, but I knew our friendship would require healing.

Lily and a beleaguered Reverend Brock stood separate from the gathering. Earlier I'd asked him if he'd wanted to say anything on Vikki's behalf, but he'd shaken his head. Lily said he was too choked with emotion.

And guilt, I thought. Had he sensed Karen had killed Vikki?

The ski patrolwomen, snowboarders, and avalanche crew were on hand to pay their respects. Neighbors, including Garrett Thompson, stood clustered to one side.

Gazing at them all, I wondered if Vikki had realized what a big family she'd had.

Something sputtered. On the highway, a beaten-up Ford truck pulled near the chain-link fence. It idled for a short time and drove on. Minutes later, Vikki's adoptive parents appeared. They shuffled to the beach and stood at the back of the crowd, he in his dungarees and winter jacket, she in a black pantsuit that looked new. Lily joined them. Though tentative at first, she finally hugged them.

I took my place next to a small table upon which I'd set a small cross as well as Vikki's locket and Bible. Attached to a leg of the table was a bouquet of white balloons.

Shaper and Candace stood at the front of the crowd. I smiled at them and clapped to get everyone's attention. As I looked out at the sea of faces, I thought about what Max had said: *Family isn't always a direct relation.* Vikki's family—her extended family—had congregated on the beach to kiss her goodbye.

To begin the service, I told a couple of stories about her. One, when she'd dropped her camera in the hot tub. Another, when she'd gotten bats stuck in her hair while exploring a cave near Mount Rose. Many laughed and murmured. I spoke about Vikki's dream of becoming a professional photographer. When I finished, a few others shared anecdotes of their own.

After all of the attendees who'd wanted to speak had done so, I returned to the front. "If you'll join me in singing one of Vikki's favorite songs, 'Amazing Grace.'"

When the singing ended, Ed Brock joined me. "May I?" he asked. I nodded. He raised his hands overhead and intoned, "Oh, Lord, bless Grace Victoria Brandon Carmichael and take her in your arms. Rock her gently until we meet again."

Using scissors, I cut the balloons' ribbons. For a long moment, they hovered in the sky and then floated away.

About the Author

Daryl Wood Gerber is the Agatha Award–winning, nationally bestselling author of the Cookbook Nook Mysteries, featuring an admitted foodie and owner of a cookbook store in Crystal Cove, California, as well as the French Bistro Mysteries, featuring a bistro owner in Napa Valley. Under the pen name Avery Aames, Daryl writes the Cheese Shop Mysteries, featuring a cheese shop owner in Providence, Ohio.

As a girl, Daryl considered becoming a writer, but she was dissuaded by a seventh-grade teacher. It wasn't until she was in her twenties that she had the temerity to try her hand at writing again . . . for TV and screen. Why? Because she was an actress in Hollywood. A fun tidbit for mystery buffs: Daryl co-starred on *Murder, She Wrote* as well as on other TV shows. As a writer, she created the format for the popular sitcom *Out of This World*. When she moved across the country with her husband, she returned to writing what she loved to read: mysteries and thrillers.

Daryl is originally from the Bay Area and graduated from Stanford University. She loves to cook, read, golf, swim, and garden. She also likes adventure and has been known to jump out of a perfectly good airplane. Here are a few of Daryl's lifelong mottos: perseverance will out; believe you can; never give up. She hopes they will become yours, as well.

To learn more about Daryl and her books, visit her website at DarylWoodGerber.com.

Made in the USA
Middletown, DE
18 September 2019